Drama
Queen

Drama
Queen

La Jill Hunt

www.urbanbooks.net

Urban Books
10 Brennan PL.
Deer Park, NY 11729

Copyright © 2003 La Jill Hunt

ISBN-13: 978-1-60162-021-7
ISBN-10: 1-60162-021-7

Fifth Mass Market printing October 2007

Printed in the United States of America

10   9   8   7   6   5   4   3   2   1

Submit Wholesale Orders to:
Kensington Publishing Corp.
c/o Penguin Group (USA) Inc.
Attention:
405 Murray Hill Parkway
East Rutherford, NJ 07073-2316
Phone: 1-800-526-0273
Fax: 1-800-227-9604

Dedication

This book is dedicated in loving memory to Sis. Sheila Artis, who taught me courage by living it and to my godmother, Mrs. Faith Peck, who taught me beauty by being beautiful inside and out.

To Marshall Hunt, Sr., who in spite of all my mistakes, told me I never disappointed him.

I love and miss all of you dearly.

Acknowledgments

Wow! Writing the book was easy, trying to remember everyone to thank is hard. I have to start at the very essence of my being and thank God Almighty for not only the gift and talent of writing, but for His favor in everything I have ever stepped out on faith and done. Lord, I praise You and rejoice in Your might and omnipotence. Thank you for putting me at the right place at the right time, even when I didn't even know it. To You be the glory!

To my husband, Charles Corey Williams. Thank you for your love and support. I know this hasn't been an easy process, but know that I appreciate you and your patience. I love you, Mi Corbello!!!

To my daughters, the Jr. Drama Queens, as they are affectionately known. You are the reason Mommy works so hard and tries even harder. I love you, love you, love you more than you will ever know.

To my parents, Charles and Martha Smith, and my "Ma" Minnie L. Hunt, for supporting me in everything I have done in life. All the years of fussing, lecturing, punishing, encouraging, praying, loving, helping, paying, driving, praising, guiding, and not giving up on me paid off!!! I love you and hope that I can influence my children in such a way as you have influenced me.

To my sister La Toya Smith, James Turner and my brother Chaz, thanks for the little things. You know what I mean, so I don't have to say any more. I appreciate you all.

To Marshall Braxton Hunt, III, the first "little brother" I ever had. You have always been there for me, even though I was older. I thank you for your "pep-talks" and advice over the years! I apologize for the beatings I caused, LOL. I love you.

To my extended families, Mr. and Mrs. Caroll Williams, the Smith family, my Uncle Marshall and Aunt Liz, Gloria Scott, Karis and Kendall, Joycelyn W. Hunt, Gabriel Peck, Jr. and Gabriel Peck, III (DJ QueTip, ATL), the Lindseys, the Yorks, and Lynne Westbrook; Stone Street Baptist Church, Bishop Rudolph Lewis and First Lady Lewis and New Light Full Gospel Baptist Church, thank you as well.

To my true friends, the ones that I can call anytime for anything, and there is never a complaint—Yvette Lewis, Joycelyn W. Ward, Shantel Spencer, Saundra White, Norell Smith, Tracy and Troy Lee, Roxanne Elmore, Tonya Kabia, Torrance Oxendine, and Theodore Wingfield, in no particular order. You are the greatest and I love each and every one of you.

To Pastor Kim W. Brown and Sister Valerie and the Mt. Lebanon Missionary Baptist Church family, I can not put my appreciation into words. I thank you for looking out for me and my family from day one, before we became "official". Pastor Brown, I have never, nor will I ever question why you do the things you do and just praise God for you and your uniqueness (You never try to be like anybody else's church). Thank you for your courage and your guidance in addition to your awesomeness. (Hey Rev. Mitchell, remember Sarah and her blessing, LOL!)

To St. Paul's College, especially Mrs. Rebecca Akers who took her own time and money and provided some struggling students with nothing but the best to read. Don't think it went unappreciated. If it wasn't for you, a lot of us never would have read, LOL.

To My Verizon family, Joya Boone, Cherie Johnson, Vonda Majette, Donnise Batton, Milly Avent, Denise Green, Tomeica Bynum-Shelton, Yolanda Stanislaus, Frieda McNeil, Danita Manley, Toney Black and Bonita Coins, thank you for helping a sister out on the job.

To my publicist Robilyn Heath. Girl, you give the phrase "work it" a whole new meaning. This is it, the ball has started rolling!!! Thank you for doing your thing and working the connects. "Love ya like a bestseller"!!! To Blessed Child Web Design. Ju Joyner, with your crazy self, thank you for just being you and hooking me up!!!

To my editor, Martha Weber. THANK GOD FOR YOU!!! You made the magic happen and I just have to give you all the props in the world. You are the best person in the world to work with. Thank you for your insight!!! (Ha, I didn't use any contractions in your shoutout, LOL)

To Dwayne S. Joseph and Angel Hunter. Thank you for taking a naïve wanna-be from VA Beach and making me feel a part of your world. Thank you for all of your encouragement and advice, even when my questions were crazy. You two have always looked out.

And now, to Carl Weber, all I can say is THANK

YOU for opportunity, for guidance, for friendship, for influence, and for faith. I will forever be grateful and I hope I can be to someone what you have been to me. See you on the bestseller list, keep my spot warm for me!!!

I think I remembered everyone else this time. Hold up, I forgot to thank the haters, the disrespecters, the drama causers and the disbelievers who gave me so much material to write about. I was gonna call names, but there is no need. Smile, you know who you are. Just read the book while I enjoy the fame. Jeremiah 29:11.

e-mail me at mslajaka@aol.com

Prologue

Kayla drove home, slightly buzzed from the mixture of alcohol and the contact smoke from her girls who were smoking weed while they put together favors at the house of one of her bridesmaids. As Ice Cube put it, today had definitely been a good day. Hell, it had been a good year. She and Geno, the love of her life, her Boo, her sweetheart for the past two years, her best friend and the best lover she had ever been with, to say the least, were getting married in two weeks. She smiled at the thought of being his wife.

She met him her junior year of college. They were both transfer students and both majored in English, which meant they were in a lot of the same classes. They hit it off instantly. She was attracted to his rugged body and intellectual mind, a ruthless combination in her book. He was funny and kept her laughing, and she loved being around him. He called her his pro-bono tutor and they did homework together. Study sessions turned into dates and dates turned into overnight rendezvous, and senior year she moved into his small apartment. After graduation, she began teaching and he began working at the local radio station, and they got a bigger place. It was inevitable that they would be married, she knew it. Geno was her soul mate, and everything was looking up for them. Life was good.

She pulled into the driveway and decided to leave the wedding favors that she and her brides-maids had finished in the trunk of her car. She was too sleepy to even bother with them. She fumbled with her keys and unlocked the door, giggling to herself as she stumbled into the dark apartment. Geno was probably passed out in a hotel room somewhere. His bachelor party was tonight and she had the entire place to herself.

As she made her way past the kitchen, she thought she heard a noise and stopped, listening closer. It was coming from the bedroom. She inched her way to the room that she and her fiancé shared and stood in the doorway, amazed at what was going on. The room was completely dark, but she could make out two shadows in their bed, illuminated by the glow of the streetlight coming through the window. The first shadow, was without a doubt a fe-male. Her body was rocking back and forth, breasts bouncing, hair flowing as her head rolled in ec-stasy, riding as if she was on one of those mechani-cal bulls that Kayla had seen in commercials for country western bars. The dick must have been good, because whoever she was, she could barely moan. Every time she tried to catch a breath, the second shadow would put it to her with quickness, causing her to gasp again. But Kayla knew the dick was good because it had been thrown to her on a regular basis. She knew what the girl was feeling because she had felt the exact same way that very morning. The second shadow was Geno's. She could tell from the moans and the way he was gripping the headboard with his thick fingers. He liked to grip it when she rode, because he said he could get more leverage that way.

She stood for a few moments, too shocked to move. She had heard stories of men sleeping with the strippers from their bachelor party, but this took the cake. *I know this nigga ain't bring home one of those tricks from his party and fucking her in our house, in our bed. This nigga must be high on crack,* Kayla thought to herself. She got her thoughts together and ran into the kitchen. Making sure she was extra quiet, she pulled a big pot from under the cabinet and filled it with scalding water. When it was full, she struggled back into the bedroom and closed her eyes. Her grandmother had once told her about two dogs that were screwing in her front yard and got stuck together. The only way that they got them unstuck was to toss hot water on them. Well, Kayla was about to get two bitches out of her bed. She groaned as she lifted the heavy pot and tossed the hot water on the two shadows.

"Sssshhhit!" the female screamed as the water hit her on the back. Geno was dazed by what was happening until the liquid hit his arms and upper torso.

"What the fuck?" he screamed in pain as the girl rolled from on top of him onto the floor, writhing in pain.

Satisfied with her handiwork, Kayla finally flicked the light switch. Everyone squinted as their eyes adjusted.

"You bastard! You brought a trick home and did her in my bed? Our bed? What kind of shit is that?" Kayla screamed and jumped on the bed, swinging at him.

"Kayla, what the hell is wrong with you? What are you talking about?" he said, looking at his burnt skin.

"Don't play crazy, Bitch! How could you do this to me?" She clawed at his face and he grabbed her arms, still looking confused.

"Kayla, calm the fuck down!" he warned. They had never gotten physical in all the time they had been together. It was Geno's rule never to push each other to that limit. He had seen his parents fight his entire life, and told Kayla that would never be him. But he had gone beyond that limit this time, and she didn't care what the rule was; she was out for blood.

"Calm the fuck down? Calm the fuck down? I know you ain't in here fucking another bitch and you telling me to calm the fuck down! Where are you at, Bitch? I ain't forgot about your ass, either!" Kayla yanked away from Geno and jumped onto the floor, standing over the still whining woman. The woman whimpered as Kayla yanked her by the hair so she could look into her face. A combination of nausea, betrayal and pain came over her as she realized who was looking back at her.

"Kay . . ." the woman began. She could not finish because Kayla slapped her so hard that she fell back onto the floor.

"What the fuck is going on?" Geno sat up and looked at the crumpled body next to his bed. He shook his head as sobriety set in and it became apparent that it wasn't his fiancée he had been making love to as he thought, but another woman.

"I can't believe you would do this to me, Geno. Her, I could, but you?" She looked at him with hate in her eyes. Never in a million years would Kayla have thought that Geno would cheat on her. It was the one thing she told him from day one that she wouldn't stand for, and he assured her he'd never do.

"Kayla, I swear. I don't know how this happened. I was drunk and I thought it was you. She was in the bed when I got here." He tried to explain.

"You thought she was me. My God, Geno, then your perception of me ain't that great, is it?" She looked over at the woman and shook her head. "I'm not surprised by you. I just thought you would have pulled something like this after me and him got married."

"He came onto me. I was in here 'sleep and he seduced me!" the woman cried.

"Bitch, what the hell were you doing in my bed? Why the hell were you even in my house? You know what? It don't even matter. You fucked him, you marry him, you slut. At least the same parents will have paid for the motherfucking wedding," Kayla told her. She wiped the tears forming in her eyes before they had a chance to fall.

"Kayla, don't do this. Wait a minute." Geno scrambled for his sweats as he got up. His head was throbbing and his arm began to blister, but he paid it no mind as he tried to get Kayla to listen to him.

"Let her go, G. She better be glad I don't call the police on her for assault. Look at my back. Payback is a bitch, you'd better believe that!" Kayla's sister pointed at her red, swollen back. Kayla ignored her and began to snatch clothes out of the closet and stuff them into her duffel bag. She knew she could not stay in that house another moment.

"Get dressed and get out, Anjelica!" Geno yelled, "Kayla, listen to me. Don't throw this away. I love you and I wanna marry you. This is all just a big misunderstanding."

Geno tried to take the bag from her but she slapped him.

"I advise you to stop talking. The more you try to explain, the worse you make this already fucked up situation. She doesn't have to get out. Y'all can pick up right where you left off after I get my shit!"

"Where're you going, Kay?" he pleaded. He knew he had messed up big time and Kayla was gonna need some time to think. But he wanted her to understand that what happened was not his fault. He needed to know she would still marry him.

"None of your fucking business! I'll get the rest of my stuff later, when neither of you is here! But good luck to you both." She took off the engagement ring she had been wearing with pride for the past year, and threw it at Anjelica. "You can have this and him!"

She stormed out of the house with Geno calling after her and Anjelica still whining about her back. The stupid bitch still didn't have the sense to apologize. Kayla checked into a hotel, not wanting to face her family or friends.

In the two weeks leading up to Kayla's wedding date, she moved into her own place and sent out cancellation announcements, telling everyone that she and Geno decided they just weren't ready. On the day they were supposed to wed, Kayla boarded a plane to Jamaica, their honeymoon destination, by herself. She called Geno from the plane, telling him that she would never forget how he hurt her. He told her that she was totally overreacting and he still wanted to marry her. That they could get through this. She told him she didn't want to get through it because she was already over it. She had decided to go on with her life and so should he. She hung the phone up, vowing to never again trust another man.

1

Whoever said it's better to have loved and lost than never loved at all was a ign'ant ass, Kayla thought as she checked herself in her rearview mirror. It had been a year since her breakup with Geno and she still felt like shit. She had tried to throw herself into teaching and becoming a better person, but even that wasn't helping to mend her broken heart. Her girls had discovered this new sports bar called State Street's and actually convinced her to come. She wasn't all that enthused, but hell, maybe a night out was what they all needed.

All of Kayla's girls were single with no kids. They were hard working, smart, educated black women who were attractive both inside and out. Any man would have been blessed to be with one of them, but they found themselves man-less at the present. Kayla had affectionately named them the Lonely Hearts Club and they had fun, nonetheless, just hanging out, living the single life. Their group consisted of Roni and Tia, two of Kayla's college buddies, and Kayla's co-worker, Yvonne.

The club was not overcrowded, but there were quite a few people. Kayla had just arrived and was looking for Yvonne when she felt someone grab her hand, startling her. When she turned around, she had to do a double take. For a moment, she thought it was Geno, but it wasn't. Although they had the same caramel complexion and similar features, this guy had a bald head, where Geno kept his thick curls cut close. He wore a mustache and goatee, as did Geno, and they had the same athletic build.

"Oops, my bad," he said when he saw the confused look on her face. "I thought you were someone else."

He checked out Kayla with her cocoa brown skin, dimpled smile, curvaceous figure and short-cropped hair cut. It was no doubt he liked what he saw.

"Oh, no problem." Kayla finally found her voice. "Excuse me."

"At least let me buy you a drink. I know you wanted to slap me for grabbing you like that." He smiled at her and extended his hand. "Craig."

"Kayla, and you don't have to do that, really, it's okay," she answered, shaking it. She quickly turned and spotted Yvonne and Roni coming toward her. She maneuvered past him and shook her head, forcing herself not to turn back around.

"Who is that, Geno's cousin or something?" Roni asked.

"I don't know. He accidentally grabbed me; thought I was someone else or something. His name is Craig." Kayla shrugged.

"He looks just like Geno, except he got a bald head and he got the thug thing going on. Better watch out," Yvonne said. Yvonne thought all hard looking guys were criminals, and she and Roni always had comments about drug dealers and jailbirds.

They found a table near the dance floor and were having a ball drinking and laughing. Soon, Roni and Tia were on the dance floor as Kayla and Yvonne watched. The deejay was spinning old school jams that they had not heard in years. Kayla could not stop rocking to the beat. Then, as if on cue, Craig pulled her out of her chair and onto the floor. He had some moves. She could not help but laugh and demonstrate moves of her own. For the first time in a long lime, she was enjoying herself.

"How about that drink?" he asked when the deejay decided to slow it down. She didn't think twice as she followed him to the bar. He seemed like a nice guy and they vibed for the remainder of the evening. She was surprised when she looked at her watch and realized it was after midnight.

"I gotta go," she told him reluctantly.

"The club doesn't close until three. What's the rush?" he asked. "You got a man at home waiting for you?"

"No. If I had a man, do you think I would have let you up in my face all night?" She laughed.

"Oh, I was all in your face, huh? That's how it is? Well if that's the case, can I at least get your number so I can stay up in your pretty face?" He looked at her with such intensity she felt a chill down her spine.

"Let me get your number and I'll think about

it," she said. He asked a passing waitress to borrow her pen then grabbed a napkin off her tray, writing his number on it.

"Well you do that. But at least call and let me know you made it home safely." He placed the napkin in her hand.

"Won't you still be here until three?" Kayla put the paper in her pocket without looking at it.

"I put my pager number on the top. Call and put in code o-o-one. I'll know it's you."

"Oh, no. I pick my own code. And you'll know it's me. I don't want some code you probably give to all your club chicks." Kayla gave him a quick hug and went back to the table to bid good-bye to her girls.

"I thought you and him went to get a room or something," Tia joked.

"Girl, please. I just met him. I didn't even give him my number." Kayla smirked.

"But I bet you got his," Yvonne threw at her. "I guess you won't be going home pining away for Geno tonight, huh?

"Why? She met the next best thing tonight. He looks just like him," Roni said. "I ain't mad at you, though. You know my motto. The best way to get over a nigga is to get under another one."

"All of y'all are sick. I'm out," Kayla said and headed out of the club. As she turned to leave, a familiar face in a crowd of females caught her attention.

"Kayla, isn't that—"

"Yeah, that's her." She cut Roni off before she could finish her question. She wanted to walk by and pretend she didn't recognize her, but the pretty woman waved and headed in her direction.

"Kayla! Didn't think I'd run into you!" She smiled.

"Anjelica. I should say the same thing." Kayla didn't even try to fake a smile.

"Well, some friends and I drove up this afternoon. It *is* my birthday."

"Happy birthday, Anjelica." Roni raised her eyebrow at what could be Kayla's twin.

"Thank you, Roni. At least you can acknowledge it, unlike some people. But what can I expect from someone who blames me for every nigga that did her wrong?"

"Whatever, Anjelica. If I were you, I'd get outta my face, you jealous trick. Green was never a good color on you." Kayla turned to leave.

"Geno thought I looked good in green." Anjelica smiled wickedly. She knew that would get a rise out of her sister.

"Don't play with me. I already owe you an ass whooping. And I have no problem giving it to you on your birthday," Kayla growled as she stepped into Anjelica's face. She knew that although her sister talked a good game, she was weak and would never fight her.

"Whoa! Hold up, ladies. I think you two need to separate." Kayla felt a hand on her arm and looked up. It was Craig. He led her out to the parking lot and walked her to her car. She let her girlfriends know she was okay as they stood and talked for a few more minutes.

"Who was that?" he asked.

"That was my sister, the bitch." She smiled at him. She felt so safe next to him; it was somewhat arousing.

"Damn, I thought y'all was about to throw down in there." He laughed. "That was your sister?"

"Yep and today's her birthday. I shoulda gave her ass some licks. That is the tradition, isn't it?"

"I like you. You got spunk. I think that is so damn sexy." He leaned near Kayla.

"I'll call you and let you know I made it home." She winked at him as she got in her car and drove off, leaving him standing in the parking lot.

She thought about Craig all the way home. After all the crap Geno had put her through, maybe she deserved a little uncommitted fun. Maybe Craig was just what she needed. While sitting on the side of her bed, Kayla looked at the piece of paper Craig had given her, wondering if she really should call. Her eyes fell on the picture she still had on the dresser. She and Geno had taken it the day they graduated from City College. Although she hated to admit it, she still loved him. Probably always would. But he had moved on and so should she. Reaching on the nightstand, she grabbed the cordless phone from the charger. She dialed the pager number and after the series of beeps, she entered her cell number along with the numbers six and eight. Smiling, she climbed under her covers and went to sleep.

2

The next morning, she had a message waiting for her. "I'm happy you made it home safe, and even happier that you called me. I really want to get together later. If you're interested, give me a call." Craig's voice sounded so sexy on the phone.

"Call him, girl," Roni advised her. "He was cute and you can have some fun. Don't be all serious. He can be your rebound man."

Kayla should have known not to ask Roni, but she had popped up at the music store to meet Kayla for lunch and she couldn't resist telling her about the message.

"What do I say?" Kayla asked her. Out of all her friends, Roni was considered the wild one. She always had a trail of guys who she had on call, so if there was an event she wanted to attend that required an escort, she had an abundance of men to choose from. She never got too serious or "caught up" and always said she would never get married.

Because of this, Kayla thought, she had never had her heart broken.

"Come on, Kay. Say you're interested. Go out. Have fun. Get some. Girl, you are young and free. Enjoy it," she said between bites.

"I don't know, Ron."

"I know you ain't still dwelling on that nigga Geno. Kayla, he's had no problem getting footloose and fancy-free. I know you heard about his new girl. You better get real. How long has it been? A year?"

"A year and some change. But you're right. I do need to get on with my life." Kayla nodded. She didn't dare tell Roni that she had hooked up with Geno last month on a whim. They had talked occasionally and run into each other at the music store.

"Get out and get some, Kayla. Call him. Go out. What's the worst that can happen?" Ron reached for the check. "It's on me, girl."

"Which one of your suitors hooked you up this weekend?"

"Trey. He got his income tax check and he won't be here next weekend for Valentine's. He feels bad." Roni laughed. "I guess I'll have to go out with Darren so *I* won't feel bad, huh?"

"You are crazy. You give the word player a whole new definition. I can't wait for the day you fall in love."

"Never that, sweetheart. I got too much game."

"Okay, game. Let's go before I get fired," Kayla said and rose to leave.

"So, when are you gonna call?"

"After I get off."

"Handle your business, girlfriend. And let me

know how it goes." The two women parted ways and Kayla went back to work. She decided to return Craig's call during her last break. She found the paper that she put in her pocket before she left for work and again paged him with her cell number and the code sixty-eight. She hoped he would call back as soon as she paged him because her break was only fifteen minutes long.

I can't believe I'm doing this. The vibration of her phone startled her to the point that Kayla nearly jumped out of her skin. She looked at the caller ID and recognized the other number Craig had written on the piece of paper. She took a deep breath and let the phone ring twice more. *Don't want him to think I'm sweating him.*

"Hello," she answered.

"So what's with the sixty-eight, Beautiful?" Craig asked in his deep voice.

"I'll always leave you wanting more. What's up with you?" She was trying to sound nonchalant.

"I'm doing better now that I've talked to you. You sleep a'ight?"

She could hear him stretching and wondered if he had just gotten up. *Maybe I should have called later.* "I slept fine. Thanks for asking. You busy?"

"No. I'm 'bout to hit the gym and then grab me some food. Would you care to join me?" he asked. She didn't know if he meant the gym or dinner.

"No, I have to work until four. As a matter of fact, my break is almost over. I did want to return your call, though."

"Well, can I take you out later? After you get off? I mean, that's still early. We can catch a movie or something." He seemed really interested in her and she was flattered.

"Okay. What if I call you around seven and we can meet somewhere?"

"A'ight. I'll talk to you then. Bye, Beautiful."

"Bye." Kayla couldn't help smiling as she put her phone back in her pocket.

They met for drinks and a movie that night. Kayla had to catch her breath when she saw him for the second time. The resemblance to Geno was still noticeable; there was no denying the boy was fine. But Craig had a hardness about him that Geno didn't have. He told her he was a chef at a local hotel. He took much pride in his cooking skills and offered to demonstrate them the following weekend, which was of course, one Kayla was dreading. It was Valentine's Day.

"I have to think about it and let you know," she told him as he walked her to her car. She looked at him and still could not deny the attraction she held for him. It wasn't that he looked like Geno. Craig had that same sparkle in his personality that made her laugh, something she hadn't done in a while.

"What's there to think about? You already got plans? I know it's the day for lovers, but it can be for friends, too." He grabbed her hand and held it for a moment as he looked into her eyes. She immediately felt self-conscious and looked away. "Do you know how beautiful you are?" he said.

This totally took Kayla by surprise. She'd been told before how attractive she was. She had even been called beautiful before, but Craig said it with such intensity that it stunned her. She looked up at him and as if on cue in a romance film, he pulled her to him. He kissed her so passionately that time seemed to stand still.

That kiss stayed on her mind for days. It was on

her mind Monday when she woke up and got dressed for work. It was on her mind when she was stuck in traffic, leaving school and headed to the music store listening to Musiq sing about "love." It was on her mind as she listened to the messages Craig left on her voicemail at home and on her cell phone.

"Hi, Kayla. I know you're at school, but I woke up with you on my mind and I wanted to hear your voice. So, your voicemail will just have to do until I talk to you, if you decide to grace me with a phone call. Have a great day, Beautiful."

Kayla could not help but smile as she hung up the phone late that Thursday evening. She still had not decided what she would do for Valentine's Day. Yvonne wanted everyone to go out, but Roni of course had plans and so did Tia. Kayla figured she would play it by ear. She had a long week and didn't really feel like going out and seeing other couples all hugged up, knowing that this time last year she was happily involved herself. *Geno. Wonder what he'll be doing tomorrow? Probably with his new trick*, she thought. At that moment, the phone rang and she was surprised to see Geno's cell number on the caller ID.

Taking a deep breath, she answered with a low, "Hello."

"Hey, Kay. How's it going?" He sounded great, as usual. The sound of his voice caused waves of memories to come flooding back.

"Great, G. And you?" she asked, monitoring her breathing.

"I've been good. I just called to check on you. I mean, it's been a while since we talked and I just wanted to make sure you were okay."

"I'm fine, G." She didn't know what he wanted to hear at this point.

"You weren't busy, were you? I mean, you sound kinda distant. Am I disturbing you or something?"

"No. I just got in from work. But I do have some papers I am about to grade. And I gotta get these gift bags together for my kids." She sighed, still wondering what brought this phone call on. She and Geno had not parted on the best of terms, but they had gotten to the point where they were at least friends. It still hurt her to know what he had done, but it hurt even more that they were no longer together.

"Well, I'm not gonna keep you long, Kay. I just wanted to wish you a happy Valentine's Day and make sure you're doing alright," Geno said quietly. She could hear him fumbling in the background.

"Where are you, Geno? You sound muffled," Kayla asked him, straining to decipher the background noise.

"The door is locked!" She heard a female voice yelling.

"I'm picking my friend up from work. Hey, it was nice talking to you. I'll call you back later," he quickly said and the phone went dead.

That nigga had the nerve to call me while he was picking up some other chick from work. She shook her head and threw the phone on the bed. She had to remind herself that they were no longer together so she had no right to be mad. Again, she told herself that he had moved on, so it was time for her to do the same thing. The kiss again was on her mind as she picked up the phone and dialed Craig's number.

3

"He's cooking you dinner?" Roni asked her as she put the hot curling iron in Kayla's hair. They were in Kayla's cluttered bedroom and Roni was helping her get ready for her big date.

"That's what he says. I mean, he *is* a cook. That's what he does for a living," Kayla answered as she tried not to flinch from the heat.

"Um, the way to a woman's heart is through her stomach." Roni smiled smugly.

"Ron, I thought that was the way to a man's heart."

"No, girl. The way to a man's heart is through his head, and I ain't talking about the one on his shoulder with two ears, either." Roni laughed and almost burned Kayla's forehead.

"Girl, you'd better chill. You know I ain't got enough hair to wear bangs." Kayla swatted at Roni.

"I can throw some tracks right in there. You know I can." Roni tilted Kayla's head and kept curling. It was a well-known fact that Veronica Jett was one of the best hairdressers this earth had ever seen; a talent inherited from her mother, Ms. Ernestine Jett, the owner of Jett Black Hair Salon on the south side of the city. But Roni decided that doing hair wasn't steady enough to be her thing, so she taught at the alternative school instead. She did her girlfriends' hair and occasionally went to work at the shop when she was strapped for cash, which was rarely, since she had enough male compadres to help her out whenever that occurred.

"Did I tell you Geno called me last night?" Kayla acted like it was no big deal.

"What the hell did he want?"

"I don't know. The girl he was picking up from work came to the car before he had the chance to tell me." Kayla shrugged.

"What girl?" Roni sucked her teeth as she reached for the spray bottle.

"I don't know." Kayla sighed. Roni reached for the makeup kit on Kayla's dresser and began making Kayla's face.

"Close your eyes," she said and Kayla felt her applying the eye shadow. "Look, Kay. I want you to do me a favor. Go out tonight, have fun, don't even think about Geno. Let it go and move on. You are a beautiful, intelligent black woman with so much to offer. Forget that nigga. It's over. Okay? All done. You like?"

Kayla opened her eyes and was amazed at the transformation Roni had done. Her big brown eyes seemed brighter and her full lips were glossy and sensual. There was not a hair out of place on her perfectly curled head.

"Damn. I *am* a diva." Kayla smiled and hugged her girlfriend.

"Now hurry up. You don't wanna keep your chef waiting. And here." Roni reached in her purse and placed a small item in Kayla's hand.

"What's this?" Kayla asked and looked down at the small plastic wrapper. "Oh hell, naw. I don't need this. You know I don't get down like that. I just met this man, Roni. He ain't getting nothing from me except maybe some tongue action— and that's only on his lips."

"Take it, Kayla. It's Valentine's and you might get lucky. You never know, girl. Better safe than sorry. I gotta run. Darren is picking me up at nine. Love you, Kay. Call me in the morning and let me know how it goes," Roni said as she left. Kayla looked at the condom and put it in the top drawer of her dresser.

"That girl is a fool," she said out loud and proceeded to get dressed. She decided to dress down, but cute. Craig told her that he would cook dinner and they would get to know each other better. She liked him more and more every time she spoke with him.

Pulling on her black silk shirt and fitted Parasuco jeans, Kayla took one last look in the mirror. She turned and noticed the photo of Geno and her. *Time to move on,* she thought as she picked it up. She placed it in the top of her hall closet when she grabbed her leather coat.

The drive to Craig's house only took twenty minutes, but to Kayla it felt like hours. The neighborhood was fairly new and she took notice of the perfectly manicured yards even though it was dark. She found his townhouse nestled at the back of the cul-de-sac, his blue Honda parked right out front. As she parked behind it, she saw the lights go dim and the porch light come on. Checking herself in the rearview mirror, she touched up her lipstick and opened her car door.

"My, my, my. You look too good to stay in, Kayla. Maybe we should go to State Street's so I can show you off." He grinned and gave Kayla a hug.

"You are so silly." Kayla could smell his Calvin Klein cologne as he pulled her close to him. She took notice of how sexy he looked dressed in the simple wife beater and blue sweat pants, white socks on his large feet.

"Come on in. Dinner's almost ready." He led her into the sunken living room and she was immediately impressed. Sounds of jazz filled the room. There was a brown leather sectional surrounded by African artwork and statues. They were all beautiful. On the wall was a huge print of a warrior, standing with staff in hand in the African jungle. The coffee and end tables were adorned with carvings and hand blown glass. Kayla had never seen anything like it.

"Make yourself at home."

"This is gorgeous. I mean, absolutely gorgeous," she told him.

"Thanks. I try," he answered. "Have a seat. I gotta check on something in the kitchen."

Kayla took a seat and continued to admire her surroundings. *This brother has taste.* The mahogany entertainment center held a 32-inch television and a stereo system. There were what looked like hundreds of CDs and DVDs on mahogany shelves.

"Did you find my place okay?" he called from the kitchen.

"Yeah. Your directions were easy to follow. This is a nice neighborhood," she answered. "How long have you lived here?"

"Almost a year," he said. She turned around and saw he was walking toward her with a glass of wine.

"Thank you," she said, taking the glass from him. "Something smells delicious."

"Chicken. It's finishing up. Would you like a tour while we wait?"

"Sure." She shrugged.

"Let's start upstairs and work our way down." He took her by the arm and led her up the Berber-carpeted steps. At the top there was a loft with a small office, outfitted with a desk, computer, file cabinet and a bookshelf full of books. The wall held framed photos of Miles Davis, Dizzy Gillespie and Etta James. There were also jazz statues on the shelves.

"You read?" she asked him, impressed by the titles, including historical greats such as Zora Neale Hurston, James Baldwin and Richard Wright.

"Jazz and reading, my two favorite hobbies." He smiled. They continued further and he showed her a bedroom, which was modestly decorated in taupe. There was a full bed and a dresser, but not a lot of artwork, as had the rest of the house. "This is the guestroom."

"Nice."

"It's a'ight. I haven't got it finished yet." They returned to the hallway and he opened a second door across the hall. "Now this is the master bedroom." He grinned as he opened the door.

Kayla's mouth dropped as they entered the huge room. It looked like something off *MTV Cribs*. The grand lair was an ivory dream. The king-sized bed was raised in the center of the room. There was a separate sitting area with a cream leather love seat and matching ottoman. As she inhaled, Kayla smelled vanilla and noticed candles burning in each corner of the room. On the far wall, she was stunned by a flat screen television.

"Wow," was all she could say. As she walked closer to the bed, she had to blink several times to make sure she was seeing clearly.

"It's mink," Craig informed her as she touched the bedspread.

"Cooking must really be paying well," Kayla commented. She could feel Craig's hand on the small of her back and she turned to face him. As he reached and touched her face, there was a beeping noise coming from downstairs.

"Saved by the bell. Sounds like dinner is ready. Shall we eat?"

Kayla took one last look around the room, still amazed at its beauty. "May I use your restroom?" Kayla asked.

"Yeah. You can use the one downstairs," Craig answered. She followed him down the steps and he showed her to the bathroom. Like the rest of the house, it was an impeccable array of browns and beige with gold detailing. She stood in the bathroom a few moments, just looking at herself in the mirror. *Maybe* he *is worth more than a little harmless fun,* she thought.

"You okay?" Craig tapped on the door, startling her.

"Yeah. I'm coming out right now," she called. She washed her hands and opened the door where he was waiting for her.

"Right this way, Madame." He looped his arm

through hers and guided her into a beautiful dining room. He had dressed the elaborate table with flowers and candles. He pulled a chair out for her to be seated and out of nowhere, presented her with a long-stemmed white rose. "For you."

"Why thank you, kind sir." She laid the rose in front of her.

"Dinner is served." He imitated a formal waiter and bowed as he went into the kitchen. She could not help giggling to herself as she drank the remainder of the wine in her glass.

Craig returned carrying two plates. He placed one in front of Kayla and the other at the empty seat near hers. She looked at the salad, which she could tell was freshly prepared.

"I didn't know what type of salad dressing you like, so I have a variety to choose from. I like this one myself. It's raspberry vinaigrette. Sweet, yet tasty." He licked his lips sexily at Kayla.

"I'll bet," she said, blushing.

They feasted on a fabulous dinner which Craig had prepared, consisting of salad, shrimp cocktail, Chicken Alfredo, garlic bread, and cheesecake. He amazed her not only with his culinary skills and witty conversation, but he even went so far as to grind fresh Parmesan over her pasta and butter her bread. By the time he placed the strawberry-topped dessert in front of her, she was too full to eat it.

"I'm stuffed," she whined as she looked at the thick slice of cake he gave her.

"At least take a bite and save the rest for later," he pleaded.

"Okay. Just a taste." Kayla took a small bite and closed her eyes. "Oh my God. This is the best."

"Naw, I got some better recipes if you wanna try 'em." He winked and continued to clear the table. "Excuse me for a moment. I need to run upstairs."

Kayla looked at him inquisitively, but Craig just kissed the top of her head and left her sitting at the table, the sound of Boney James serenading her. *I wonder what he's up there doing?* She didn't even want to think about it. She poured herself another glass of wine and gulped it down. She heard him coming down the steps and regained her composure.

"Wanna come upstairs for a little while?" he asked.

"Uh, I don't think that's a good idea." She could feel her heart beating faster as he walked closer to her.

"I have something for you." He looked deep into Kayla's eyes. She wanted to look away but couldn't. "Please, it's not what you think."

A million thoughts seemed to go through Kayla's mind, including Roni telling her to live it up and have fun. Curiosity won over apprehension and Kayla smiled at him.

He reached for Kayla's hand and she followed him up the steps and into his bedroom. She was surprised when he continued past the bed and opened another door. He motioned for her to come inside. Kayla slowly walked in and gasped. It was the biggest bathroom she had ever seen. There were candles everywhere and she could hear Brian McKnight coming from a wall mounted CD player, asking her if he ever crossed her mind anytime. Craig pulled her closer, pointing to the jetted tub.

"I took the liberty of drawing you a milk bath,

with rose petals, of course. Your towel and wash-cloth are right here. It's a pair of shorts and a T-shirt on the counter for you to put on when you get out. I can bring you another glass of wine if you'd like. This is a time for you. A brother ain't trying to be all up in here or nothing like that, unless you want me to be." He laughed.

"I . . . uh . . ." Kayla was at a loss for words.

"Water's getting cold. Enjoy. I'll check on you in about forty-five minutes. Tub jet button is right here." He pointed to the switch on the wall. "I'm going back downstairs to finish cleaning up the kitchen. Holla if you need anything." He closed the door before Kayla had a chance to respond.

Alone, Kayla put the top down on the commode and sat down to think. She looked at the steaming tub of white liquid with the flowers floating on top. *What have I gotten myself into?* She wanted to call Roni, but remembered her phone was in her purse, downstairs. S*tuff like this happens to Roni and Tia, not me. What, what, what?* As if prompted by Kayla's thoughts, Phyllis Hyman began singing through the speakers that she was "moving on." *Why not? Me too!*

Kayla removed her clothes and stepped into the Jacuzzi. *What if this nigga is some kind of freak with a camera hidden somewhere?* She quickly looked around for a red light hidden somewhere and then smiled at being so paranoid. The soft, hot water felt like heaven on her skin as she submerged her body. She reached and flipped the jet switch and the tub began to massage her body. She relaxed like she never had before. The candles reflected in the bath-room mirror and caused an ambiance that whispered, "Let go and enjoy." She closed her eyes and obeyed.

"You need anything?" Craig quietly tapped, causing her to wake. She looked at her watch and saw that forty-five minutes had passed.

"I'm fine. I'm getting out right now," Kayla replied. She stood up and got out of the tub. Drying off, she realized that her skin was soft and supple. She looked at her reflection and smiled. Maybe it was the wine, but she looked and felt damn good. She decided to scrub all of her makeup off and get a little more comfortable. She bent over to pick up the shirt and shorts Craig had laid out for her. Usually conscious of what her grandma called an "onion butt," Kayla turned around in the mirror and admired herself. She ran her hands along her full breasts and down her flat stomach, resting them on her hips. Bottle shape; blessed with it and worked hard to keep it. She pulled the T-shirt over her head and the shorts over her hips. She slowly opened the door expecting to see Craig, but his room was empty. She looked at the magnificent bed and decided to see how it felt. She sat on the side and rubbed her fingers across the bedspread. *Mink. Go figure.* Kayla laid back and closed her eyes.

"I think you got a little too relaxed."

She sat up when she heard the deep voice. "Oh my. Sorry. I just wanted to sit down for a few moments. I'm sorry," Kayla said, embarrassed.

"Ready to go back down?" Craig looked amused.

"I don't think I can make it." Kayla smiled.

"I'll help you." Craig reached and gently pulled Kayla up. When they got to the top of the steps, he got in front of her and put her on his back.

"What are you doing?" She giggled.

"Told you I'd help. Jump on." He laughed. Kayla hesitated then climbed on Craig's back. She could feel and see his muscles through the thin T-shirt he wore and noticed part of a tattoo on his left shoulder. She looked closer and saw that it was a cross with a rose wrapped around it.

Somehow, they made it back into the living room. Craig had lit the fireplace and had a huge blanket lying in front of it. Kayla got off his back and stood in the middle of it.

"You're amazing," she told him.

"It's Valentine's. I wanted it to be special." He pulled her to him and kissed her like he had before. Kayla responded, for it was what she had been waiting for all night long. She could feel him leading her to the floor and she obliged. They kissed for what seemed like hours. Exploring each other's mouths, tasting each other, neither one wanting to be the first to pull away.

"Turn over," he whispered.

"Huh?" Kayla stopped and realized what he said.

"Turn over. On your stomach."

"Hold on, Craig. Maybe I need to let you know up front," she began.

"I wanna rub your back. Come on." He began rubbing her neck in a circular motion. Kayla's eyes began to close and her head fell forward. "I told you I'm good with my hands." He reached under one of the end tables and pulled out a bottle of oil.

Kayla lay on the blanket and Craig massaged her back and shoulders. His hands worked their way along her body, picking up where the tub jets left off. His touch was firm yet gentle, and there was something about the way his fingers lingered along certain spots that sent a chill down Kayla's spine. She began to feel heat in places she hadn't felt in a while. She heard herself moan as Craig's hands kneaded her lower back.

"Feel good?" he asked her. She could feel him shifting and suddenly she felt his breath in the small of her back as he began nuzzling. Kayla's body tensed, shocked by what he was doing. "Relax," he told her.

He pulled her shirt up, began nibbling his way back up her torso, and licked her shoulders.

"Craig," she whispered. She did not want it to feel this good. It was too hard to say stop. *Tell him you want him to stop,* her mind told her. "What are you doing?" were the words that came out of her mouth.

This was too much for Kayla. Somehow she managed to roll over, but once again got lost in his alluring eyes. Craig continued to sing as he removed her T-shirt and kissed her neck.

Don't do this, her mind said. Her back arched, reaching for his kisses as his mouth found her hard nipples. He kissed each one gently and continued down her stomach, stopping only to pour more oil.

"You are so fine," he paused long enough to say. Before she could thank him, she felt him kiss the inside of each thigh, bending her legs, nibbling her calves.

This is wrong. You don't even know this man, her brain warned her. It was as if her body and mind were at war, but the physical was determined to beat out the mental. When Craig poured oil on each of her feet and began sucking her toes, Kayla knew that her mind had lost all control of her body. She could not remember taking the shorts off, but she knew they were not there when she felt Craig's fingers opening her dripping canal. She gasped as she felt his tongue going where only Geno's had gone before. Craig licked and sucked her like she was one of his sweet recipes that he had perfected. She could hear him moaning and it turned her on to the point where she thought she was gonna lose her mind totally. Her legs began to shake as he buried himself between her legs. And at the moment when she had reached the pinnacle of the voyage he was taking her on, he stopped.

"Not yet. I want to come with you and feel it," he said. He removed his sweats and her eyes widened at his long, thick penis. His hand never left her clitoris, continuing to stroke it, and before she knew it, he had entered her, taking her even further.

"Oh God, please don't stop," Kayla groaned from the back of her throat.

"I won't, baby. I wanna come with you. How long you want me to ride, baby?" He looked deep into Kayla's eyes.

"Forever," Kayla answered. He pleasured her and stroked her with a rhythm like no other and as she felt herself gushing while he pumped into her, they came with a fierceness that shocked the hell out of both of them.

"Dang, Kayla. You certainly had a better night than mine," Roni commented. It was a little after nine in the morning and Kayla had to be at the music store by ten. She had been home since seven, having fallen asleep in Craig's arms as he entertained her with stories about growing up in Mississippi. He had to be at work by six-thirty and told Kayla she could stay as long as she liked, but she chose to leave when he did.

"So you see my little package I gave you came in handy, huh?"

"What package?" Kayla asked as she lay across her bed, not wanting to go to work.

"Uh, the condom." Roni said it like Kayla was slow.

"Oh, yeah it did. Thanks," Kayla said, not wanting to tell her friend her night of sexual pleasure had been an unprotected one. "Look, Ron. Don't tell anyone about this. I just want this one to stay between me and you, okay?"

"Sure." Roni was surprised. Kayla usually shared everything with Yvonne. "They don't know about the date?"

"They don't even know we went out last weekend. I just wanted to keep it on the DL. You know how Yvonne is, and Tia has been wrapped up in some guy named Theo. Hold on, I got a beep." Kayla hit the flash button and answered the other line. "Hello."

"Good Morning, Beautiful. You up yet?" Craig asked her.

"I never went back to sleep. I have to be at work at ten, remember?" she responded.

"Oh yeah. I forgot you were a teacher by day and a CD bootlegger by night," he said, trying to be funny.

"Ha ha. I get off at five, though. What time do

you get off today?" Kayla questioned, trying to feel out whether he was trying to hook up later.

"Uh, I gotta work a double so it'll be pretty late," he said quickly.

"Okay. Well, I gotta get ready and get out of here." She sat up and noticed how late it was.

"I'll call you later. And Kayla, thank you for a great Valentine," he said sexily.

"No, I should be thanking you. Talk to you later." Kayla smiled as she hung up the phone and threw it on the bed. It quickly rang again and she answered it. "Hello."

"Why was I on hold forever? It must have been a man. What did he say?"

"He has to work a double and he'll call me later, nosy," Kayla replied. "But I gotta get out of here."

"At least he's sending you to work with a smile on your face," Roni yelled before Kayla had a chance to hang up.

That was the one and only time Kayla ever slept with Craig. After that night, she only talked to him a few times, nothing serious, and she would see him occasionally when she and the girls went to State Street's. She learned early on that he was full of crap. He would say he was coming over and wouldn't show, but it was all good with Kayla because although the sex was off the hook, it made her realize she still wasn't over Geno, and a relationship wasn't what she needed right now.

4

I need a drink, Kayla thought as she looked down at her vibrating cell phone. Unfortunately, Craig was calling her for the third time in the past fifteen minutes. Kayla hit the end button and sent the call to her voicemail. She had experienced the day from hell and was in no mood for lying, no-good niggas. She had a fight break out in her classroom and her boss actually insinuated that it was her fault, her car was acting like it had an attitude and most importantly, she was stressed as hell working two jobs and still being broke. This is not how her life was supposed to be working out.

"TGIF, girl," her girlfriend Yvonne said as Kayla walked to the school's parking lot.

"You can say that again, girlfriend." Kayla sighed.

"You ready to go? You look worn out," Yvonne said as she unlocked her car.

"Yeah, just frustrated."

"Girl, you need a drink. You wanna go by State Street's for happy hour tonight?" Yvonne asked.

"I don't know. I'm tired, Von."

"Come on. Roni has been calling my cell and I know that's what she wants. Let's go for a little while. At least get our eat on for free." Yvonne smiled and Kayla couldn't help but laugh. "Besides, you may even meet Mister Right."

"More like Mister Right Now." Kayla giggled. "I am not staying all night, Von."

"Cool. You know I'm not gonna be in there for long either, Kay." Yvonne told her friend. "You're taking your car?" she asked as Kayla unlocked her car door.

"I might be ready to leave before you are. I told you I'm tired," Kayla answered and got into her car.

She pulled out of the parking lot behind Yvonne and opened her sunroof. The air felt good on her face and she immediately felt rejuvenated. She turned on the CD player and let the mellowness of Jill Scott relax her as she drove. Her cell rang and recognizing Tia's number, she answered it.

"Hey, ho!" Tia sang into her ear.

"Hey, girl. Where you at?" Kayla asked. Tia was a fitness trainer and she worked varied hours, depending on her clients.

"On my way to da club to meet y'all." She laughed.

"I know you are all diva-fied, so let me warn you that I am not. I have on my jeans, a black shirt and some casual shoes."

"But I know you got your spare pair in your trunk, trick, and you'll probably mousse that good hair and make that face up before you step up in there, so I ain't even worried," she answered. She knew Kayla too well. Kayla did have a spare pair of shoes in her trunk, as well as a full makeup kit, complete with extra hair products.

"I'll see you in a minute. We're almost there. Ms. Yvonne is leading the way."

"Alright, I'm pulling into the parking lot right now, so I'll get us a table," she said and hung the phone up. Kayla's cell immediately rang again and this time it was Roni.

"What up, Ron?" she answered.

"What's wrong with you? Von said you don't feel good."

"Just tired, I guess. Dealing with them bad-ass kids is wearing me down."

"You need a vacation. I don't know why you don't call out sometimes."

"Unlike you, I don't teach public school. We don't have a million subs to come in when we call out. We are short staffed. And even if I call out at one job, I have another one to go to," Kayla replied.

"What you need to do is find a guy that's paid to help you out for a minute. Geno is over and done with. You need to find another to step in and take over," Roni continued. Just the mention of Geno's name made Kayla's heart beat faster. Despite everything, she still missed him.

She pulled into the club parking lot, parked beside Yvonne and noticed Roni walking toward them. She shook her head at her and put the cell into her purse. "That's why you got a two hundred dollar cell phone bill. Why didn't you tell me you were already here?"

"I was caught up in the conversation." Roni shrugged. They gave each other a quick hug and Kayla opened her trunk to change shoes. She set up her big mirror and touched up her hair and makeup. Times like this she was glad she opted to cut her shoulder length hair to the short, funky style. She had surprised everyone when she did it, but she was going through a lot and decided it was time for a change. Roni and Yvonne watched as she handled her beauty business.

"You ready, Diva?" Yvonne asked.

"Yep. Let's go." Kayla turned and smiled a weak smile as she closed her trunk.

"'Bout time," Roni joked as they joined the line that began to form outside of State Street's Sports Bar. It was becoming well known that they had one of the best happy hour buffets in the city, and each time the Lonely Hearts Club visited, the crowd seemed to get bigger and bigger. After a few moments waiting in line and getting their ID's checked, they made their way inside.

"You see Tia?" Yvonne said loudly above the sound of Craig Mack's "Flava in Your Ear."

"No, let's look over by the wall." Kayla pointed to the round tables lined along the side of the club. "You know she's not far from the dance floor."

"I'll call her." Roni reached for her cell but Kayla snatched it before she could dial. Yvonne laughed at her two friends who always provided her with comic relief.

"Put that phone down! She's right over there." Kayla pointed to Tia who was waving her arms to get their attention. She was decked out in a black linen pantsuit and heels. She had her braids pulled to the top of her head and looked like she had just stepped off the cover of a magazine with her beautiful face.

"Hey, Ms. Thang," Roni said as the ladies made their way to the table.

"Hey yourself. Everybody ready to get their groove on?" She raised her glass toward the bar where a nice looking gentleman was smiling at them.

"Cute. Friend of yours?" Yvonne asked Tia.

"Too early to tell, girl. But he did buy me a drink and he hasn't been all up in my face. That's a good sign," she told them. They all took their seats and a waitress came over to take their drink orders.

"Blue Malibu," Roni said.

"Apple Martini," Yvonne added.

"White Zinfandel," Kayla murmured. She felt drained and really didn't feel like hanging out. The thought of having to be at the music store the next day from nine in the morning until four, was not helping her mood.

"What's wrong with you?" Tia frowned at her.

"I'm okay, just tired," Kayla said to her friend.

"I told her she needs a couple days off," Roni said. "That's why they give you vacation and sick days."

"Not at our school. We are so short staffed that it is not even funny," Yvonne told them. "Mrs. Warren guilt trips employees into not calling out."

"Well, maybe you'll feel better after you've eaten. Let's hit the buffet," Tia said as she led the way to the soul food buffet the club offered every Friday night. Usually, Kayla could not get enough of the chicken wings, but she didn't even have an appetite. She watched her girlfriends pile their plates up as she put a dab of 'this and that' on her own plate and maneuvered her way through the crowd, returning to her seat. Suddenly, she felt someone put his arms around her and whisper in her ear.

"I knew you'd be here. Why didn't you call me back?" the husky voice said.

She tried not to smile, but could not help herself. "Because I knew you would give me some lie about not being here, so I figured why bother?" She turned and faced him.

"Come on, Kayla. Why you wanna treat a brother like that?" Craig asked her.

"Geno, I'm tired. I've had a long day and I don't feel well," she said.

"Yeah, you must really be sick, because my name is Craig, not Geno. Call me when you feel better." He turned and walked away. Kayla could not believe she had called him Geno. She knew it was time for her to leave.

"What's wrong with him?" Yvonne asked. She knew Kayla talked to Craig every once in a while, but from what she saw across the room, it looked like Kayla had hurt his feelings.

"I accidentally called him Geno," Kayla said as she sat at the table and took a big gulp of her wine.

"You what?" Tia laughed out loud, causing Kayla to smile.

"I called him Geno."

"Oh, no you didn't. What did he say?" Roni was tickled to death.

"He told me to call him when I could get his name right, basically," Kayla said. She picked over her food, watched her girls dance and flirt, had a second glass of wine and decided to call it a night. As she stood up, she nearly lost her balance.

"Are you alright, Kayla?" Yvonne reached out to grab her before she could fall. Roni took notice and rushed over to the table.

"How much did she have to drink?" Yvonne glared at Roni.

"Two glasses, and why are you rolling your eyes at me? It was your idea to meet here, if you recall. Kayla never gets lit," Roni threw back at her.

"I'm okay. Dang. I just got a little light headed. I'm fine." Kayla regained her composure and gathered her purse.

"I'm gonna drive you home," Yvonne said and looked for her keys.

"Von, I am fine. I told you I'm tired. I'll call you and let you know when I get home." Kayla hugged Yvonne and Roni and waved at Tia as she left. Her eyes met Craig's as she watched him dance with another female on the dance floor. *Good, let him find someone else to lie to for a change.*

5

As broke as she was, Kayla called in and didn't go to work the next day. After a full week of teaching, she was too tired to even move. When Roni called, Kayla told her that she had the flu and assured her that she would be fine. She got up to get some water and a wave of nausea came over her. Grabbing the side of the toilet, she threw what felt like her entire insides up. Then she remembered she had missed her period. Hell, she had missed two periods. Beads of sweat began to form around her brow and she crawled back into bed. *Please God, let me just have the flu.*

She slept until Sunday afternoon and somehow found the strength to make it to the drugstore and get a pregnancy test. She sat on the side of her bed and looked at the pink line, thinking that it must be wrong. There was no way that she could be pregnant. She had been on the pill for years, ever since her mother took her to the doctor when she turned fifteen and told her to take them "just in case." Her mother. She was going to be so pissed. She and her father had worked so hard for her and Anjelica, giving them a good home. Her dad worked as a city bus driver for the past thirty years and her mother was a secretary. Both still worked hard. She had never even told them the truth about Anjelica and Geno. She didn't want to cause conflict within the family, even though it wasn't her fault. Kayla hated to disappoint her parents. Their respect was too important to her. But she knew that her having a baby would be a letdown for them, because she had let herself down.

Kayla needed to talk to someone, but she was too embarrassed to tell her girlfriends. She hadn't told anyone that she had slept with Geno a few months ago. It wasn't anything that was planned. She was working at the music store when he walked up to the counter.

"Do you all have any Go-Go?" he asked, so focused on the sales paper that he didn't look up.

"G?" she asked, looking at him and smiling.

"Kayla. What in the world are you doing here?"

"What does it look like? I work here," she said.

"For real? You get a discount?"

"Only for my family and friends. You don't fit either category." She smirked at him.

"That is real cold, Kay. You act like you ain't got no love for a brother."

"When I did have love for you, you did my sister. What are you doing on this side of town anyway?" she asked.

"Funny. I came to visit my moms."

"You here alone? Where's your new woman I

heard so much about?" She couldn't resist asking. Rumor had it that he was living with some older chick.

"Jealous?"

"Please. I just hope she doesn't have any sisters. The Go-Go section is this way," she said and led him to the right aisle.

"You are a real comedian, you know that?"

"Whatever. You'd better hurry up because we close in ten minutes." She turned and went back to her register. He returned with three CDs and she rang them up.

She handed him his bag, adding sarcastically, "Thanks for shopping. Have a great night."

"I really want to talk to you, Kayla. Can we go somewhere after you get outta here?" he asked.

"I don't think that would be a good idea, G," she answered and watched as he reluctantly walked out of the store. She tried not to admit it, but she missed him terribly.

Her manager locked the store up and Kayla quickly braved the cold wind and ran to the parking lot. When she got there, Geno was standing next to her car.

"What do you want?" Kayla inquired. It was cold and she wanted to go home.

"Kayla, can we just go somewhere and talk?" Geno asked her.

"About what, G?" She unlocked her door and hopped in her car. Geno remained standing in the cold. She cranked the engine and rolled down the window enough to hear what he was saying.

"Shit, Kayla, I don't care. I just want to talk to you. I miss you. I miss hanging out with you. We used to have fun, Kayla. I ain't saying we gotta talk about what happened, but let's just go out and chill for old time's sake. Please?" She could see the mist coming out of his mouth as he talked.

"Are you begging?" she asked.

"What?"

"I said, are you begging?" She knew Geno hated to be played like a sucker, but she wanted to see how far he would go to talk to her.

"Don't play with me, Kayla. It's cold as hell out here." He blew into his hands and rubbed them together. "Yeah, Kay, I'm begging."

"Where you trying to go?" She couldn't help but smile.

"Follow me. And you need to get this raggedy car of yours checked out. It sounds like a moped." He laughed.

"Don't push your luck, Geno. I ain't followed you yet," she warned.

She followed him to an old hangout spot that they used to shoot pool at back in the day. They laughed and talked like old times, taking shots of tequila and drinking beer. She got caught up in the moment, enjoying just being with Geno. She didn't resist when he suggested they get a hotel room. The good feeling ended when she awoke, curled by his side with his arms around her, to the sound of his cell phone ringing. He nuzzled against her and kissed the top of her forehead while she pretended to be asleep.

Geno slipped out of bed and quietly retrieved the ringing phone out of his pocket. He looked over at Kayla again and went into the bathroom. She could hear him mumbling through the door, lying about where he was and who he was with. Knowing that this had been a mistake because she still had feelings for him, she quickly got dressed and left him without saying a word.

Now here she was facing a situation she never thought she'd have to face. They were no longer together and the night they shared had just been one of physical pleasure, not emotional. She threw the white plastic entity in the trash and went back to bed, too depressed to think about her next move.

Somehow, Kayla made it to work by seven o'clock Monday morning. She knew she looked a horrid mess with her hair barely wrapped the night before and not a drop of makeup on other than a little foundation, but she had to get to school early and talk with the principal, Mrs. Warren. Kayla dreaded telling the woman that she needed the day off, because it was a well-known fact throughout the staff that unless you were dead, Mrs. Warren expected you to be at work—no exceptions. It was one of the few things Kayla hated about her job.

"Mrs. Warren. I need the day off," Kayla told her.

"What seems to be the problem, Ms. Hopkins?" she asked.

"I think I have the flu. As a matter of fact, I was sick all weekend. I really need to go to the doctor and maybe take a few days off," Kayla pleaded.

"Ms. Hopkins, you know we are extremely short staffed and subs are hard to come by these days. Why don't you at least get started this morning and then we'll see how you feel. Get your class settled and I will work on finding someone to cover your class this afternoon," she told Kayla. Kayla dragged herself to her classroom and Yvonne stopped in to see how she was doing.

"You look like death warmed over. You still don't feel well, huh?" She placed a cup of hot tea on Kayla's desk.

"Thanks, Von. No. I'm trying to go to the doctor this afternoon, but Mrs. Warren swears she can't find a sub for me. Go figure, but she can go and get her hair done every Friday morning with no problem." Kayla stirred the hot liquid.

"I can cover for you today. No one has anything scheduled in the library, so I don't think that would be a big deal," Yvonne suggested.

"Thanks, Von. Can you go and tell her?" Kayla greeted her students half-heartedly as they entered the classroom. Once Yvonne had cleared with Mrs. Warren that she would cover for Kayla and her students were settled, Kayla went home.

I need to make an appointment with Dr. Bray as soon as possible," Kayla told the receptionist at her doctor's office.

"I'll be happy to see what we have available. Name?"

"Kayla Hopkins."

"Okay, Ms. Hopkins, let's see. She has a cancellation at ten-fifteen. Can you make it then?" she asked.

"Yeah. That's fine," Kayla mumbled.

"Ten-fifteen it is. And what is the nature of your visit?"

"I think I failed a pregnancy test," Kayla told her.

* * *

Sitting in the examination room, she waited for the doctor, trying not to throw up. *I have finally done it. I have ruined my life. My dad is gonna have a heart attack. How am I gonna have a baby and work two jobs? What am I gonna do? What is Geno gonna say when he finds out he's gonna be a father? Me and Geno are having a baby. This can not be happening to me.*

"Kayla, Kayla, Kayla. How you doing, girl?" Karen was her usual chipper self. She had been Kayla's doctor since her junior year of college and she always made her feel comfortable.

"Hey, Karen. I'm not doing all that great. I failed a home pregnancy test." Kayla sighed.

"You failed an office pregnancy test, too, sweetie. But let's not look at it as failing. I know many women who would love to have these positive results." She washed her hands and read Kayla's chart.

"I wish it was them rather than me. I can't believe this."

"Believe it. Well, let's check you out. Lie back." Kayla lay back on the table and Karen began her examination. Kayla closed her eyes and tried not to think about why she was there. For a moment, it felt like a regular exam until Karen pulled out an odd looking probe and said, "Now, how about we take a look and see what we're working with?"

"What's that?" Kayla almost began to panic.

"I'm gonna do a vaginal ultrasound and see exactly how far along you are. It may be a little uncomfortable, but no pain." She could see Kayla was worried.

"I been on the pill for years. How did this happen?"

"Well, even the pill isn't one hundred percent

foolproof. Women get pregnant on the pill too, Kayla."

Karen wasn't making Kayla feel any better. She didn't know what she wanted to hear, but she knew that it wasn't what Karen was saying.

"How far along am I?" Kayla asked. She figured that she had been with Geno about three months ago.

"Well, the ultrasound puts you at around ten weeks. That would give you a due date of about November twenty-first. Thanksgiving Day. I guess that would give you a conception date of, uh, February fourteenth, Valentine's Day," Karen said matter-of-factly as she calculated.

"Dear God, no." Kayla sat stunned and could not move.

Kayla went home, called both her jobs and took the rest of the week off. She turned the ringer off on her phone and climbed into bed. She thought about the baby she was carrying and what she should do. Here she was single, not even able to make ends meet while working two jobs, and now she may have another mouth to feed. And she didn't even want to think about the father. That bastard couldn't even commit to a movie date, let alone a baby. She had barely even talked to him in a few weeks, now she was gonna call him and tell him she was knocked up? Be for real. Kayla didn't even want to think about her parents' reaction. Everything she had worked so hard for could now be ruined by a fucking one-night stand. There was no way she was gonna keep this baby. It made no sense.

I can't have this baby, she thought as she drifted off to sleep. She woke to the sound of her doorbell ringing. "Hey, girl," she said and opened the door for Yvonne.

"I see you're not feeling better." Yvonne followed Kayla into her bedroom and watched her climb back into bed. "I tried to call you but you didn't answer. Mrs. Warren just left a message that I would be subbing for you the remainder of the week, so I decided to come by. Did you go to the doctor?"

"Yeah."

"And?" Yvonne sat at the foot of the bed.

"She said I have a virus and it has to run its course." Kayla slid deeper under the covers. She wasn't ready to share the truth with anyone, especially after she decided to have an abortion. She knew that would be one decision she'd take to her grave.

"I figured you did. You know it's been going around the school. I'm surprised I haven't gotten it yet," Yvonne told her.

"This is one virus you don't want to catch," Kayla murmured.

"Let me get you something to drink." She took Kayla's empty glass off the nightstand and went into the kitchen. When she came back, she gave Kayla a cup of tea and a bottle of water, then filled her in on her students. "Do you need me to do anything else while I'm here?"

"No. I just wanna sleep." Kayla managed a weak smile. "But can you let Tia and Roni know that I am okay? I turned my ringer off and I don't want them to worry."

"Done."

"Thanks, Von." She sat up and took the saucer holding the steaming liquid.

"Okay. Call me if you need anything." Yvonne gave her tired looking girlfriend a hug and made sure the door was locked behind her as she left.

She was lying back in her bed trying to watch *Law and Order* when there was another knock. She grabbed her robe and hobbled to the door. She looked through the peephole and saw Roni standing outside.

"Didn't Yvonne call you?" Kayla shook her head at her.

"Yeah, but I wanted to check on you myself. And since you're not answering your phone, here I am. What's wrong with you?" She followed Kayla back to the bedroom.

"I got the flu, that's all. Damn." She could not look at her as she answered. Roni knew her too well. The two shared a sisterly bond that she and Anjelica never had.

"The flu, Kay?"

"Yeah, Roni. The flu. Let it go, okay?"

"You're the one on the defense, Kayla. I just asked what the hell was wrong with you. Now it would be something else if you were lying, wouldn't it?"

Kayla tried to brush her friend off, but it wasn't working. She was scared and had to tell someone. Roni was her best friend, but she was embarrassed. Shit, it was Roni who gave her the condom that she didn't use. How could she tell her that she was that irresponsible? All of the questions and feelings that Kayla felt overwhelmed her and she began to cry.

"Kayla, talk to me. What is going on?" Roni

hugged her girlfriend and tried to comfort her. Kayla told Roni about her unplanned pregnancy. She even told her about the night she spent with Geno, and how it made her feel even worse knowing that he had moved on, but she was still harboring feelings for him.

"Kayla, it's okay. Geno is gonna be a good father. He still loves you and he will love this baby too."

"But, Ron. You don't understand. I can't have this baby. You don't get it. Geno isn't the father. Craig is," she admitted to her best friend. She had finally said it. She even felt somewhat relieved.

"Damn."

"Exactly. I *cannot* keep it. It makes no sense."

"Kayla, it doesn't have to make sense in order for you to keep it. You don't know what you're saying. You have never believed in abortion, Kay. But now because the man you wanted to be your baby daddy *ain't*, you want to get rid of it? That's not even you, Kay. You don't even think like that." Roni sat up and looked at her.

"But Ron, I don't have no money to take care of a baby. And what about Mama and Daddy? They are gonna be pissed too. And Craig, don't even get me started on him," Kayla cried.

"You know that if you want to have this baby for real, Kay, it's gonna be taken care of. Your mama and daddy are still gonna love you no matter what. And we can let the child support judge take care of that nigga if he don't wanna act right. I just want you to see all the sides of this before you decide to do something I know you don't want to, Kayla. Take it from someone who's been there. It's not an easy thing to do. But I am here for you no matter what you decide to do."

"Ron, I . . ." Kayla began, but Roni cut her off.

"Senior year, sweetie. Remember? But I did what was best for *me* at the time. Why do you think I stay on y'all about condoms? A lot of good it did *you*, I see."

Kayla could not help but laugh. She was glad she had decided to confide in Roni. They talked a little while longer and then Roni stood up to leave.

"Know that I love you and support you, and so do a lot of other people, Kay. Unconditionally, no matter who your baby daddy is." She hugged Kayla and said good-bye.

6

For three days Kayla's routine consisted of sleeping, taking showers, drinking tea and water, eating crackers and throwing up. On Thursday morning, she rolled over and looked at the alarm clock. The numbers read eleven twenty-one. *November twenty-first, my due date.* Kayla did the only thing she knew how; she began to pray.

Okay, God, I am finished having my pity party. It's just you and me now. What I did was wrong, and I am asking you to forgive me. But I know that what has come out of it is a blessing, not a curse. Please, God, guide me and tell me what to do. Give me the strength to make it through this, because I can't do it without You. She closed her eyes and did not realize that she had gone back to sleep until she checked the time, and this time it read two-fourteen. Kayla knew what her next move had to be. *Okay, God, here goes,* she thought as she reached for the cordless phone and dialed the numbers.

"Hey, beautiful. I was hoping you would call me," Craig said when he answered.

"Hi. Are you at work?" she asked him. She could not remember his schedule.

"I get off at three. Why? What's up?"

"I need to talk to you. Do you think you can stop by on your way home? Or maybe I can meet you at your house?" Kayla felt that this was something she should tell him in person rather than over the phone.

"No! I mean, I'm not going straight home."

"Then can I meet you somewhere?"

"What's the deal? I guess I can swing by your place. Is this gonna take long, because I have somewhere to be."

"No. I just need to talk to you." Kayla tried not to be irritated by his covertness. She gave him directions to her apartment and got up to prepare for what she was about to do.

"Nice place." Craig gave her a quick hug and kissed her lightly.

"It's not quite as lavish as yours. Have a seat. Would you like something to drink?" She remembered to be cordial. *He is a guest*, she reminded herself.

"No, no thanks." He looked down at his watch, "So is this just a ploy to get me into your bed?" He smiled his sexy smile; always the flirt. He sat on the soft, hunter green sofa that Kayla had inherited from her parents' den.

"Definitely not. That's the reason I'm in the shape I am in now." Kayla tried to say what she needed to say without coming straight out and telling him.

"Um, you look like you're in great shape to me, Beautiful."

"Not for long." She chose to sit in the chair across from him so she could look him right in his face.

"Alright, Kayla. What is this all about? Come on. I told you I gotta be somewhere."

"Okay. You know I've been sick, right?" she began.

"Yeah. I know you called me some other nigga's name at the club last week. You said you were tired. What's wrong?" He began to look worried.

"I'm pregnant," she told him quietly. She looked in his face for some type of reaction. He just nodded his head.

"Okay." He shrugged his shoulders.

"By you," she whispered.

"What? Me? Are you sure? We were together only one time." He responded like she had made a bad menu choice, rather than told him she was carrying his child. She thought it would go a lot worse than it was. Kayla had heard horror stories from other women when they told guys they were pregnant and it was unplanned.

"It only takes one time, Craig."

"Alright. So, how much you need?"

"What do you mean?" She was confused.

"For the procedure. I mean, you want me to pay half. Isn't that why I'm over here?"

"What procedure?" the realism of what he was talking about sunk in. "The only procedure I'm having is a full-term delivery," she said angrily.

Craig looked down at his watch. "Look, Kayla. Obviously you haven't thought this all the way through. I ain't in no position to have a baby. I mean, you said so yourself you gotta work two jobs to make ends meet. How you gonna take care of a baby?"

Now, this is the reaction Kayla was expecting. She felt the anger rise in her body. "I plan on doing what I need to *and* do a hell of a job taking care of *my* baby! I mean, it is *my* body!"

"This baby might not even be mine. I ain't even gonna get into this with you, Kayla. But if it is, I'm telling you that I *can't* take care of a baby. Not right now. I just can't. Now you can be a superwoman and do what *you* want to do because it's *your* body or whatever. But I'm just trying to tell you up front. I ain't trying to have a kid right now!"

"Then your ass shoulda considered that when you went raw dog on me. And furthermore, you ain't my prime choice to be the father of my child. Nigga, ain't nobody trying to trap your ass if that's what you're thinking!" Kayla got up and stood in his face, taking him by surprise.

"The only thing I'm thinking is that you done lost your damn mind!" He took a step back for fear that she would swing on him.

"I ain't lost my mind yet! Look, I did not call you over here to argue. I'm just trying to talk to you about the situation at hand." She took a deep breath and rubbed her temples, trying to calm down.

"The situation at hand is this, you are not trying to hear nothing I have to say right about now and I gotta go. I'll call you later once you've calmed the fuck down and are rational." He stood up and walked out, leaving her stunned, wondering what she was supposed to do next.

7

It was May and Kayla was now three months pregnant. She still hadn't told anyone, with the exception of Roni and Craig, because she didn't feel ready yet. She was still trying to convince herself that she was making the right decision by keeping this baby. She hadn't talked to Craig since the night she'd told him about the baby. She didn't call him and he didn't call her; not that she expected him to. She figured that she wouldn't really start to show until after school was out, so she wouldn't have to do a whole lot of explaining to her parents or her students until the start of the new school year, *if they let her return.*

Kayla was sitting at her desk, grading papers as her students worked on their Mother's Day cards. *Next year, I will be celebrating Mother's Day,* she thought. Suddenly, David, one of her students was on the ground.

"Stop!" She heard him yell out. She stood just in

time to see another student, Nate, snatch something out of his hands as he tried to get up.

"Gimme my glue stick, punk!" he responded.

"It's not yours!" David began. The remainder of the class began to crowd around to get a front row view.

"Nate! David! What is going on?" Kayla rushed over to stop whatever was about to start.

"This punk took my glue stick! I just took it back!"

"It's mine, Ms. Hopkins. Look at the bottom. My mom put my initials on it. He picked it up when it rolled on the floor," Dave explained.

"Give me the glue." Nate stood, looking at her like he wanted to kill her, but Kayla was determined not to bend. She looked at him just as hard and yelled, "Now!"

"I hate you!" Nate yelled as he picked up the desk and hurled it at her. The students began to duck and scream as Kayla watched it fall in front of her.

"Pick it up," she told him calmly. He looked confused, so she told him again, "Pick it up. You missed the first time. Now this time I need you to hit me so I can sue your parents for your house *and* their cars, *and* I can sue the school, too. Now let's try it again. Pick it up."

"No!" He spat at her.

"I'm giving you another chance. Pick it up. If you're gonna get suspended for it, at least get the satisfaction of knowing that you hit me, Nate. Now pick it up."

"I ain't getting suspended," he laughed. "Don't you know how much money my parents donate to this school? Mrs. Warren ain't suspending me, 'cause if she do, my parents are gonna pull me out. Can't you see? I rule this school."

"We'll see. Well, I gave you a chance and you didn't take it. Don't even bother taking your books. I'll bring them down when I bring your referral." She walked back to her desk and went back to grading her papers.

Her students were still stunned by the incident and were not moving. "Finish your gifts so you can take them home," she announced. Nate stormed out of the room, slamming the door behind him.

Kayla waited about fifteen minutes before she went down to the office, giving Nate and herself some time to cool off. She was so mad she wanted to smack him. She was going to demand expulsion for him. Nate was more of a problem than the school deserved to deal with, and she was no longer going to tolerate his behavior. She walked into the office and found him sitting in the waiting area.

"Where is Mrs. Warren?" she asked the secretary.

"Giving a tour. She should be right back. Did he really throw a desk at you?" She looked shocked.

"Yep," Kayla answered and looked at the crude little boy, sitting like he owned the joint. "I've gotta go back to the class. Tell Mrs. Warren she can buzz me if she needs me." Kayla proceeded down the hallway.

"Ms. Hopkins?" She heard Mrs. Warren's voice and looked up. "We just left your classroom."

"You did?" Kayla commented, not realizing who "we" were. She hated the dimly lit hallways of the school.

"Yes, this is Mr. and Mrs. Coleman. They are enrolling their son, Nigel, in the fall." Mrs. Warren introduced the couple. As Kayla extended her hand, she looked at the gentleman's face and nearly passed out.

"Ms. Hopkins is one of our best teachers." Mrs. Warren beamed.

"Avis Coleman." The dark skinned woman with the bad weave job shook Kayla's hand. "This is my husband, Craig."

"Nice to meet you." Kayla did not look at them. She kept her focus on Mrs. Warren. "I hope my students were on their best behavior?"

"Of course. They have made some beautiful gifts for their mothers. They will be so pleased on Sunday," Mrs. Warren said to her.

"Your classroom is so nice," Bad-weave Wife commented.

"Yes, it was beautiful," Craig had the audacity to say. Kayla wanted to punch him in the forehead. The motherfucker was actually smiling at her.

"Thank you. Well, I have to be getting back to help them finish up. Enjoy the rest of your tour." She quickly returned to her classroom and sat down. Her head was going in fifty million directions and she felt like she wanted to throw up. Somehow, Kayla made it to the restroom in the teachers' lounge and stood over the sink to splash cold water on her face.

Married. How can he be married? I have been to his home, in his bed. He cannot be married. Kayla tried to think of every detail of the house and could not come up with anything that might have indicated that a woman lived there, let alone a wife and a family. *All the times he couldn't make it when we were supposed to go out, the supposed 'double shifts' he had to work—all lies.* Kayla was furious. She didn't know who she was angrier with, Craig for being so damn deceitful or herself for being so damn naïve. *And this nigga smiled at me in front of his goddamn wife.* Kayla thought about marching into the principal's office and telling the ghetto woman about her husband who tried to come off as so fucking polite. But then, there was no way she could look into his face without smacking the shit outta him, so she decided to chill, *for now.* The sound of the bell startled her and she caught a glimpse of her reflection in the mirror. She quickly got herself together and returned to the classroom. Sitting at her desk, she remained motionless, unable to think.

"Ms. Hopkins?" She looked up to see Mrs. Warren standing in the doorway. "Can I speak to you in the hall?"

"Yes, ma'am." Kayla tried to think of a way to explain to Mrs. Warren that she had no idea Craig was married.

"I wanted to talk to you before Nate's parents got here," Mrs. Warren said when Kayla reached the hall.

Nate. The desk. Kayla had almost forgotten about the incident.

"Okay." Kayla shrugged.

"What brought this on, Ms. Hopkins?" Mrs. Warren walked closer to Kayla.

"Nate took David's glue and when David took it back, Nate pushed him. When I told him to go to the office, he picked up the desk and threw it at me," Kayla told her.

"Did David aggravate Nate in any way?"

"No." Kayla was confused at this point.

"Did you say anything out of the way to Nate?"

Kayla could feel heat rising to her neck and she had to tell herself to remain calm. "Are you asking me did I somehow provoke this incident, Mrs. Warren?"

"I know that you have had some conflicts in your classroom a few times these past couple of weeks involving Nathaniel. I just want to hear your version before I speak with his parents." Mrs. Warren began to read the bulletin board. Kayla could not believe what her boss was trying to say. *She don't have my back,* she thought. *She is trying to make this my fault and keep that bad-ass boy in school. Nate was right.*

"Mrs. Warren, Nate bullies others, he doesn't get bullied. He harasses his classmates and he is disrespectful to the staff. We give him chance after chance and he does not improve. And now, you're still not kicking him out, are you?" Kayla said incredulously.

"Ms. Hopkins, Nathaniel Morgan has been at this school since he was four years old. His parents are some of our biggest contributors and support this school in all of its endeavors. Now, I know that Nate has been going through a rough time of it, but his parents and I feel that it would not be in his best interest to remove Nathaniel from school at this time."

"You mean he is not even being suspended?" Kayla was appalled at what Mrs. Warren was saying. "He could've hurt me or another child with that desk. You've gotta be kidding me, right?"

"It's near the end of the school year and he will need to prepare to take his final examinations, Ms.

Hopkins. This school is in the habit of solving problems, not expelling them. That is one of the goals of Academy."

"Okay, Mrs. Warren. But it's in my best interest to educate my students without having a menace in my classroom trying to prevent that from happening. And since the *Academy* and I don't have the same goals or interests, I quit!"

Kayla went into her room, gathered the remainder of her things and strutted out of the classroom, pausing before she left. "You may have the pleasure of letting Nate's parents know that I won't be provoking him anymore, because I am no longer their son's teacher. I will let my other parents know personally. Good-bye, Mrs. Warren. Good luck finding a sub!"

8

It can't get any worse than this. Kayla looked on the caller ID as her phone rang later that night and then realized it could.

"Hello."

"Kayla Denise Hopkins, why haven't you called me?,,

"Hi, Mama. I'm sorry. I've been busy. You know I work two jobs," Kayla answered. She knew her mother was mad because she used Kayla's full name. She wanted to call her mother, she really did, but she just couldn't bring herself to do it.

"I don't care how many jobs you work. Your Daddy and I been worried sick. I know you know I been calling because you got caller ID. Did you get the message I left for you last week? And don't lie to me, either."

"Yes, Ma. I told you, I've been working." Kayla sighed.

"Are you coming home this weekend?" her mother asked.

"No, Ma. You know my car has been acting up." That was the truth. Her car had been acting crazy over the past couple of weeks.

"I can send Anjelica to pick you up Friday night," her mother offered.

"No! Do not do that. You know I don't want her doing nothing for me, Mama," Kayla told her mother.

"Kayla, that is your sister. Now I don't know what has happened to cause you two to become so distant, but that fact will never change and don't you forget it. You understand?"

"Yes, ma'am." Kayla felt as if she was a little girl again the way her mother scolded her. She could not stop the tears from falling down her cheek.

"Kayla, what is wrong with you? Why are you crying, Baby? I know your feelings don't get hurt that easily."

"I quit my job, Mama." Kayla told her mother about the desk incident that had happened in her classroom.

"You'll find something else, baby. What the Devil means for bad, God always means for good. That is with every one of your *situations*. There's no point in crying about it. You know what you have to do. Get yourself together and get another job," her mother told her. "Just know that you have our love and support."

When her mother said that, Kayla began to cry even harder.

"Kayla. Something else is going on. Tell me." She could hear the worry in her mother's voice and decided that telling her would be the right thing to do.

"Mama, I'm pregnant," she said in barely a whisper.

"Oh, Kayla." Her mother sighed.

"Mama, I am so sorry. I didn't mean for it to happen, I mean, I swear, I . . ." Kayla could not go on. She was sobbing. She knew that her mother was devastated by this news. She had raised Kayla to be a respectable young woman and now look what had happened.

"How far along are you?" her mother asked her.

"Three months. I'm due Thanksgiving Day." Kayla sniffed.

"So, you *are* having it?"

"Yes."

"Good, and the father? What does he have to say about this?" Her mother questioned. What little relief Kayla had begun to feel now left her. She began to whimper again.

"That's what makes it even worse, Mama. I had a one-night stand and we really don't even have a relationship. I am so sorry."

"Stop apologizing, Kayla. You are a grown woman, not some fifteen-year-old high school student. Granted, I *am* sorry that this happened under the circumstances, but you'll be okay."

"I just wanted you to be proud of me."

"Your father and I are proud of you, Kayla. Let me let you talk to him."

"Mama, no. Please, not now. I can't tell him now."

"Kayla, he's gonna find out sooner or later."

"I know. But I just need a little more time."

"Suit yourself. But please don't dwell on us being mad or thinking that you are a failure because of this. We love you Kayla, no matter what. Do you need anything? You have enough money?"

"Yes, Mama." Kayla laughed a little.

"How're you feeling?"

"Better. I was really sick, but now I'm over it, I guess."

"I got a beautiful Mother's Day bouquet from Geno. Have you talked to him lately?"

Kayla could not believe he sent her mother flowers. "I saw him a few weeks ago," Kayla told her. "I still love him, Mama."

"You always will, baby. I wish I could tell you that your feelings for him will stop, but I can't lie to you. I just don't understand what happened."

"Things just happen, Mama. Look at what has happened to me. I am now knocked up and unemployed on top of that."

"But you're gonna be fine. I know that. But, you need to tell your daddy. You owe him that much."

"I will, Mama. I promise." Kayla felt as if a ton of bricks had been lifted from her shoulders. "I'll call you on Sunday and wish you a Happy Mother's Day."

"No, this year I can call you." Her mother laughed. "I love you, Kayla."

"Love you too, Mama." She lay back on the bed. The sound of the doorbell caused her to jump. She looked over at the clock and saw that it was after eight.

"Hey, Kay. Am I intruding?" Kayla was stunned as she opened the door and saw Geno standing there. He looked good. He had let his facial hair grow out to a full beard and it was trimmed perfectly, reminding her of a built Craig David. His thick arms protruded from his SeanJohn T-shirt and in his perfect hands he held a plastic bag.

"Geno. No. Come on in." She opened the door and followed him into the living room. When they reached it, he turned around and faced her.

"Can't a brother get a hug?" He reached and pulled her to him, laughing. It was a sound she hadn't heard in a while and until then, she didn't realize she missed it. "You cut your hair again. And you filling out. Damn, Kay. You look good."

"You grew a beard. And you working out. You look good, G." She quickly pulled away from him for fear that he may figure out why she was filling out.

"Still crazy. How you been?" He looked at Kayla and sat on the sofa.

"Okay. How is everything with you, Geno?" Kayla sat on the other end of the couch and they faced each other. "Wait a minute, how did you find out where I live?"

"I have my resources." He smiled at her.

"Okay, *resources*. They do have laws for that now. I believe it's called stalking."

"Damn, that's cold. I figured after our last encounter you'd be glad I found you." He took her hand and looked at her curiously. "Ma sent me over here to invite you over Sunday. You know whether we are together or not, you are still a part of my family. She says she hasn't talked to you in a minute. That's not like you, Kay. What's going on?"

"Nothing, G." Kayla tried to lie but she could not keep the tears from falling. She missed Geno and hoped they would somehow get back together. Now the reality of carrying another man's child, a married man on top of that, had wrecked that possibility. Geno had always said he would never date a woman with children because it was too much drama.

"Kayla, come here." He reached for her and she cried into his arms, imagining for a moment that she was his again. "What's wrong, baby?"

She mentally began to panic. For a second, she started to be honest and tell him the truth in its entirety, but she thought better of it and blurted out, "I quit my job."

"You quit?" He wiped her tears and stood up. She watched him go into the kitchen with the bag and when he returned, he had two glasses of wine and a wet paper towel. She took a sip of the drink so he wouldn't question why she wasn't drinking, then wiped her face.

"Yeah, I quit," Kayla continued and told him about Nate, the desk and Mrs. Warren's reasons for not suspending him.

"That's crazy. So she would rather endanger the other students and staff members because his parents give the school money?"

"That's what it seems like," Kayla answered.

"Where's the remote to the stereo? I made you some CDs." He reached into his pocket and pulled two CDs out. She pointed to the bookshelf and he opened the player. He put a CD in and smiled as Brian McKnight began to sing about what's going on tonight.

"So, now what am I gonna do?" Kayla shrugged.

"Find another job, Kay. That's what. One with some decent pay and some real benefits." He grinned at her. "It ain't that deep."

"I missed you, Geno." She smiled back at him. "So what's going on with you? How is your job?"

"It's cool. You know I like what I do."

"And the older woman?" Kayla dared to ask him.

"She's just a friend, despite what everyone thinks. Rent is expensive, Kay, and she had a room for rent." He looked down at her hands in his.

"It's okay, Geno. Even though we aren't together, we will always be friends. We can still talk. Are you happy?" Kayla asked him.

"Her name is Janice and she's cool," he said nonchalantly. Kayla knew that he was lying. If she was just a friend, they wouldn't be living together. Rent wasn't that damn expensive and Geno made decent money. She decided to ask the inevitable.

"You love her?" Kayla had to know. *You got a lot of nerve, knocked up with a married man's baby and you asking him if he's in love,* Kayla scolded herself.

"I don't know, Kay. I mean, she is so good to me. She's smart, intelligent, funny. She has her shit together. Know what I mean?" he said

"Yeah, she's perfect." Kayla smirked.

"No, Kay. Not perfect. I don't feel the same way about her as I feel about you. That's what scares me. There was never any doubt that I loved you, Kay. That's how I know it was real. Hell, Kay, I still love you. You're still my best friend," he said.

Kayla couldn't respond to what he had just said so she just sat. The doorbell broke the silence.

"Were you expecting company?" he asked.

"No, I wasn't even expecting you." Kayla went to the door and looked through the peephole. She closed her eyes and wished the tall figure on the other side away. She looked again, but obviously the wish did not come true.

"Kayla, open the door. I need to talk to you," Craig yelled out.

"Go away! I have nothing to say to you!" Kayla hissed.

"Open the door! At least let me explain. Please," he moaned.

"I don't need an explanation and furthermore, I don't want one. The only thing I want from you is for you to get the hell away from my door," Kayla answered. Suddenly, Geno nudged by her and opened the door before she could stop him.

"Is there a problem?" Geno asked Craig. They both had strange looks on their faces as they looked at one another.

"Naw, Bruh. I just needed to talk to Kayla for a minute. You mind?" Craig took a step back.

"*Naw, Bruh.* I don't mind at all, but evidently she does. So I think you need to leave." Geno flexed and crossed his arms, standing protectively in front of Kayla.

"Who the fuck are you?" Craig looked suspicious. He and Geno stood about the same height and were the same size, so neither one seemed intimidated.

"None of your fucking business!" Geno answered with a growl.

"You here with my girl, nigga, so obviously it is my business." Craig feigned a callous smile and stepped toward Geno.

"Your girl? I think you got that all wrong." Geno didn't back down.

"Look, both of you need to back the fuck up! Now!" Kayla stepped between the two men.

"She carrying my mothafuckin' seed. According to her, it's mine!" He looked accusingly at Kayla.

"What?" Geno looked at Craig like he was crazy.

At that moment, Yvonne, Roni and Tia walked up to the door.

"Oh, snap!" Roni jeered as she realized both Craig and Geno were in front of Kayla's door.

"Geno!" Tia shrieked.

"So you're that punk nigga Geno?" Craig leered.

"Craig, you need to leave." Kayla faced him.

"Naw, this nigga is the one that needs to be leaving," he continued.

"I ain't going nowhere!" Geno retorted to him. The two men were squared off and she knew they were about to rumble. Kayla knew she had to do something.

"Craig, I asked you to leave. Now, if you don't get your married, thug ass off my property, I will call the police and have you removed and then call your wife and tell her where to find your ass."

"Oh, shit!" Kayla heard Roni say.

Kayla's comment must have hit home with Craig because he stepped back.

"Fuck both of you!" he said as he left. Kayla closed her eyes and took a deep breath.

"What the hell?" Yvonne asked as she pulled Kayla into the house. Geno, Roni and Tia followed.

"I'd like to know the answer to that myself," Geno murmured.

"Geno and I were sitting here talking and Craig just showed up. The same way you guys did, I might add." Kayla flopped onto the couch and shook her head.

"She's right. We were just sitting here chilling and this nigga came banging on the door. He looks familiar. I just can't figure out where I know him from," he said. The girls looked at each other knowingly. *He looks like your twin,* is what they were all thinking, but no one said it.

"I think we need to be leaving, too," Roni said to Tia and Yvonne. "Call us tomorrow, Kay."

They left Geno and Kayla standing in the living room.

"Who the fuck was that, Kayla?" Geno asked. "And what the fuck was he talking about when he said you carrying his seed? You fucking that nigga?"

"G.," Kayla looked down.

"Don't tell me you're pregnant by that wanna-be, hard mothafucka for real, Kayla." He looked at Kayla like he was disgusted. "I can't believe you."

"Hold up! You *living* with a broad and you going off on what I'm doing?" Kayla could not believe the nerve of him. It was she who looked at him like he was a fool this time.

"I know you're smarter than that. You don't even know this nigga."

"And how long have you known the woman you're living with, G.? You know what? We really don't even need to be discussing this. You can leave, too. Go home to your woman." Kayla opened the door for him and he left without saying another word.

9

"So that was it?" Roni asked.

"Yep. That was it," Kayla answered. She had gotten up early and gone over to Roni's and told her what happened after they had left the night before. They were sitting at her small kitchen table.

"Girl, when we walked up and saw Craig and Geno, I almost died. I thought they were gonna throw down."

"Me too. I can't believe Geno had the nerve to be mad, can you?"

"You were mad when you found out about him and that other woman. It's a natural reaction. You two are still in love with each other. Face it," Roni told her.

"I am not in love with Geno. I still care about him, yeah. But I ain't in love with him." Kayla reached into Roni's refrigerator and grabbed a piece of fruit.

"So, you decide what you're gonna do yet?" Roni asked her.

"About what?"

"Don't play, you know what I'm talking about."

"Honestly, Ron, I don't know. I have so many messed up situations right now to decide on. A job, Geno, Craig, my car." Kayla leaned back in her chair.

"About the baby, Kayla," Roni interrupted her.

"Oh, I was gonna get to that situation eventually, but you jumped in. I'm gonna have it, I guess."

"Really? I think that's a good decision." Roni hugged Kayla.

"I told Mama."

"Ooh, what did she say?"

"Nothing, really. She wasn't even upset as I thought she was gonna be."

"And your father?"

"He doesn't know. I told Mama I would tell him later. I'm not ready to tell him yet, Ron."

"Tell who what?" Tia asked as she and Yvonne came in. Roni looked at Kayla and she looked back.

"What are y'all talking about?" Yvonne sat in the chair across from Kayla.

"Nothing. Have either of you heard of knocking?" Roni asked quickly.

"For what? I got a key." Tia shook her head. She looked too cute in a white cotton short set. "You got any juice, Ron?"

"In the fridge. I think it's some in there. Use one of the glasses on the top shelf."

"What aren't you ready to tell, Kayla? Geno and Craig obviously already know about each other."

Yvonne giggled. Kayla decided she would just go ahead and tell them about the baby. There was no point in keeping it from them. They were, after all, her best friends.

"I'm pregnant," she announced. The sound of breaking glass startled all of them.

"Tia!" Roni yelled, looking at the broken pieces on the floor.

"Sorry." Tia continued to stare at Kayla as Roni picked up the mess.

"What did you say?" Yvonne wanted to make sure she heard correctly.

"I'm having a baby," Kayla confirmed.

"Wow. Is that why Geno was at your house?" Tia questioned.

"No, it's not his baby." Kayla knew what the next question would be, so she answered before it was asked. "It's Craig's."

"Kayla," was all Yvonne said.

"Okay, I'm confused. When did you sleep with Craig?" Tia reached for another glass.

"Valentine's night," Kayla told her.

"Where was I?" she continued.

"Obviously not having as much fun as *she* was," Roni laughed. Tia gave her a high five.

"What are you gonna do?" Yvonne had been quiet the entire time. Kayla expected this reaction from her.

"I am gonna be a mother," Kayla told her. She fought the urge to look away from her girlfriend; she knew she had to keep her pride.

"So, you're gonna have a baby by *him*? You don't even know him like that, Kayla." Yvonne continued, "You mean you slept with him without using protection, Kayla? That's so irresponsible."

"I know it is and I'm not trying to make any excuses, Yvonne. I'm accepting responsibility now, though." Kayla felt the tears swell in her eyes.

"It's too late to be responsible. You're about to have a baby by practically a stranger you met in the *club*, of all places."

"Hold up, Yvonne. You're outta line, girl." Roni stopped her.

"She's right, Von. You can't judge her like that." Tia added, "You're out there living it up too."

"The only difference between you and her is that *she* got caught. Shit happens. But that doesn't mean I love her any less or think I'm better than her. I thought I knew you better than that, Von," Roni frowned.

"I'm so sorry, Von. My life is so screwed up right now that sometimes I feel backed into a corner with nowhere to turn." Kayla cried.

"That's your choice, Kayla, because you can always turn to us. We have always been there for you." Tia reached out to Kayla.

"And I need *you* to be there for me, Von. Be here for me right now. Please." Kayla put her head in her hands.

"I am here for you, Kayla." She felt her friend reach and rub her back. The women embraced each other and Kayla knew she would be okay.

"Happy Mother's Day, Mama."

"Hi, Baby. I told you I'd call you. How you feeling?"

"I'm fine, Ma. I wanted to call because I'm about to go to the store and I didn't want to miss you. You know how you think I'm dodging your calls." Kayla laughed.

"That's because most of the time you are." Her mother laughed. "Your father just asked had I talked to you. Hold on, I'll get him."

"Mama, no. I told you I'm about to leave out. I will talk to him later," Kayla said quickly. "I just wanted to tell you Happy Mother's Day and I love you."

"Love you too, Kayla. But you better talk to your father soon. No use putting it off."

"I will, Mama. Bye." Kayla hung up the phone and headed to the door. She wanted to get a paper and go through the classifieds.

"What do you want?" Kayla asked as she flung open the door.

"I been trying to call you, Kayla. I called your house, your cell. You gotta talk to me. Where you going?" Craig asked her as she closed the door behind her.

"No you didn't! What business of it is yours? I certainly ain't going to see your wife and your son, though maybe I should." She walked toward her car, Craig right on her heels.

"Kayla, I am so sorry. I was gonna tell you, but . . ."

"Save it, Craig. I don't even wanna know what you were *gonna* do. I can't believe you got a wife and a kid! Where the hell were they on Valentine's, huh? What? Did you take down all their pictures and hide all the toys?"

"No, I mean, that wasn't my house, Kay. It was my brother Darryl's crib. He's a sport's agent and he was working. Avis and Nigel were gone out of town for the weekend." He looked down as he confessed. "But we are having problems. We are actually filing for a separation. It's over between her and me. I promise."

"You don't have to promise me anything, Craig. What we had wasn't even that deep. Believe me, there is no love lost here." Kayla looked at him like he was crazy.

"I need for you not to say anything about this, though, Kayla. Now do you see why I don't need the stress of a baby? You are gonna be teaching at the academy and . . ."

"You can stop right there. Not that it's any of your business, but I no longer teach at the academy, so me running into your wife at the school is the least of your worries." Kayla folded her arms and glared at him. She could not believe she liked him at one point. He was pathetic.

"But I don't need for you to tell anybody, either. If she finds out, she's gonna haul my ass to court for real. I'll do anything, Kayla. Please rethink this shit. Don't do this to me. Don't have this baby." He began to shake his head at her. "I can't take this stress."

"Get the hell away from me, Craig. What you should be worried about is how you're gonna pay child support to two different baby mamas. If you gonna be stressed, be stressed about that. Because you are really gonna have to pay me to keep our 'little' secret." Kayla got into the car and pulled off, leaving Craig standing in the middle of the driveway with his mouth hanging open.

10

Kayla was determined to get a job and get one quick. She knew that it would have to be one with benefits because she would have to be out on maternity leave, preferably with pay. Theo, who was Tia's new boyfriend, worked for an insurance agency and told her they were hiring. He passed her resume on, but Kayla had not heard anything and it had been a week. She found out the Human Resources person's name and decided to go see her in person.

"Good morning. Hunter Davis, please," Kayla told the elderly security guard.

"Okay. And you are?" He smiled and reached for the telephone on the cluttered desk.

"Kayla, Kayla Hopkins," she answered.

He mumbled into the receiver and then hung the phone up. "She's in a meeting. Leave your number and she'll call you back."

Kayla looked at her watch and saw that it was quarter to ten. She didn't feel like leaving her resume anywhere else or filling out any more applications. She took a deep breath and walked back over to the desk. "If you don't mind, I'll wait until she has a moment to speak with me."

"No, I don't mind. You can sit right over there." He pointed to a leather sofa in front of a table full of well-worn magazines. Kayla went and picked up a subscription of *Better Homes and Gardens*. The lobby was pretty much empty and remained that way with the exception of an occasional courier dropping off or picking up a package.

"You want me to try her again?" the security guard asked her for the third time since she had been waiting.

"No, you've already left two messages. I'm sure she will be out soon," Kayla told him.

"Well, it's twelve o'clock and I'm about to go to lunch. I'll be back in a half-hour. You need anything?"

"No, thanks. I'll wait."

"Suit yourself, ma'am." He came from behind the desk and went through the glass doors separating the lobby from the remainder of the building. At one point, Kayla thought about calling Tia and having her call Theo to let him know she was in the lobby. *No, he did what he said he'd do. Now it's up to me.* She sat back and reached for another magazine. Soon, the guard returned and found her still waiting. Several employees began entering and exiting the building. Checking her watch again, Kayla's stomach began to growl. *Maybe I should go and get something to eat and come back.*

"Ms. Davis, this is the young lady that has been waiting for you all day," the security guard quickly said to a tall, attractive brunette as she came through the doors.

"Ms. Hopkins, you're still here? But it's after two." She looked surprisingly at Kayla.

"I decided to wait until you got a moment. You can go to lunch. I'll wait."

"Nonsense. By all means, you've waited long enough. Come on back." She used a keycard and she and Kayla stepped through the glass doors and onto the elevator. They rode to the third floor, walked down the corridor, entered a door labeled Human Resources and then went into Hunter's office. "Have a seat. Can I get you anything? Coffee, soda, water?"

"Water, if that's okay." Kayla took a seat and hoped her stomach was not growling loudly.

Hunter reached into the small refrigerator located beside a file cabinet and took out two bottles of water, passing one to Kayla. "Believe it or not, calling you is on my to-do list for this week. But our district manager came into town and announced that we will be developing a new division and that has the entire place going crazy."

"I can imagine." Kayla nodded.

"I have reviewed your resume and I see you are a teacher. I am a former teacher myself, but I got burnt out." Hunter sat down and opened a file folder on her desk.

"That is the point where I am now," Kayla explained. "I definitely need a change. " Kayla looked deep within herself and told Hunter everything she thought the woman wanted to hear. She had prepared herself mentally for this interview and she was determined to get a position. She had to.

She had to get herself together. Getting a job was just the first step in that direction.

"Well, Ms. Hopkins, you certainly are what we are looking for here at Atkins and I will definitely be calling you in the next month or so," Hunter said.

"In a month? I need a job now, Ms. Davis. I can't wait a month." Kayla felt her heart beating faster and her breath quickened. Tears began to well into her eyes.

"I'm sorry, Ms. Hopkins. The hiring for the new division won't be until then. As a matter of fact, our last training class starts on Monday afternoon and it is full."

God, please help me. I have a child to provide for. Open a door for me. I need this, Kayla prayed in her heart.

"I can start Monday, Ms. Davis. Please, just give me a chance," Kayla pleaded.

"But today is Thursday. You would need to have a drug screening and security clearance. That takes about a week to complete and today is Thursday. The head of security works half days on Friday and he does not take kindly to being rushed." She looked at Kayla sadly.

"Please. I will take care of everything I need to by Monday." Kayla was beginning to cry at this point.

Hunter looked at her and Kayla could see the wheels turning in the woman's head. She stood and reached into the file cabinet, passing Kayla a pack of papers. "Call this clinic and see if they can take you this afternoon or first thing in the morning. You need to be back here by noon tomorrow for your security paperwork."

"Huh? You mean . . ." Kayla began.

"I respect your resilience. You have the courage to go after what you want. We need that here at this office. Welcome to Atkins." Hunter stood and extended her hand to Kayla. Kayla threw her head back and laughed. *Thank you, God.*

"Thank you, Ms. Davis. I won't disappoint you," she said as she shook her hand.

"I'm sure you won't," Hunter told her.

The next day Kayla looked around the small security office as she completed her paperwork. There were several TV monitors transmitting different entrances to the building and the parking lots as well. She watched employees pass by the screens and was grateful that she would be among them. She had rushed over to the clinic, completed her drug screening and made it back to the Atkins Agency at precisely twelve o'clock.

She looked over onto a small table and noticed other pictures with names on them. There were several other women and a few men; one in particular was a big, cheesing, dark-skinned man wearing a sweater vest with a paisley bow tie. The name on his picture was Terrell. *He looks happy to have a job,* Kayla laughed to herself.

"In your haste to accept the job, I didn't get a chance to tell you exactly what department you would be in, the hours, your salary or your benefits. I guess we should take care of that, huh?" Hunter said as she collected Kayla's paperwork.

"I think we should." Kayla smiled.

Hunter told her about the customer service position that she was hired for and went over the thick benefit packet. "Now here's what the starting salary is, but there is a ten percent night differential because the hours are from noon until nine. After a year, you will be reviewed for an additional salary increase based on merit."

"I need to tell you something," Kayla said quietly.

"What's wrong?" Hunter looked concerned.

"I'm pregnant."

"Congratulations. When is your due date?" She smiled.

"November twenty-first."

"Well, that works out perfect for you. Your ninety-day probation will be up and you will be entitled to two months paid maternity leave. Now you can take up to a year, but only the first two months are paid. We love giving baby showers around here. Gives us a reason to eat cake."

"Wow." Kayla thanked Hunter for all she had done and walked out of the building happy that she was once again fully employed.

11

"I can't believe you quit one job last Friday and you got a new one on this Friday," Yvonne said as she looked through the sale rack. It was Saturday afternoon and she had taken Kayla to brunch to celebrate her new job, and then they had made their way to the mall.

"Believe it, girl. I just got it like that." Kayla faked a vogue pose.

"So, what about the music store?"

"I had to quit. The hours were conflicting. But with the new job, I make more money than the two jobs I was working anyway. Do you like this?" Kayla held up a cute, green sundress.

"I sure am gonna miss that discount. Yeah, that's cute."

"I'm gonna miss it too. I think I'm gonna try it on." Kayla took the dress and went into the dressing room.

"Let me see it?" Yvonne called out to her as she was trying on her fashion disappointment.

"No. It's too small," Kayla pouted.

"Too small? But isn't that a twelve? I thought it would be too big."

As Kayla was coming out, she bumped into a woman coming in. "Oh, excuse me."

"You need to watch where you going," the familiar woman said as she brushed past Kayla without looking. *Oh, no she didn't. And I know that trick from somewhere, too.* Kayla tried to remember where she knew her. *Avis, Craig's wife.*

"Do you have this in a bigger size?" she heard her call out to the salesperson.

"I'm sorry, ma'am, a twenty-two is the largest that comes in."

"This must be mislabeled or somethin'. It ain't fittin' right."

She came out of the dressing room and Kayla saw that they were holding the same dress. She could not resist walking up to the counter next to the woman. *I wonder why she didn't recognize me? It doesn't matter, but it's a good thing she doesn't.* Kayla decided to have some fun.

"I think she's right, ma'am. I know I'm a size ten and this eight is too big for me. I think they are cut big. Come on, Yvonne, let's go over to the petite section."

"You are crazy. She looked mad as hell."

"She ain't mad as she gonna be. I can't believe her fat tail. Try to disrespect me 'cause she weigh nearly three hundred pounds and can't fit in the dressing room. I see why Craig leaving her big behind. Let's get out of here and go get some ice cream." Kayla grabbed Yvonne's arm. She looked around to make sure Avis was gone.

"That's why that dress was too little." Yvonne laughed and followed her girlfriend out of the store.

The following Monday, Kayla entered the training room and sat at the round table. There were a few people already seated and she smiled as she spoke to them. There were snacks, soda and water in the center of the table and the guy whose name she remembered was Terrell, was sitting across from her. The training class was scheduled to begin at twelve-thirty and it was quarter after. As other people came in, she recognized them from their pictures. The trainer entered and introduced herself and they began. Finally, after about two hours, the trainer called for the first break. Kayla gathered her bag and went into the break room along with some of her classmates. She found a quiet spot outside and sat down. She looked up and saw Terrell looking at her.

"You can come and sit with me, Terrell. I promise I won't bite." Kayla smiled.

"I know how you women are. I ain't trying to get caught up in a harassment charge. You know I'm a prime target, being the only brotha in the class." She laughed as he sat down, and they talked until he looked at his watch and announced, "We gotta get back."

The first week of training went by fairly quickly. Kayla and Terrell hung out together during breaks and lunch. He kept her laughing and amused her with his tales of being a mack, or so he said. Every time she talked to one of her girlfriends, she had to tell them what Terrell had said or done. He was intelligent, funny, street-smart and respectable. He knew when to speak up and when to shut up. A lot of guys hadn't mastered that skill nowadays. And to be as thick as he was, he could dress his tail off. The boy had style and class.

"Okay, is there something going on between you and this Terrell dude that I should know about?" Yvonne asked her one night on the phone.

"No, Von. It's nothing like that. We are just real cool, that's all. Come on, now. I'm pregnant. What do I look like trying to holla at another nigga? That's like adding fuel to the fire. I got enough problems with Geno and Craig."

"I was just asking. You seem awfully excited when you talking about him. And as sneaky as your ass is, I have to ask or I'm the last to find out." Yvonne smirked.

"Terrell and I are just friends, Von. He's like the male version of me. I mean, we think alike, and he always has a story to make me laugh," Kayla explained. It was like everyone assumed that she had something going on with Terrell. The truth was, he was just what she needed right now: a friend.

12

"What's up for tonight, Ms. Kayla? You know it's Friday and the club will just be getting jumping when we get off. You down?" Terrell asked.

"I'm going home and fall out. It has been a long week and I am tired to death," Kayla said.

"Let's hit Dominic's. The deejay that's gonna be there tonight is off the hook!" He started singing, "Can I get a what, what?"

Kayla could not help joining him and started dancing. "It sounds like fun, but I am too tired."

"Come on, Kayla. Let's go. You can sleep all day tomorrow."

"Okay, for a little while." Kayla shook her head. "I'll call my girls and see if they wanna come too."

"Bet. Hold up, are they fine?" Terrell asked.

"Of course they are." Kayla grabbed her cell and left a message for Roni, Tia and Yvonne, inviting them to Dominic's. Everyone agreed to meet at the door at ten-thirty. By the time they got off from work, the adrenaline was flowing and Kayla was just as hyped as Terrell to go out.

"Hey, you! Look at you. You look good!" Roni ran up to Kayla and hugged her.

"You are so silly, Roni. You act like you haven't seen me in months." She laughed and hugged her girlfriend.

"It seems like it. The job must be agreeing with you. You are glowing," she said and they went to join Tia, Theo and Yvonne in the line. Dominic's was a new club but it was packed. The line was wrapped around the building and seemed to go on forever. They had waited about twenty minutes when Terrell walked up and beckoned for them.

"Where are we going?" Kayla asked.

"Come on, let's go." He motioned for her to follow him.

"But what about the line? And I have my friends . . ."

"Come on and follow me. Bring 'em with you," he said. Kayla shrugged and she and her crew followed Terrell right up to the door. Other people waiting in the line did not seem too thrilled that they passed them. The bouncer saw them coming and immediately opened the door for them.

"What up, Terry," he said and gave Terrell a pound. "How are you all doing?" He greeted everyone else and let them in.

"How much is the cover charge?" Kayla asked, reaching for her small Coach bag.

"I'm a baller, girl. And you are my guests. Come on." He grabbed Kayla and ushered her into the huge club. She was taken aback when they made it all the way in. This was the biggest club she had ever been in. There were two floors, the second overlooking the first and the huge dance floor had tank-like columns at each corner, filled with water and lights. The bar spanned the entire wall on one side. The deejay booth was mounted from the back wall and the lighting system was fierce.

"This place is incredible!" Theo said over the loud music.

"Come on, we can get a table up here," Terrell called out.

"But that's the VIP section," Yvonne said.

"I *am* a VIP." He smiled, and greeted the security guy who held a red velvet rope. The guy opened the walkway and they made their way to an empty table.

"Okay, you a player." Kayla laughed and sat down. She was suddenly exhausted. Although she was no longer nauseous, she tired very easily these days. But she was determined to have a good time and not let her friends see any changes in her behavior.

"This is so fly," Roni said. "Now *this* is how a sister is supposed to go out."

The waitress came and took their drink orders and Yvonne and Roni didn't waste any time hitting the dance floor. A couple of females came to the table to speak to Terrell and he seemed to be in his element. After finishing their drinks, Theo and Tia headed to get their dance on, too.

"You wanna dance, yo?" Terrell asked Kayla.

"No thanks. You go ahead." Kayla shook her head.

"Well, I was asking to be polite. I didn't want to show you up on the dance floor anyway. You know a big brother got some moves." He nudged Kayla.

"Whatever, Terrell. Why don't you ask one of your adoring fans that have been flocking to you?"

"Do I detect a hint of jealousy?" He grinned.

"Hell, no."

"Dag, I was just playing. But you know how it is. You never dance with anyone you meet when you first arrive. Then they expect you to be with them for the rest of the night. You understand?"

"Oh, but you can dance with *me*, huh?" Kayla was beginning to enjoy this quick lesson in club etiquette. She looked around and all of a sudden she spotted Geno. She could not believe it. She stood, but quickly turned when she realized he was not alone. She couldn't resist turning around to get another look.

"I've already introduced you as one of my home girls, so the chicks know that we are just cool. Friend of yours?" He stood to see who Kayla was looking at.

"Huh? Oh, nobody special." She tried not to seem disappointed, although she knew Terrell could read her face. He looked and saw her watching a guy at the bar, hugged up with an attractive woman, whispering in her ear.

"Come on, yo. Let me make you look good on the floor." He grabbed her and they made their way in front of the deejay booth, jamming to TLC singing "Scrubs." Terrell was right about one thing: he had some moves. That boy could dance and she fell right into rhythm with him. Before she knew it, there was a circle formed around them and the deejay was pumping them up even more by screaming, "Go Terry!" into the mike. She decided she couldn't take anymore and signaled for Roni to take over. She eased her way back to the side of the floor and watched. She forced herself not to look for Geno.

"Whew, girl. Y'all were tearing that floor up!" Theo said as he and Tia joined her. "Big boy can go."

"I know. He told me he could dance, but I didn't know he was like that," she responded.

They joined the rest of the crew at the table and Terrell whispered in her ear, "What's up with your friend? She is fine as hell. You think I can holla?"

"No offense, Terrell, but she is a little out of your league. She's just as much a pimp as you are," Kayla whispered and laughed. She looked at Roni, who was focused on the dance floor. She slid next to her friend to see what she was finding so engrossing. "Who are you looking at?"

"Girl, the deejay is the bomb. Did you see him?" Roni leaned further over the balcony, pointing him out to her girlfriend. Kayla saw the sexy, chocolate brother as he was whispering into a scantily clad female's ear, giving her what Kayla assumed was a business card.

"He is fine, Ron. But he's been all up in females' faces all night. You know he's a ho." Kayla scanned the small tables on the opposite wall of the bar.

"You're probably right, Kay. And you know I don't sweat no nigga. But it's something about him." Roni continued to look at the fine brother as he did his thing.

"Kay, I gotta tell you something. While we were coming upstairs I saw . . ." Tia began and put her hand on her girlfriend's shoulder.

"I already saw them." Kayla didn't let her finish. She didn't even want his name to come out of anyone's mouth.

"You wanna leave, Kay?" she asked, looking at Theo for assurance.

"It's still early. We can hit State Street's or another spot," he suggested.

"No. I'm cool. Seriously, everyone is having a good time, including me. Come on. Let's go back to the table." Kayla turned to go back down the steps when she heard the sound of Teddy Riley coming from the speakers. She turned around and looked into the eyes of Geno. His date was pulling for him to dance with her but he could not move. For a moment, both he and Kayla were frozen, remembering the first time they had made love. From that moment, Blackstreet's "Stay" had been their song. She looked at him, daring him to break the stare, but he was just as determined as she was.

"Geno, come on. I love this song." The woman was grabbing his shirt by now. "What is wrong with you?" She turned and saw him looking at Kayla.

Geno did not move.

"Is that her, Geno? Geno?" She grabbed Geno's face and he pushed her hands away. The woman looked at Kayla with fire in her eyes.

"Let's go," he said to the woman and turned to walk away, pulling the woman by the arm.

"I want to know if that's her. Are you Kayla?" She stepped toward Kayla, snatching away from Geno.

"Yes, I am," Kayla answered daringly. "And you are?"

"Janice. Geno's girlfriend."

"Let's go, Janice. I need a drink." He reached for her arm again but she pulled away.

"You can go to the bar, Geno. I'll be right here when you get back, chatting with your ex." The girl continued to look Kayla up and down.

"I don't think we have anything to chat about, *Janet*. Is that your name?" Kayla asked her sarcastically.

"Janice, bitch. Get it right."

"Geno, you better check your girl. And do it quick." Kayla glanced past the crazy woman and straight at Geno. She gave him a look that let him know she meant what she was saying. He took heed and stepped between the women.

"Come on, Janice. You're making a fool of yourself," he told her quietly in her ear.

"What? Geno, I will whoop her ass in here. I know you don't call yourself shutting me up, do you?" The woman was yelling at this point. Without warning, she tried to swing around Geno at Kayla, but he grabbed her arm. Kayla prepared to defend herself. She wasn't no punk.

"What the hell are you doing?" Roni yelled and jumped in front of Kayla.

"Who the hell are you?" Janice tried to swing at Roni this time. Geno pulled Janice and forced her out, kicking and screaming. By this time, a crowd had formed and everyone came to see what the commotion was.

"You okay, yo?" Terrell asked Kayla.

"I'm fine. She's the crazy one." Kayla smiled at him.

"Everything okay over here, Terry?" one of the security guards asked.

"Yeah. It's cool," he informed him.

"I'ma get that ho. Messing wit me, she'd better watch out!" they heard Janice scream.

"Yo, Kayla. Why was she tripping?" Roni asked as she and Terrell stood by her.

"I don't know. She just flipped out." Kayla began to ascend the steps.

"If your nigga was looking at another female like she was his wife, you'd be pissed too," Terrell told her and smiled.

13

"Can I get my hair like that?" Kayla asked Roni, pointing to a girl in the nail salon. It was the Friday before Father's Day and Kayla had to be at work in an hour. She decided to get her nails and feet done because she knew the salon would be packed tomorrow.

"Those are tracks, Kay," Roni said.

"I know. But you can do tracks, Ron." Kayla picked out a pretty lavender polish for her hands and feet.

"I know I can do tracks. I'm just surprised you want some. I thought that was the whole point of you cutting your hair."

"I just feel like something different. Will you do it for me?" Kayla sat down in the princess chair in front of the nail technician.

"You gotta come to the shop tomorrow if you want that done. And you know it's gonna take a minute to put in. I don't wanna hear your mouth, Kayla," Roni warned her.

"I know, Ron. I'll come and I won't complain." Kayla smiled.

"I'll pick your hair up tonight. Be at the shop by noon. On time."

"Thanks, Ron. I know you love me."

"I'll love you even more if you come with me to Dominic's," Roni pleaded.

"Ron, I can't. I am so worn out that I can barely drive home. I can't be hanging out at the club in this condition. Besides, I am getting too fat to fit into any of my clothes."

"You're barely showing, Kayla. It's just for a little while. I just want to check out the deejay. Please, Kay."

Kayla could not believe her girlfriend was sweating the deejay from Dominic's. This was a total change for Roni. She had the guys looking for her. And what made it worse, Roni still had yet to meet the man. Every time they went to the club, he had a flock of chickenheads lined up at the booth.

"Ron, he is a straight dog. You of all people know the type. I am not going to Dominic's so you can fantasize about a man who has just as many women as you have men."

"Fine, Kayla. But you have got to admit that is the sexiest brother you have seen in a while. I think he is my type. I am so attracted to him," Roni said as she blew her wet nails.

"No, you're attracted to him because he is a challenge. Unlike every other nigga you meet, he is not all up in your face."

"Not yet, anyway." Roni winked at her girlfriend who shook her head.

Kayla made it to the shop at twelve fifteen the next day. She tried her best to be on time, but she had been having these funny feelings in her stomach. She prayed that nothing was wrong as she looked at her tummy getting bigger. She took her time getting dressed and stopped to pick up a doughnut. She craved sweets to no end. The shop was pretty full when she got there.

"Hey there, stranger. Roni didn't tell me you were coming in here today." Ms. Ernestine greeted her as she came in the door.

"Hi, Ms. Ernestine," Kayla greeted. She put her bag of goodies down on the table in the waiting area and walked over to Ms. Ernestine's station. "Where's Roni?"

"Back here. Mama got me washing hair," Roni called from the shampoo bowl.

"Kayla, is that you?" a voice called from under the dryer. Kayla turned to see who it was. It was Geno's mom, Ms. Gert.

"Come here, girl, and give me a hug." Ms. Ernestine reached and gave Kayla a big hug. All of a sudden she stood back and looked at Kayla strangely. "Girl, Roni ain't tell me you were having a baby! When are you due?"

Kayla felt her heart beating and looked into Ms. Ernestine's eyes. She looked from Ms. Ernestine to Ms. Gert, but knew there was no point in lying to either one of them.

"Baby? Kayla's not having a baby," Ms. Gert said as she lifted the dryer all the way up. "She would have told me."

"Thanksgiving Day," Kayla said and took a deep breath. She could not turn around and face Ms. Gert, so she walked back to the waiting area and sat down. It was so quiet in the shop that even the dryers seemed to have stopped humming.

"Kayla, you're having a baby and didn't tell me?" Ms. Gert came and took a seat next to her.

"I'm sorry, Ms. Gert. I just didn't know how. I mean, it's not Geno's, and . . ."

"That doesn't matter to me, Kayla. You do. I love you like you are one of my own children. Does Geno know?"

"Yes."

"He still cares about you, Kayla. You do know that, right?"

"We were engaged, Ms. Gert. Geno and I will always care about each other."

"So you still love him?"

"Ms. Gert, I'm pregnant by another man and Geno is living with another woman. I don't think how we feel about each other is relevant. It's over. We have both moved on." Kayla looked at the woman she had grown to love over the years. They were as close as she and her own mother at one point, and like everyone else, she could not understand why Kayla and Geno broke up.

"I understand, Kayla. And if that's how you feel, I respect that. But you will always be a part of my family and nothing will ever change that." She reached over and hugged Kayla as a chorus of "awww" was heard in the shop. The women looked up and saw that everyone had stopped and all eyes were on them.

"Are you two finished with your Hallmark moment so Roni can get some work done?" Ms. Ernestine smiled at them.

"Mama, I know you ain't trying to rush nobody when they working for free!" Roni put her hands on her hip.

"Free? Child, you still owe me for that college education I paid for. You just lucky I don't garnish your wages like the student loan people do."

"What is you doing, dawg?" Terrell asked her Monday afternoon when she got to work.

"What are you talking about, Terrell?" Kayla knew she looked fly. Her white rayon outfit was perfect from her manicured hands to her perfect feet, which wore Kenneth Cole heeled sandals. Roni had hooked her hair up and it was flowing down her back. Her eyebrows were arched and she had put on her MAC makeup like a professional artist.

"You are trippin' for real." He sighed as he sat at his desk.

"Terrell, what are you talking about?" Kayla knew he would have a smart comment. She was prepared for it.

"You can not, I repeat *can not* leave on Friday night with a short bob and return on Monday with hair down to your behind." He touched Kayla's tracks and acted like he was gonna pull them.

"You can if you're a diva." Kayla batted her eyes at him and stuck out her tongue. The rest of the class laughed as he took his seat, smiling.

During lunch break, Kayla bought a honey bun and a bottle of Pepsi. She sat at their regular table and pulled out the *What to Expect When You're Expecting* book that Roni had dropped off to her that morning. She was determined to find out why she kept having those strange feelings in her stomach. The book confirmed that the butterflies in her stomach were called flutters. Kayla smiled as she realized she was feeling her baby move for the first time.

"Who's having a baby?" Terrell asked as he sat down and looked at her book.

"I am." Kayla smiled.

"Yeah, right. When?"

"In November." Kayla opened the honey bun and decided to put it in the microwave for a few seconds to get it soft. She returned to the table and saw Terrell flipping through her book.

"You having a baby for real, Kayla?" he asked.

"For real," Kayla said and prepared herself for the sweet, gooey food she had sitting before her. She picked up the warm honey bun and was about to bite into it when Terrell snatched it from her and tossed it into the trash.

"What is your problem?" Kayla stood up and asked him angrily.

"You can't be eating that stuff. It's not good for you," he answered and went back into the cafeteria. Kayla wanted to cry. She had been thinking about that honey bun all day and now his big behind had thrown it away. She sat back down, too furious to move.

"Here," Terrell said, placing a tray in front of her. On it were a grilled chicken sandwich, some baked chips, an apple and a glass of milk. As bad as Kayla wanted to stay mad at him, she couldn't.

"You know I wanted to stab you, right?" Kayla told him.

"Whatever, diva. You wouldn't dare if you want that hair to stay pretending like it's yours," he joked.

"You're just mad because I won't let you touch it," Kayla threw at him.

"My uncle has a stable down South. I know what it feels like."

Kayla stuck her tongue out at him and began to eat her food.

"Man, you don't even look pregnant," he said.

"Coming from anyone else I would take that as a compliment, but from you, I don't know." She looked up from her plate.

"Was that your baby daddy the other night at the club?" he asked as he reached on her plate and grabbed some chips. Kayla raised the fork over his hand and pretended to stab him.

"If you must know, no, that was not my *child's father*. That was my ex-fiancé and his new girlfriend," she told him.

"He's still feeling you. Does he know you're pregnant?"

"How do you know he's still feeling me?"

"Because I saw the way he looked at you. That's the reason ol' girl was mad at him, because he was more interested in you."

"Well, we're over."

"Where is your baby daddy?"

"That's a whole 'nother story and he's out of the picture too." She finished her sandwich and gave him the remainder of the chips. He didn't hesitate to take them and she laughed.

"What happened to him?"

"I didn't appreciate the fact that he was married," she informed him. He gave her a surprised look.

"You, somebody's mistress? I underestimate you

and your *playerability*." His shoulders shook as he laughed at her. Kayla was not amused.

"I am *not* anybody's mistress. I didn't know he was married and, like I said, he's out of the picture. I'm all alone," she said sadly. Kayla realized that indeed she was alone. She thought about having to go to birthing class and doctors' appointments by herself. There wouldn't be a proud father with her in the delivery room waiting with a camcorder in one hand and a digital camera in the other. She looked down at the empty tray, reminding her of her empty heart.

"Hey, you're not alone. You got your girls. I know they got your back. And you got me. You're my dawg." He gave her an encouraging look and Kayla shook her head at him. Over the past few weeks, she had learned that Terrell was a great listener. They would share stories and thoughts with each other and he always seemed to understand what she was going through. Although he acted like he was a player, she knew he had issues of his own. Even so, to her, he was genuine in his own way.

"Your *dawg?*"

"My ace, my buddy, my girl, you know . . . my dawg! Now come on, before we're late," he told her and pulled her up from the table.

14

The June heat was bearing down on Kayla as she sat on the hood of her car. She was traveling along the interstate when it went dead. She got out and popped the hood as if she knew what she was looking for. She called Roni, but got no answer on her cell or Yvonne's. She knew Tia was at work and she wouldn't be able to reach her. Luckily, her father had her on his AAA account and they came and towed the car to her house. The tow truck driver told her that her transmission was gone and it would take about two thousand dollars to repair. *Where the hell am I supposed to get two thousand dollars?* She wondered as she rode home in the tow truck. *I don't even have two hundred dollars in my savings account.* Her situation was going from bad to worse. *How am I gonna raise a baby with no man, no car, and no money?*

She slammed the door as she went into her house and sat on the sofa. The phone rang and she picked it up on instinct.

"Hello."

"Hey, Beautiful. I was calling to see how you were doing." The sound of Craig's voice pissed her off even worse.

"Why the hell do you care? All you wanted was for me to have an abortion, right? I didn't and I haven't told your wife, *yet*."

"I know you didn't. That's why I'm calling. I appreciate that, for real. How are you feeling?"

"Not good. My car broke down and I don't have the money to get it fixed. Are you gonna help me out?"

"How much you need?"

"Two thousand."

"Dollars? Hell, you can buy another car for that much."

"Are you gonna give me money to buy another car then?"

"I don't have no money like that. I mean, I can get you some loot, but it ain't gonna be no two thousand dollars," he told Kayla. She was totally surprised. She didn't think he was gonna offer her any help.

"How much can you get me?" she sat up and asked him.

"Let me check some stuff out and I'll get back with you," he told her. She had heard this from him before and she wasn't even falling for it this time.

"Whatever, Craig. Don't lie to me. I know you ain't gonna call me back," she told him.

"I am, Kayla. I just gotta check on something and then I'll call you back." Craig sounded as if he meant what he said.

"I need for you to call me tonight so I'll know what I need to do," Kayla told him.

"Okay. I'll talk to you then," he said and hung up the phone. That was at quarter after seven. At twelve-fifteen, Kayla went to bed. *I knew he was lying.*

She woke up early the next morning. She had to figure out how she was gonna get to and from work. She couldn't very well ask her girls to be her personal taxi service. She went on line and found a bus schedule and mapped out her route. She made it to work twenty minutes early. *At least I know I can make it here on time everyday,* she thought, relieved. The only bad part was catching the bus home at ten o'clock at night. But Kayla knew she had to do what she had to do. Walking to the bus stop after work, she tried not to panic when she saw a car pull beside her.

"What are you doing, dawg?" she heard Terrell call as the window rolled down.

"Going home. The same thing you're doing," she answered.

"Where's your car?" he asked.

"My electrical system went out. Costs almost two grand to fix."

"I'll give you a ride. Come on. Get in." He reached and opened the door. Kayla looked at him, hesitating.

"Where do you live, Terrell?"

"Do it matter? I'm the one taking *you* home. Get in, girl." He smiled.

Kayla got in his Altima and they pulled off.

"So, where am I taking you?" He fumbled with his radio.

"Terrace Gardens, the townhouses." She sat back.

"That's not far from where I live. As a matter of fact, it's on the way. Why didn't you say anything about your car being broke, yo?"

"Because that's my problem. I don't want to be airing my issues to everyone," she said.

"So you were just gonna catch the bus to and from work, not expecting me to offer you a ride? Come on, we peoples. You know that by now. This is my joint right here." He turned up the volume on the radio and began to nod to the music. "You don't know nothing about that, girl."

Kayla laughed and directed Terrell to her house. "Thanks, Terrell."

"No problem, Kayla. I'll see you tomorrow. Be ready at eleven-thirty. I'll blow the horn. And have me some lunch ready." He smirked.

"Imagine that." She got out and closed the door, shaking her head.

"Well, at least be ready on time. I'll let you slide with the lunch part. Tell your girl Roni I said what's up, though."

"She's out of your league, Terrell. Besides, she's caught up with another guy right now. I will give her the message, though." She started to go in the house.

"Peace, Kay. And eat something healthy before you go to bed," he called out as he pulled off. Kayla shook her head and was grateful that they had become friends.

15

"So what are we gonna do to celebrate the Fourth of July, Prego?" Tia asked Kayla as she flipped through the CDs.

"I don't know," Kayla answered. They were having a Lonely Hearts Club night at Kayla's and while they drank wine, Kayla sipped on a Pepsi and they listened to music.

"What did your dad say when you told him you were pregnant, Kay?" Yvonne passed her a bowl of tortillas and she dipped one in the guacamole.

"I haven't told him," Kayla said between bites.

"He doesn't know?" Roni sat up on the sofa.

"He knows. If your mother knows, then he knows," Roni and Tia looked at each other and said, giggling. There was a knock and Kayla went to answer the door.

"Hey, Terrell. What's up?" Kayla opened the door and he followed her into the living room where the other ladies were.

"Now this is my type of party. Four beautiful

women, all shapes, sizes and flavors." He grabbed a handful of chips and sat beside Roni. Kayla looked at her and laughed. She had told Roni of Terrell's crush, but as she suspected, Roni was not even trying to go there.

"What? You don't have one of your hot dates tonight?" Yvonne asked him.

"Yeah, I did. But she began to bore me so I decided to check on Kay while I was in the neighborhood. If I would have known y'all were over here chillin', I would've cancelled it and came here from the jump." He laughed.

"What are you doing tomorrow for the Fourth, Terrell?" Tia asked.

"I am making my rounds. I got some dates lined up, but my brother is having a nice little cookout at his spot. You guys wanna come?" he asked. "You got something to drink?"

''Yeah, look in the fridge. It's wine, juice and soda," Kayla replied. Terrell got up and headed for the kitchen.

"Anybody else need something while I'm in here?" he asked and picked up Kayla's almost empty glass.

"I'm good."

"No thanks."

"I'm cool."

He returned with a glass of wine for himself and a glass of juice for Kayla. She looked at him and frowned as he took her can of Pepsi away.

"I'm not having my godchild come out all hyper. I told you about that," he informed her.

"Your godchild? That's my godchild." Yvonne threw a pillow at him.

"Correction. Theo and I have already claimed that child as our first joint venture." Tia laughed.

"Well, I'm glad it's my niece or nephew. Kayla is my sister, even if it's no blood between us," Roni aimed at all of the other claimants.

"Well, if anyone deserves to be the godfather of this child, it's me. If it wasn't for me, the poor kid would be trying to survive on Kool-Aid and Now n' Laters. You'd better want me to be the godfather, because then the kid is straight. Because I am a *pimp*," Terrell joked.

Roni punched him in the arm and told him, "My niece or nephew will not have a *pimp* for a godfather."

"If Kayla's baby is your niece or nephew, yes it will. Now are y'all coming to my brother's crib tomorrow or what? It's gonna be plenty of food, plenty of drinks and plenty of fun." He looked around at the beautiful women.

"Are there gonna be plenty of men?" Roni asked.

"I'm gonna be there. I'm more than enough. It's plenty of me to go around." He moved closer to her.

"You can say that again." Roni laughed and moved further away.

"I'm down. What time?" Tia asked.

"It's supposed to start at three. But you know how black folks are. I'd say get there around four, four-thirty. It's gonna be off the hook, for real. My brother *can* throw a parry. He learned from the best."

"I'm afraid to ask who that might be," Yvonne said.

"Me, of course." His cell phone began to ring and he looked at it. "Well, ladies, duty calls and I must leave you now. I'll meet y'all here at four and you can follow me to his crib. That cool?"

"That's cool," Tia said.

Kayla got up to walk him to the door. "Thanks, Terrell."

"Be on time. You know how you can get." He smiled as he closed the door and left.

"You look so cute," Tia said as Kayla opened the door. Kayla had on her first maternity outfit. She wanted to wear some cute shorts and a midriff top like she usually wore on the Fourth of July, but her condition this year did not allow it. Kayla had on some red maternity shorts and a red and white striped sleeveless top along with some white socks with a red ball on the back and a fresh pair of white Classics.

"I look like a strawberry." Kayla frowned. "Hey, Theo."

"You look cute, Kay," he said as he came inside.

"I can't believe your stomach. It's so cute," Tia continued and touched Kayla's somewhat noticeable belly.

"Shut up, Tia." Kayla laughed and slapped her hands away.

"Roni and Yvonne just pulled up," Kayla said as she looked out the front window. "And there's Terrell. Go tell them I'm ready. But I need Roni to come put my hair in a ponytail. *Don't* tell Terrell. Just tell Roni I need her."

"Okay. But you know Terrell is gonna be fussing," Tia said. "Come on, Theo. Talk him to death to distract him."

"What are you trying to say,?" she heard Theo ask as they departed.

"What's up, Kay?" Roni asked as she came in the door.

"I need you to pull my hair up, Ron."

"I thought something was wrong. Come here, girl." Roni twisted and twirled Kayla's hair until it was perfect.

"I don't see how you do this." Kayla smiled at herself in the mirror.

"Come on, let's go!" They heard Terrell's voice booming from the front. Kayla grabbed her purse and sunglasses and they left.

"Wow. It's a lot of cars here," Kayla told Terrell as they parked in front of the pretty condo. "These are big."

"Yeah, they got three floors," Terrell commented and got out of the car. He took the time to fix his shirt and made sure his pants fit perfectly over his Timberlands.

"Anybody ever tell you you're vain?" Roni said as she joined them. She was touching up her lipgloss.

"I know you not talking, yo." Terrell smirked.

"Both of you take vanity to a whole other level," Kayla said and they followed Terrell to the house. He opened the door and there was a crowd of people. They were sitting in the well-decorated living area and there was what sounded like a live deejay coming from the backyard.

"Terry! What's up, man?" They greeted Terrell like he was a superstar.

"What's up? Yo, where's Toby?" he asked.

"He's out back working the grill," a tall red-bone told him.

"Come on, y'all. Let me introduce you to your host." Terrell led them through the living area, down a hall past the dining room and kitchen to the huge backyard where a live deejay was set up. A huge grill was filling the air with the smell of barbecue. Theo nodded toward the fully stocked bar and beer keg. There were long picnic tables full of food—salads, fruit, breads, and vegetables, anything you could ever imagine at a cookout. Kayla looked to her left and saw one guy holding a beer, frying fish in a deep fryer. Yvonne nudged her and pointed to another table with a big container in the middle. Kayla looked at her and they knew what the other was thinking—Crabs!

"Now this is a cookout!" Roni nodded. "What does your brother do again?"

"Here he is now. Yo, Toby!"

"Terry. I knew you was gonna be late." The voice came from behind the grill. The cover closed and Kayla saw Roni's jaw drop.

"Hey y'all, this is my brother Toby, otherwise known as Deejay Terror. You know, at Dominic's."

"Nice to meet you. Terry has told me a lot about you all." Toby came and shook all of their hands, stopping at Roni. "I'm glad you could make it."

"Thank you. I'm glad we were invited," Roni said, her eyes never leaving Toby's.

"Toby, I think the meat is ready," a big girl with long hair called from the grill. She did not seem too pleased that he was in Roni's face.

"Well, eat, drink and be merry. Please have a

good time. Let me know if you need anything. We'll talk more later," Toby said.

"Toby!" the girl called again.

"A'ight, Darla. Gimme a break. If it's ready, take it out!" he growled at her as he returned to the grill.

"Do you think that was directed at all of us or just Roni?" Tia laughed.

"I think the last part was for Ron," Theo replied.

"Why didn't you tell me that was your brother?" Roni fumed and asked Terrell.

"You never asked. I mean, I don't go around saying my brother is Deejay Terror. That's some gay type stuff."

"I can't believe this." She shook her head and tried not to look at Toby.

Kayla decided to look for her. The brother was beyond fine. He was dark chocolate in color and at six three, two hundred forty pounds, he was cut just right. Because he was always standing behind the deejay table, they had never known he was bow-legged until now. His chiseled face had deep set, amber eyes and he had deep dimples when he smiled. *I see why she's digging him.*

"Well, let's eat," Terrell announced. They set out to fix their plates.

"Hi, I don't think we've met. I'm Darla, Toby's girlfriend," the heavy-set girl who had interrupted them earlier walked up and said to Roni.

"I'm Roni," she said mildly, staring the girl in her face. She was never one to be intimidated by anyone.

"And you are?" she directed at Kayla.

"Kayla."

"You here with Terrell?" she asked, looking at Kayla's stomach.

"He invited us." Kayla looked Darla up and down.

"That's cool," she said.

"Darla! Go to the store and get some more ice," Toby yelled from behind the bar.

"Okay." She scurried away, leaving Roni and Kayla standing.

"If she's Toby's girlfriend, why is she worried about if I'm here with Terrell?" Kayla laughed to Roni.

"She better chill, because she messing with the wrong one. Let me get her *boyfriend* to fix me a drink." Roni smiled and headed to join Toby at the bar.

Kayla and her crew feasted and more than enjoyed the food. The deejay, although not as tight as Toby, did an excellent job mixing old school and current favorites. They ate and ate and laughed and joked and ate some more. Soon the sun began to set and Toby joined them at their table, sitting next to Roni.

"I don't think your girlfriend would appreciate you sitting over here with me." Roni smiled at him as he brought her another margarita.

"What girlfriend?" He looked at Terrell, confused. Terrell just put his head down and shrugged.

"What's her name, Kay?" Roni turned to Kayla.

"Darla," Kayla answered.

"Darla? I don't have a girlfriend, and if I did, it definitely wouldn't be *Darla*. That's just my STD." He and Terrell looked at each other and laughed.

"What's a STD?" Tia asked.

"Something To Do. You know. If I get bored and

want someone to come over and cook, I'll call her. I need my dry cleaning picked up or someone to wait for the cable man, I know she'll do it. She hangs around me at the club, helps me load my equipment in the car."

"Gives you some," Roni interrupted.

"I didn't say that." He smiled.

"You didn't have to," Roni replied and sipped the frozen beverage seductively through a straw. Toby tried not to stare. He glanced down at his watch and checked the time.

"Hey, you know y'all can see the fireworks from back here. They're about to start in a little while." Everyone was kicked back, having a good time when Kayla caught a familiar face from the corner of her eye.

"G! What's up, baby?" Toby called out.

"Deejay Terror!" Geno started for their table and stopped before he made it, noticing who was sitting there.

"Kayla," Geno said.

"You two know each other? Cool!" Toby got up and offered Geno a seat. "Let me get you a beer, man."

"Hey, Geno," Roni offered.

"What's up, everyone? I didn't think I'd run into you all here," he said. Kayla spotted Janice talking to Darla at the opposite end of the yard. Obviously, she didn't see Geno talking to her. Although he didn't seem too worried about being caught.

"Where's the bathroom?" she asked Terrell.

"Come on, I'll let you use the one upstairs," Terrell told her. They went inside and walked up to the second floor. He showed Kayla the bathroom and told her he'd wait for her. She went inside and sat down on the toilet, relieving herself. As she washed her hands, she looked at herself in the mirror. *What the hell is Geno doing here? I'm not even in the mood to deal wit' no ignorance tonight.*

"You a'ight, Kay?" She heard Terrell tapping on the door.

"Yeah. Give me a few minutes, okay?" she called out.

"Okay. Take your time. I'll wait for you downstairs," he said. She could hear him talking to someone down the hall. She washed her face and hands again and opened the door. She found Geno waiting outside the bathroom.

"I told Terrell I needed to talk to you. He said we could use the room at the end of the hall." He grabbed her hand and led her into the bedroom. She sat on the bed in the middle of the massive room.

"What do you want, Geno? Ain't your psychotic girlfriend gonna be looking for you?" she asked him.

"I need to know something, Kayla," he asked, ignoring her question.

"What?"

"When is the baby due?"

"November."

"We were together that night, Kayla. That would be nine months."

"You can't go by months, Geno. It takes forty weeks from conception to birth. I got pregnant on Valentine's." She looked at him.

"But it still might be . . ."

"It's not, Geno." She stopped him. As bad as she

wanted him to be, she knew she couldn't make
Geno the father of her child.

"Look, I know you are mad about me and Janice."

"You and Janice? I don't give a damn about you
and her," Kayla fired at him.

"Chill out, Kay! Don't act like the thought of me
being the father never crossed your mind!" he
yelled back at her.

Kayla sat on the side of the bed and tried not to
cry. The door opened and Terrell stuck his head
in.

"You a'ight, yo? Everything cool, man?" he
asked, looking at Kayla and then Geno.

"Yeah, man, we just talking," Geno answered
him.

"Try to keep it down. Y'all don't want everybody
up in your business. Know what I'm saying?" He
nodded as he left out and closed the door behind
him.

"You wouldn't lie about this, Kayla. Would you?
Please, tell me."

"I wouldn't lie to you period, Geno. You know
that. Your being with Janice has nothing to do with
it. I've never lied to you," she told him.

"Then I guess I owe you an apology, Kay. I
mean, I remember that night, and . . ." He smiled
weakly, but she knew he was hurt. They sat silently
for what seemed like an eternity, just looking at
each other. "You look . . ."

"Big as hell." She finished the sentence for him.
He smiled weakly. "No, you look beautiful."

"Come on, we'd better get back downstairs. The
fireworks are about to start." She struggled to get

up. He reached his hand out and helped pull her to her feet. They giggled as they went into the hallway.

"What the hell are you two doing?" an icy voice said. Kayla and Geno turned around and Janice was standing at the top of the steps looking at them like she could spit daggers. Kayla could tell that she was drunk.

"We were talking, Janice. That's all. Come on, let's go back down," he said and tried to get past her, but she blocked him.

"Oh hell, naw!" she yelled. "You come out the bedroom wit' your ex-bitch, who by the way is knocked up, and you wanna act like it's all good? You gotta come better than that, Geno!"

"You know what? I ain't even gonna entertain this bullshit." Kayla laughed as she went to walk by them. "Excuse me."

"Don't run. What the hell were you doing wit' my man?" she slurred. Kayla looked over the rail and saw a crowd had begun to gather.

"Janice, you're drunk. Come on, let's go." He pulled her arm and she spun around and looked him in the face.

"You still love her, Geno? Is that it?" She waited for him to answer.

"Come on, Janice. Let's go home." He reached for her arm again and she stumbled as she stepped back.

"Tell me. Tell me in front of her, while she standing here, big belly and all. Do you still love her?" This time, she pointed to Kayla.

Kayla looked down at the floor so he wouldn't have to look at her face. As bad as she wanted to know the answer to that question, she dreaded hearing the answer. Either way, it wouldn't matter. They were over.

"Answer me, dammit!"

Suddenly, Geno bent over and picked up a screaming Janice, carrying her down the steps past the audience that was observing the moment. He looked back at Kayla but didn't say a word. She watched as the door closed behind them.

"Man, that was better than the fireworks," Terrell said. "That was the highlight of the party."

"Shut up, Terrell! You okay, Kayla?" Yvonne ran next to her girlfriend to make sure she was all right.

"Yeah, girl. That bitch is crazy," Kayla said as they went outside.

"No doubt. What were you and Geno doing up there anyway?" Tia asked.

"We were just talking, that's it," Kayla answered.

Everyone had made their way back outside and the party had picked up where it left off. Soon, the sky was lit up with bright, colorful fireworks. Kayla looked up and felt her baby kicking; she couldn't help but smile. *Next year, I'll be watching the fireworks with you.* She put her hand on her belly.

"I got a date this weekend," Roni whispered in her ear.

"I'm not surprised." She smiled at her friend. She looked around and saw Tia and Theo hugged up and Yvonne laughing with a guy by the beer keg. Everyone seemed so happy and content, their lives predictable and settled. Kayla felt the movement in her stomach again and told herself that one day, she and her baby would be happy too.

Despite all the drama earlier, the evening's festivities continued well into the night. Everyone was having such a good time that no one wanted to leave. Kayla tolerated the merriment for as long as she could and then decided she couldn't take it anymore. At ten after eleven, she looked for Terrell. She went inside to check the kitchen where she found him kissing Darla.

"Oops, my bad," Kayla said, embarrassed as she quickly turned around.

"That's okay. You ready to go?" He pushed the plump girl away and she excused herself, walking by Kayla with a smile.

"I'm tired. I can see you're not, though. I'll just get Tia and Theo to drop me off. You go handle your business, Terrell." She smirked at him. They went back into the backyard.

"It ain't even like that. But naw, we can go. I think I might hit a few spots tonight and get my dance on. Is she rolling with us?" He motioned toward Roni who was dancing with Toby.

"I'll go and ask." She shrugged. She waved at Roni and pointed to her wristwatch. Roni nodded and whispered something into Toby's ear. They walked over to her.

"I'm sorry, Kay. I didn't even know it was that late," Roni told her.

"No, I'm sorry, Ron. You can stay if you want. I'm sure Theo will give you a ride. I think Yvonne left, though. I can't find her," Kayla replied.

"I can take you home. That is if you don't want to spend the night." Toby rubbed Roni's arm, smiling.

"You must think I am one of your STD's, huh? don't think so." Roni pushed his hand away.

"I heard that. Well, let's roll, then," Terrell announced.

"Terry, you not gonna help me clean up?" Toby asked his brother.

"Sorry, bro. I'm quite sure Darla got it under control for you. You know I chauffeured these ladies tonight. I gotta get 'em home, too." He laughed and motioned toward Geno who was walking back into the yard, alone. "I think your boy wanna talk to you."

"I'ma go tell Theo and Tia we're out," Roni said. "You gonna be okay?"

"Yeah." Kayla nodded. She sat back down and watched as Geno walked toward her.

"I'll meet you all out front," Terrell said and waved toward Geno. "We outta here, G!"

"I wanted to come back and apologize for earlier, Kay." He sat beside her.

She wanted to ask him where Janice was, but kept quiet.

"She gets kinda crazy when she drinks. I'm sorry."

"You didn't do anything, Geno." Kayla shrugged. "You might wanna tell her to get some help, though. Any other time you know I wouldn't have been so nice. But I *am* pregnant."

"No, your being pregnant ain't got nothing to do with it. You are *you*. Listen, I just want to let you know that we're still cool. No matter what, okay? You call me if you need anything, you understand?"

"Yeah, G." She turned and faced him. Roni came from around the side of the house and Terrell pulled up all at the same time. "Well, take care of yourself, Geno."

He gave her a quick hug and kissed her cheek, then hugged Roni. "Look out for her, Ron."

"I always do, Geno. Hey, see where Toby's head is at for me, okay?"

"I already know where it is. You got him open." Geno laughed.

"I know that. I got 'em all open. But I gotta figure him out. Let him know I'm not your average chick," Roni said.

"He been in your face all night and he had around forty female guests that came to be in his face. It ain't that hard to figure." Geno waved as they got in the car.

Terrell dropped Roni off and then proceeded to Kayla's. As they pulled up, he noticed something sitting outside her door.

"What's that?" he asked her.

"I don't know." She opened the car door and hesitated going up the sidewalk, turning to look back at Terrell.

"Now I gotta be security too. Jeez." He commented as he opened his door and got out. He picked up the package and read the note. "It's a cake. From your baby daddy."

"Quit playing." Kayla went and grabbed the note from him.

Hey, Beautiful.
   I came by to check on you and bring you something sweet. But you weren't here—I guess it's my loss. Call me later so I can see how it tastes.

                                    Love,
                                    Craig

"I can't believe his lying ass. What did he want? And where was his wife and kid?" Kayla snatched her door open and threw the cake on the counter.

"Call him and find out," Terrell told her. "I thought you said he wasn't around."

"He's not. I haven't seen or heard from him since that day I cussed him out in my driveway." She flopped down on the sofa. Terrell wasted no time getting a knife and cutting a slice of the cake.

"Damn, this is the bomb," he said. "That nigga can cook."

Kayla tried to resist but she couldn't. "What kind is it?"

"Chocolate something," he said between bites.

"Bring me a piece," she called out sweetly. He brought her a big slice of the chocolate frosted inferno. It was chocolate with chocolate chips, nuts and caramel. "Who's pimping who, now?" She laughed.

"That's not even funny, yo." He tried not to smile. He knew she had caught him off guard.

"Oh God, this is sinful," she said as she took a bite.

"Well, you good? 'Cause I gotta be out," he said and wiped his mouth.

"Oh, that's right. You're going out," she murmured. "What was up with you and homegirl?"

"Who?"

"The one you were slobbing over." She looked at him knowingly.

"What? Darla? Please. She was trying to get back at Toby for being all in Roni's face. But what she doesn't realize is that Toby ain't her man, and will never be her man because she is too weak. Toby likes strong women. They are a challenge for him. Darla is a chicken head, a freak chicken head at that. That was nothing."

"Okay *nothing*." Kayla wrapped the remainder of the cake up.

"Yo, tell that nigga that cake is the bomb when you call him. I'll holla at you tomorrow. You a'ight?"

"Be safe." Kayla hugged him as he left. She made sure her door was locked and picked up the cordless phone. She dialed the numbers and waited for Craig to answer.

"Hey, sweetheart. Did you get your cake?" he asked as if it was the most natural question in the world.

"Don't even try it, Craig. What the hell was that all about? You popping over my house again? I thought you got enough of that the last time you showed up over here unannounced."

"There you go. Why you always gotta trip, huh, Kayla? I made that because I thought you'd like it." She could hear a lot of laughter in the background.

"I thought you were gonna call me back the other week, huh, Craig? Don't tell me, you had to work and didn't get a chance, right?"

"No, I . . ." he began but Kayla didn't give him a chance to finish.

"I don't care what happened. It doesn't even matter anymore. Nothing you tell me is the truth. The sad part is that you lie for no reason. I can take anything but a liar and a cheat, Craig, and you are *both* of those."

"Kayla, I'm sorry. I know I've fucked up and you have no faith in me. Hell, I don't blame you. But I'm telling you I'm gonna do right by you. This is a messed up situation for both of us, and I was taking all of my frustrations out on you. I'm sorry."

Craig was breathing hard into the phone and Kayla could tell that he must've changed rooms or went outside or something, because the background noise that was there earlier was gone. "Hello, Kayla?"

"I'm here," was Kayla's only response. She didn't know what to say. She wanted to believe Craig, but she knew that he was lying. She had been set up one too many times by him and her guard was up.

"I'm gonna bring you some money, Kayla. And I'm gonna take care of my baby. You understand?"

"If you say so, Craig," she answered.

"Can you call me tomorrow after you get off? I can come through whenever you tell me to. Is that a'ight?"

"I'll call you after ten. I'm 'bout to go to bed. I've had a long day." She sighed into the phone. Geno, Janice, Craig. Kayla was beyond exhausted and she couldn't think straight.

"I guess you don't feel like company then?" Kayla could hear his flirtatious grin through the phone.

"No, I don't. I'll talk to you tomorrow, Craig."

"Goodnight, Beautiful. I'm gonna do right by you, just watch," he told her and she hung the phone up.

16

"I'm so excited. My first ultrasound," Roni whispered as they waited for the radiologist to come into the exam room.

"You are so silly, Ron, You'd think you were having the baby." Kayla tried to find a comfortable position on the table. There was a light knock and the door opened.

"Ms. Hopkins? Hi, I'm Kelly and I'm gonna be doing your sonogram today. You feeling okay?"

"Fine. This is my friend Roni."

"Nice to meet you. Well, let's get started." Kelly lifted the gown and measured Kayla's stomach with her hands. "You feeling the baby move?"

"A lot." Kayla smiled.

"Now, this is gonna be a little cold," she said as she put the blue gel across Kayla's stomach. She reached for the scope and moved it around Kayla's belly. "There's the heart, liver, kidneys, all looking good. There's the head. Look at the arms, the legs."

Kayla watched in amazement as she saw her baby on the small monitor. Tears began to form in her eyes and she did not bother to stop them. This was her baby. At that moment, she knew without a doubt that she had made the right decision. She saw the form on the small screen and the love that she felt was overwhelming.

"Can you tell what it is?" Roni whispered.

"You want to know the sex?" the woman asked Kayla.

"Yeah." Kayla nodded and continued to focus on the screen.

"Well, let's see. Now I'm not one hundred percent certain because of the position, but I'd say you're having a healthy boy," Kelly said.

A boy, a son, my son.

"Yes, yes, yes. I am gonna have a nephew. He is gonna be spoiled rotten!" Roni gushed.

"I can tell. Let me print some of these out for you and then you can get dressed. Karen will see you in her office in a few minutes." Kelly passed Kayla some paper towel to wipe her stomach and helped her sit up. "Congratulations, both of you."

"A son. Wow, I'm having a baby boy," Kayla said as she got dressed.

"I gotta call Tia and Yvonne and Mama. Girl, we got some shopping to do. We are cleaning that junk room of yours out this weekend, Kayla. It's time to design a nursery."

"You are crazy, Roni." Kayla shook her head.

"What did your dad say, Kayla?" Yvonne asked as she put Kayla's college books into a box.

"About what?" Kayla reached into the closet and pulled some bags out.

"Having a grandson. I know he's excited." Yvonne closed the box up and began to go through the bags Kayla pulled out. "Why did you keep all of this stuff? What is it anyway?"

"Old bulletin board stuff. I never know when I might need it again and the storage at school was full. I brought it home and stored it in my extra bedroom." Kayla watched as Yvonne pulled out some tin foil snowflakes her class had made during her first year of teaching.

"Well, you are no longer a teacher, so it's now fresh," Yvonne told her. "Roni, can you bring some more fresh bags in here?"

"More? We already used a whole box," Roni called from the kitchen. Her cell phone rang as they were cleaning out what used to be Kayla's guestroom and she excused herself. They knew it was Toby by the way she was talking.

"So, what did he say?" Yvonne asked Kayla.

"I still haven't told him. I'm going to, though." Kayla sat on the floor and crossed her legs.

"When? At his kindergarten graduation? What are you waiting on, Kayla?"

"You know my father. This is gonna break his heart. I just don't know how," Kayla told her friends. She had tried and tried to think of the right way to tell her dad. But no matter how she tried to play the scenario out in her head, it always ended with him being hurt and disappointed.

"You'd better tell him, Kay. I'd hate for him to hear it from someone else, which would be even worse. He'll be even more upset because *you* didn't tell him."

"He's gonna be upset, period. I am just trying to keep the peace for a little while longer. Trust me, I know what I am doing." Kayla hoped she did, anyway.

The girls finally finished clearing the room out and then went out to grab a bite to eat. They were studying their menus at IHOP when a sexy gentleman approached their table. He was short, but cut like L L Cool J. He had perfect skin and the cutest smile. He was neatly dressed in a spandex T-shirt and dress pants, fitting perfectly to show off his physique.

"Excuse me, but don't I know you from somewhere?" he asked, looking at Yvonne.

"Oh, how original," Roni groaned and shook her head at him. Kayla looked at him, but she didn't recognize him from anywhere.

"I think so, but I'm trying to figure out where," Yvonne told him.

"The school. You work at my nephew's school. I pick him up sometimes," the guy said, realizing who Yvonne was.

"That's right. I've spoken to you in the hallways sometimes. See Roni, he does know me from somewhere."

"I see," Roni replied.

"I'm Darrell, Darrell Coleman." He extended his hand to Yvonne. Kayla frowned at him as she began to comprehend who he was. *It was my brother Darrell's house. The sports agent.* Craig's voice echoed in her head.

"Yvonne Majors. And these are my friends, Kayla and Roni." She pointed to her friends.

"Nice to meet you," he said and noticed that Kayla didn't seem too friendly. "Well, I won't interrupt you ladies any further. Enjoy your meal. I'll see you next time I pick up my nephew."

"I look forward to it." Yvonne smiled and he walked away.

"Cute, Von. You should have given him your number." Roni grinned at Yvonne.

"No she shouldn't have. Don't you know who he is? That's Craig's brother," Kayla hissed across the table.

"Shut up. His brother is that fine?" Roni turned to get a better look.

"Don't turn around! He's looking over here," Yvonne whispered. "Kayla, he seems nice."

"So did Craig, remember?" she muttered, trying not to look across the room at Darrell. "Oh God, he's coming back over here."

"Excuse me, Yvonne. I wanted to leave my number with you. Call me some time if you want to hang out."

"Uh, thanks." Yvonne smiled at him. Kayla was not impressed.

"When's your baby due?" he turned and asked Kayla. *Why don't you ask your brother,* was what she started to say, but thought better of it.

"Thanksgiving Day," she answered with a fake smile.

"That's nice. Well, I look forward to hearing from you. Nice talking to you ladies again." Darrell turned and walked away, leaving the ladies smirking at each other.

"Shut up and eat," Kayla warned before anyone could say anything.

They enjoyed the rest of their meals and went to the register to pay.

"It's already taken care of, ladies," the cashier said.

"What?" they asked in unison.

"Someone already paid for your meal," she said to them like they were slow.

"Who?" Roni demanded.

"The gentleman already left a few moments ago." She gave them their receipt.

"Compliments of DC," Yvonne read aloud. "Darrell Coleman."

"Now that brother has taste," Roni told her.

"You should see his crib," Kayla mumbled.

"What?" Yvonne turned to Kayla.

"Can't believe he paid the bill," Kayla lied. "If I would have known he was paying, I would have gotten dessert."

17

"A godson. My first godson," Terrell said to Kayla. They were sitting at their desks and Kayla finally told him the results of the ultra-sound. She tried to lie and say she didn't know, but Terrell in his eternal nosiness had seen her writing down boys' names on a piece of paper, so she had come clean. "Now we have to come up with a tight name."

"We?" Kayla looked across at him.

"I'm not letting you screw up his life with some cornball name."

"I am not picking cornball names, you jerk." Kayla threw a rubber band at him.

"What do you have so far?" Kenosha asked.

"Okay. How about Xachary Denzel Hopkins," Kayla said proudly. "But spell Xachary with an X, not a Z."

"ANNNN!" Terrell made the sound of a game show buzzer.

"I like it," she said.

"Hell, no. First of all, Zachary with a Z isn't even player. It's a nerd name. And then you're gonna really confuse him, his teachers and everyone else by spelling it with an X? And when he plays football, he's gonna be big Xach. That is ugly. And Denzel? Come on."

"Well what do you suggest, Terrell?" Kayla waited for him to think.

"Tyranny. Now that's player." He smiled.

"ANNNN!" It was Kayla's turn to make the buzzer noise. "What the heck? Tyranny? Doesn't that mean oppression? What about Montel Jordan Hopkins?" Kayla asked.

"His first words are gonna be 'this is how we do it'," Terrell joked. They tossed names around every day for weeks until Kayla decided on the perfect one, telling no one. She did, however, let everyone know that she appreciated their input, but they would just have to wait.

"Why won't you tell me, Kay?" Roni asked as they were painting the nursery walls a pretty shade of sky blue. It was the end of August and Kayla was getting bigger by the day. She decided they had better get this done before she couldn't get out of the bed.

"Because it's a surprise, Ron. I'm not telling anyone until he's here."

"Not even Craig?"

"No, not even Craig," Kayla told her. Kayla and Craig had come to terms on their relationship. He would come by once a week to check on her and see if she was okay, bringing her banging desserts that she began to thrive on. They would talk for a little while and he would see the progress she was making on the nursery. The entire theme was denim, and everything was OshKosh thanks to her childless girlfriends who got a kick out of outfitting the room. He agreed to purchase the two hundred-dollar stroller she wanted and surprised the hell out of her when he showed up at her door one night with it. At this point, Kayla had no complaints about him. He tried to push up on her every now and then, but she stopped that real quick. They were just cool and Kayla made sure that he and every one else knew that.

"Is he excited?" Roni began painting the opposite wall.

"I don't think so. I mean, this isn't his first child and he already has a son. It's really no big deal. Calm down, boy." Kayla rubbed her belly.

"Oh, let me feel." Roni walked over and Kayla put her hand where the baby was kicking. "Kay, it's a baby in there."

"Naw, for real? Let's take a break." They went into the living room and Roni looked out the window.

"You expecting company?" she asked.

"No, Yvonne is out with Darrell, and Tia and Theo went to the movies."

"It's a burgundy Explorer pulling up in your driveway. Oh my God!"

"Please don't tell me, Ron." Kayla closed her eyes as she thought of the only person in the world she knew with a burgundy Explorer.

"I'll open the door." Roni went up the hallway and waited for them to knock. Kayla went into her private bathroom so she could think for a minute.

"Ron, hey there girl. How you been doing?" Kayla heard the deep voice say. She tried to calm herself and took a deep breath.

"Fine. You look good."

"Thanks, where's my baby?"

"She's in her room. I'll get her." Roni went to close the door when she realized the rest of the family was getting out of the truck. "Be right back. Make yourself at home."

"Kayla, come out." She tapped on the bathroom door. She knew this was the moment Kayla had been dreading and she wanted to be there for her friend.

"I can't," she whined.

"Yes, you can. Come on, Kayla. They're out there waiting for you." She tried the door but it was locked. She turned around and was startled when she realized she was not alone in the room.

"Move!" the woman commanded. Roni wasted no time doing what she was told. She sat on the side of Kayla's bed and waited for this scene to play itself out.

"Open the door and come out right now."

Kayla opened the door slowly. "Hi, Mama."

"Your hair is growing back. It looks good," her mother said as she hugged her. "Look at you."

"Kayla! I did not drive almost three hours for you to be in the bedroom all day. Come on out here and see me." She jumped at the sound of her father's voice.

"Go on, baby. Time to face the music." Kayla's mother rubbed her back. "She's coming right out, John. Give the girl a few moments. We did show up unexpected."

"Well, if she would call home every now and then she would have been expecting us." He laughed heartily.

"Does he know?" Kayla quickly asked her mother.

"Did you tell him? He'll know in a few minutes." She pulled Kayla out the door and down the hall. "Come on, Roni."

"Hi, Daddy," Kayla said as she walked toward her father. Her dad reached out and hugged her, then quickly let go.

"Kayla? Are you . . . ?" He frowned as he looked at his youngest daughter. The one he taught to ride her bike and scramble eggs. He couldn't believe that she was having a baby, and worse, that she had kept this from him.

"Yes, Daddy." Kayla looked down, ashamed.

"Looks like we're gonna be grandparents, John." Kayla's mother put her hand under Kayla's chin and raised her head. "Don't you hold your head down. You know better than that."

"Is that why you haven't called or come home? But Jennifer, you talked to her. Did you know?" He looked at Kayla's mom.

"I smell paint. Are you painting something?" Kayla's mother quickly asked.

"We're painting the nur—I mean guest room," Roni answered.

"Well, Roni, why don't you show me and we can give Kayla and her dad a chance to talk." They disappeared down the hall, leaving Kayla alone with her father. He sat down on the sofa, still shocked.

"I'm sorry, Daddy. I wanted to tell you, but I was too ashamed. I knew you'd be mad and I wasn't ready to deal with that. Not yet, anyway."

"Mad? Kayla, you are a grown woman. Why

would I be mad? I am disappointed, but that doesn't mean I don't love you. What is Geno saying?"

Kayla really wasn't ready to tell him that the baby wasn't Geno's, but she knew that the time had come to be honest about everything. "It's not Geno's, Daddy."

"What? Then whose is it?" Her Dad was truly baffled by what she was saying.

"Craig's," she answered.

"Who the hell is Craig?" He looked up at her.

"A friend."

"So let me get this straight. You get pregnant, don't call or visit for months and the father is your friend, not your ex-fiancé?"

"That's about right, Daddy. But I'm going to be all right. I have a great job and a support system from my friends. This isn't anything I've planned, and believe me, I have gone back and forth with myself about this decision. My child may not have been conceived under the greatest of circumstances, but I *am* gonna be a great mother. You and Mama raised me to do the right thing and I am."

"Baby, baby, baby. You are doing the right thing. But you could have come to me. I could have—" Tears filled his eyes.

"I'm sorry for not coming to you, Daddy. But there was nothing more you could have done for me except what you're doing now, loving me," she said and gave her father a big hug.

All of a sudden there was another knock at the door and it opened before Kayla could answer it.

"Yo, Kay. Let's roll to the mall," Terrell's voice yelled as he came in the door. He realized she wasn't alone and began to apologize. "Oh, my bad."

"Dad, this is . . ." Kayla started.

"You don't have to tell me who this is. My daughter tells me you're the father of this child she is carrying," her dad stood up and said coldly.

"She told you what?" Terrell looked at Kayla, appalled.

"Hey Terrell!" Roni greeted as she and Kayla's mom entered the living room.

"Terrell?" John looked totally baffled. "I thought you said his name was Craig."

"No, *you* said his name was Craig. This is my coworker and friend, Terrell." Kayla introduced Terrell to her father.

"You thought Terrell was Craig?" Roni giggled.

"Who's Craig?" Jennifer inquired.

"The baby's father," John told her.

"Oh, yeah."

"Craig is the father. Terrell is the godfather. And Geno and I are just friends." Kayla sighed. "Everyone understand now?"

"I got it," Roni said.

"Me too," Terrell replied.

"Now, I see the walls are being painted blue. Does that mean I am having a grandson?" Jennifer put her arm around Kayla.

"Indeed you are." Kayla smiled at her mother.

"A grandson named Jonathan. I like that." Her dad smiled at her.

"I like that, too," her mom agreed.

"Uh-uh. I don't like it." Terrell shook his head.

"Me either. But Kayla is keeping the name a secret anyway. She's not telling anyone until after he's born," Roni informed them.

"It's gonna be Jonathan, after her father," her dad said matter-of-factly.

"Well, Kayla, you don't need to be in there

painting. Why don't we leave and let your father and Terrell finish the room and we go shopping? Maybe even register you at some stores for your shower," Jennifer said. Kayla looked at Terrell and knew he wanted to object but didn't out of respect for her parents. "You don't mind, do you, Terrell?"

"Uh, no ma'am," he answered and Kayla and Roni suppressed their laughter.

"Go get changed, Kayla. We gotta go shopping for my grandson." She pushed Kayla toward the bedroom.

"I didn't know I drove all this way to paint. And by the looks of what you're wearing, you didn't either, huh?" John asked Terrell. "I appreciate it, though. And I'm sorry about assuming you were the father."

"Happens all the time," Terrell told him. John excused himself and went out to his SUV.

"Thanks, Terrell," Roni told him.

"For what?" He looked confused.

"Making an uncomfortable situation better."

"Why didn't she tell him, anyway?"

"I don't know. She knows her parents have and always will support her. She didn't want to upset him."

"Your girl and her emotional confrontations. That's why I call her DQ."

"What's DQ?"

"Drama Queen. The funny thing is, she doesn't go looking for the drama. It just always seems to find her." He laughed. "Her parents are cool, though. But I did get pimped into painting the room."

"Hey, that's what godpimps are for," Roni told him.

"I like that. Godpimp." He nodded.

"That was supposed to be a joke."

"Now it's my new title." His cell began to vibrate on his hip and he answered it. "What up? Over here at Kayla's. Yeah. She's right here. You wanna speak to her?" He passed the phone to Roni.

"Hello. Oh, it's in my purse. Okay, that's cool. I'll check my schedule and let you know. I'll call you later. Bye." She passed Terrell his phone back, glowing.

"You know he's really feeling you, right?"

"Yeah. Me and how many others?"

"Naw, you are good for him. You don't jump when he wants you to, like all the others. He likes that. I bet he wanted you to go out tonight, right?"

"How do you know?"

"That's how it works for him. He's known since y'all went out the other night that he wanted to see you again, but he'd never tell you that then. He'll wait until the day of and call to ask you. Now, most chicks would've said yes. But you held it down and said you'd let him know. That's player."

"So he already planned to take me out? Why did he wait?"

"Because you are supposed to sweat him, not him sweat you. That's his MO How long have y'all been going out?"

"Since July, so two months."

"He's never sweated anyone that long before. Whatever you're doing, keep doing it. That is if you really like him." He nodded at her.

"I do. He's a male version of me, kinda what I been looking for."

"Then it'll work because you're a female version of him. I can see why you are so compatible. He talks about you all the time and believe it or not, the games are about to stop. You just need to make sure you're ready for that."

Roni thought about what Terrell was telling her and thanked him. She really liked Terrell because he was the realest guy she had ever met. He was a good friend and just what Kayla needed right now. She respected him because he spoke his mind, even though he was so full of himself that he made her want to throw up sometimes.

Kayla, Jennifer and Roni shopped well into the evening. By the time they returned to Kayla's townhouse, they found John knocked out on the sofa and Terrell long gone. Kayla and Roni took the bags into the nursery. They cut on the light and smiled when they saw that the room was completely done. Not only had they done the walls and trim, there was a neon moon in the corner and glow in the dark stars had been applied to the ceiling.

"Grandpa and godpimp did a good job," Roni whispered to Kayla.

"They always do," she replied and almost cried.

18

The first few weeks of September went by so fast that the days began to run together. Kayla was standing in front of her closet one afternoon when she heard Terrell blowing his horn. She looked at the clock on her nightstand, making sure she had the correct time. The clock read ten forty. She went to let him in.

"You up yet?" he asked her.

"Naw, I'm still in the bed opening the door," she retorted. "I don't feel like going to work today. Let's call in."

"What?"

"Let's call in. I gotta start looking for a car anyway. I'm gonna need one by the time the baby gets here and I got my money saved, plus my trade-in. So, you can help me find a car."

"You're serious?"

"Yeah, I'm serious. Then we can go to lunch, my treat. We need a mental health day." She picked up the phone and called their manager, letting him know she would be absent. Then she passed the phone to Terrell who followed suit.

"I think they're gonna put two and two together and see that we're both calling out."

"Why give us vacation days if you don't want us to take them?" she said. She got dressed and they departed for their day of mental relaxation. They enjoyed test-driving all the latest vehicles, although Kayla knew she couldn't afford them. But by the end of the day, thanks to fast talking Terrell and her nice savings, Kayla was driving a black Maxima.

"Now you gotta get a system and some tint. You already got rims on it. Whoever had it before you took care of that."

"No, now I gotta get a car seat." She laughed. "Thanks, Terrell. I appreciate this."

"No, thank you, Kayla. It was almost enough to make me forget my own drama for a change." His cell began to ring and he checked it. "Hello. Hey, yeah, I took the day off. Um, sounds good. I'll be there in twenty." He clicked the phone and put it back on his hip.

"I don't even wanna know. You are so pitiful."

"Don't hate me 'cause I'm a player. I'll call you later," he told Kayla as he got in his car. She opened the door of her new ride and he rolled down his window. "That car almost looks good enough for me to push."

"It doesn't have any tint or rims, jerk."

"You're right. But you look a'ight in it." He pumped up his music and drove off.

19

"You still working everyday?" Karen asked her as she completed her exam.

"Every day." Kayla tried to sit up. Karen had to reach out and help her.

"You okay with that? I mean, you only have a few weeks left. Are you tired?"

"Tired, hungry, exhausted, fat, can't breathe. But if I stay home, I'll be bored. And I wouldn't be able to stand that." Kayla put her hand on her stomach. "Is being home gonna stop him from doing pull-ups on my ribs?"

"Unfortunately, no. But look at the bright side. It's almost Veteran's Day and by Thanksgiving, he'll be out of there."

"Promise?"

"Promise. I'll see you next Wednesday." Karen smiled as Kayla left. When she got home, Craig was waiting in her driveway.

"What did the doctor say?" he asked when she got out of the car.

"She said by Thanksgiving I'll be able to breathe. What are you doing here?"

"Came to check on you, Beautiful. I swear, Kayla, pregnancy agrees with you."

"Shut up. Where is your wife? And why aren't you at work?"

"I go in at four and she's my soon-to-be-ex-wife."

"Whatever. You still live there."

"Not for long. I'm gonna move in with Darrell." He followed her into the house and she turned to face him.

"Not a good idea," she said.

"Why not? He has an extra bedroom and I definitely ain't staying there with her much longer."

"Look, I need to let you know. We bumped into your brother a couple of months ago at IHOP. He's been trying to holla at Yvonne ever since. Before you freak out, he has no idea who I am or that this baby is yours. I know you haven't told anyone about the baby."

"Really? I guess I need to let him know then, huh?"

"You're gonna tell him?"

"Yeah. That's my brother. Don't worry, Kayla. You just worry about getting my baby outta there." He put his hand on her big tummy. "I'll take care of announcing his arrival."

"You'd better make it quick. He ain't gonna be in there for long. Believe that," she warned him.

"So what are we gonna do with this head?" Roni asked the Saturday before Veteran's Day.

"I don't know. I don't care. I can be bald at this point and it wouldn't matter," Kayla whined.

"What about some braids, Kay?" Tia suggested.

"I can't sit on the floor that long. My back is already aching."

"I'll do it at the shop," Roni told her. She looked knowingly at Tia.

"That'll take all day."

"Who's doing it, me or you?"

"You."

'Then quit complaining. Come on, let's go."

"You're gonna do it now?"

"Yes, and you'd better hurry up because I have a date with Toby tonight."

"You coming, Tia?" Kayla looked at her girlfriend, who seemed preoccupied.

"Uh, no. Theo's on his way to pick me up. You two go ahead. I'll call you later, Kay."

Roni insisted on driving and they stopped at the beauty supply store to get some bags of hair for Kayla, then proceeded to Jett Black.

"Well, look who wobbled in. Hi, Kayla and company."

"Hi, Ms. Ernestine." Kayla dragged herself to the nearest empty chair and plopped down.

"Miserable, huh?" her friend's mom asked.

"Beyond miserable. And now Roni wants to braid my hair," she moaned.

"Well, at least your hair will look good in your delivery room pictures." Roni began to comb through Kayla's hair.

"What delivery room pictures? I'm not having any pictures taken in the delivery room."

"You think that I'm gonna be your birth coach and not take pictures? This is the birth of my nephew."

"She already bought a new camera, Kayla." Ms. Ernestine shrugged.

"And she can take all the pictures she wants in the hospital nursery," Kayla told them. They laughed and joked until the sun set and Roni finished the last braid.

"That looks good, Roni. Well, it was nice having you, Ms. Kayla. I guess the next time you visit us you won't be by yourself."

"I guess not."

"Do you need anything?" Ms. Ernestine asked her, helping her out of the chair.

"No, I pretty much got everything. Between my mama and the Lonely Hearts Club, I am pretty well set."

"Well, call me and let me know. No matter what time it happens."

"You know we will, Mama. I'll see you later." Roni kissed her mother's cheek and they headed for Kayla's house.

"I would invite you in, Ron, but I know you have a date. I wish you could keep me company for a little while at least." Kayla reached in her purse and pulled out her keys.

"Fine, Kayla. I'll call Toby and tell him I'll meet him later." Roni pouted as she followed Kayla inside.

"Thanks, Ron. You know I love you." Kayla went in.

"Surprise!" People yelled when Kayla turned on the light. There were blue, yellow and white balloons everywhere and what looked like a hundred people in her house.

"I'm gonna kill you, Roni." Kayla hugged her friend.

"It was Tia, Yvonne and Terrell, too," Roni told her. Kayla greeted all of her guests and looked at the big banner hanging in the living room, welcoming baby boy Hopkins. There was a long table spread with food on top of food and a huge, blue and white cake in the shape of a rocking horse.

"Thank you so much," Kayla said as she wobbled to her lounge chair and sat down.

"Surprise, baby," she heard her mother call out. She turned to find her.

"Mama! Where's Daddy?"

"You know he was not trying to come to no baby shower, although Terrell told him other males would be here." She pointed to Terrell who was talking to Theo and Toby in the corner of the room. "But your sister did come."

"What?" Kayla looked at her mother and she felt her heart pounding. Her mother walked off before Kayla could speak.

"Hello, Kayla," Anjelica said. Kayla looked at her pretty sister. She looked nice in a red, sleeveless sweater and some jeans. Her hair was pulled back off her face and fell past her shoulders. "Congratulations."

"What the hell are you doing here?" Kayla asked as her sister bent down to hug her.

"Look, I don't wanna be here any more than you want me here, but mama made me come. So calm the hell down before you embarrass you and her in front of all your friends."

"I don't give a damn. I want you outta my face, Now!" Kayla yelled. Roni quickly came over to her friend's side. She was glad the music was loud enough to drown out the two sisters' arguing.

"Anjelica, I think you might wanna go in the other room for a while, please," Roni told her.

"Fine." Anjelica rolled her eyes at Kayla as she walked by.

"I want her out, Ron. Please get her outta my house." Kayla grabbed Roni's arm.

"Your mother made me invite her, Kayla. I couldn't say no. I'll keep her out of your way, I promise," Roni assured her. She had no idea what had gone down between Kayla and Anjelica, but she knew it was deep.

Kayla calmed down and began talking to her other guests. Some of her co-workers were there, even though they had given her a huge shower at work. Ms. Ernestine arrived shortly after she and Roni did. And the most surprising guest of all presented Kayla with a huge box.

"Congratulations, my Kayla," Ms. Gert said as she gave her a kiss.

"Ms. Gert. I . . . Thank you." Kayla was lost for words.

"For what? Child, I keep telling you we are family no matter what. You are still my daughter-in-law. I love you, okay? Where's your mama? I haven't seen Jennifer in ages. Let me go find her." Ms. Gert set off to find Kayla's mother.

It was a shower like no other. Kayla got everything on her gift registry and more. She got enough diapers to last a year and even Toby surprised her with a blue stereo system for the nursery along with some classical and jazz mix CDs.

"Start him out early as a music pro." He laughed.

Terrell had purchased his first leather coat with fur trim.

"Where did you find that?" someone called out. "What size is it?"

"A small." Kayla read the tag.

"'Cause my godchild has to look player." Terrell smiled at Kayla.

Tia, Yvonne and Roni took the job of writing down what was from whom, and Theo and Toby carried armloads of gifts to the nursery.

"Thank you all for coming." Kayla stood and said as the shower ended.

"Let us know when he makes his arrival," everyone told her as they left. Her girls were busy cleaning up and putting away the food. Kayla wanted to change into something more comfortable. She passed the nursery and noticed the door was cracked. She pushed it open and startled Theo, who was pushing Anjelica away from him.

"What the hell are you doing?" Kayla demanded. Her sister stared at her and Theo wasted no time evacuating the room. Anjelica looked at her with no remorse.

"Nothing happened, Kayla. Chill," she said, running her fingers through her hair.

"What the hell is wrong with you? You try to push up on my best friend's boyfriend in my house?"

"You need to calm the hell down. I already told you nothing happened. And the key word here is boyfriend. I don't recall seeing a ring on his finger or hers. To me, he's free game."

"You really are a skank! You know Tia and him are together and you still pushed up on him? You are a trifling wench!" Kayla yelled, getting angrier and angrier by the minute.

"True words from a pregnant woman knocked

up from a one-night stand. And I am the trifling one?"

Those words hurt Kayla and she swiftly moved and raised her hand to slap her sister back to reality, but a strong hand caught her before she could make contact. She turned to see everyone crowded in the doorway watching the entire incident unfold.

"I think you need to leave," Terrell told Anjelica, turning Kayla away.

"Who the hell are you supposed to be? Her bodyguard?"

"No, I'm her friend and the brotha that's keeping her from whooping your ass, whether she's pregnant or not. Now, if you can't respect your sister or her friends, then you need to leave her house."

"Whatever! I didn't want to come here anyway." Anjelica stormed out of the room and they heard the door slam behind her. Kayla went into her room and sat on her bed. Beads of sweat began to form on her forehead and she could feel her heart beating a mile a minute.

"You okay, Kayla?" Roni asked and sat next to her friend.

"I hate her. Always have, always will." The tears fell from her cheek and onto the bed.

"Don't say that, Kay. That's just her. Always has been, always will be. She's just her."

"Ain't that the truth." Tia came and joined them on the bed. "We all know how she is."

"Can I have a moment, please?" Kayla's mom tapped on the door.

"Sure. We gotta go finish cleaning up anyway," Roni said. She and Tia left Kayla and her mother alone to talk.

"Your sister was wrong. Terrell was right. She disrespected you, your friends and your home." Her mother rubbed her back.

"Why did you even invite her? You know we hate each other. She only came to do something like this." Kayla wiped her face.

"Because like it or not, she's your sister. And she was right to come. I don't know why she does what she does. And I am not gonna make any excuses for her obnoxious behavior. Maybe she's jealous."

"Of what?"

"You."

"Why would she be jealous of me? I am single, pregnant, broke, and I don't know what life holds for me from one day to the next."

"But you accept every challenge that is presented to you, Kayla. No matter what it is. When Anjelica caught her boyfriend with that white girl, she didn't get out of bed for a week. When she found out she was pregnant, she got rid of it and then got so depressed she nearly lost her mind. She's never really had any close friends and here you have Tia, Roni, Yvonne *and* Terrell. She would never move twenty miles from home, let alone two hundred. You are a conqueror, Kayla, and she resents that."

"Mama, I know she is your child and you think you know her, but you don't. Anjelica is evil. She's done some wicked, hurtful things to me and I couldn't care less whether I ever see her again. Sister or not." Kayla went into the bathroom and closed the door behind her.

After a few minutes she came out, expecting to find her mother still sitting there. To her surprise, her room was empty. She went into the living room and found her three best friends sitting next to a pile of gifts, still wrapped.

"I thought I opened all the gifts," she said as she sat down. "Where's Mama?"

"She went to get something out of the car. She'll be right back," Yvonne answered.

"I just want to thank all of you. This really meant a lot to me. I thank you and love you, as my son will too." She told all of them. Her mom came in carrying another wrapped gift and Roni lit some candles on the mantle.

"Now, we have some things for you," Tia told her.

"I got enough things. Where did these gifts come from?" Kayla was still wondering what they were about to do.

"The shower gifts you got earlier were for the baby. Now this shower is for you," Yvonne said and handed her a box. Kayla opened it and smiled at the foot massager and pedicure set. "Thanks, Von."

"For those tired feet, girl. Walking that baby to sleep at night." She hugged Kayla and sat back down on the sofa.

"This is from me and Theo," Tia said and handed her the pretty, wrapped box. Inside Kayla found a giftset from Bath and Body Works and an envelope. She opened it and found a gift certificate to a day spa. Kayla squealed in delight.

"Do you get to bring a guest?" Von asked.

"Sorry, only good for one." Tia laughed.

"And this is from me." Roni could hardly push the big box in front of Kayla.

"What in the world?" Kayla asked. She opened the top of the box and looked down into it. "A suitcase."

"Help her take it out," Tia said. They slid the rolling bag out of the box and laid it on its side.

"Open it," Roni encouraged. Kayla unzipped the bag and her eyes filled with tears.

"Oh, my," she heard her mother say. Tia and Yvonne came closer to get a better look. The bag was fully packed with nightgowns, slippers, underwear, socks, soap, comb, brush, toothpaste, toothbrush; everything Kayla would need at the hospital, down to an outfit to wear home. Kayla could tell that Roni put a lot of thought and effort into packing it.

"Roni, I don't know what to say." Kayla did not try to stop the tears from falling. By now, every eye in the room was watery.

"Well. I guess it's my turn now." Jennifer stood and handed Kayla the gift she had gotten her. When Kayla opened it and saw what it was, she really began to cry.

"Oh Mama, it's beautiful." She held up the gold locket for her friends to see. She opened it and found her baby picture.

"Read it, baby," her mom said.

"From one mother to another." Kayla barely got the words out because she was crying so hard.

"The other side is for you to put your baby's picture. We all love you, Kayla. We know this hasn't been easy for you, but we are here for you and we just wanted to show you." Her mother sniffed.

They all gathered around Kayla and hugged her, big belly and all.

20

Kayla was two days from her due date and she was beyond miserable. She came back from lunch and laid her head on her desk. All of a sudden, she felt a pain go down her back and spread across her abdomen. It caused her to suck her breath in and sit straight up.

"You okay, Kayla?" her manager asked.

"I got a pain in my back," she told her.

"Just one?"

"Yeah, so far." She looked at her watch and mentally noted the time as six forty-two. She began work and after a while, another pain shot through her body. This time it was six fifty-one, less than ten minutes apart. She waited until she had a set of six pains.

"What's wrong, yo?" Terrell asked.

"I think I'm in labor," Kayla told him.

"For real? You want me to call Roni?"

"I wanna go now. Can you take me, Terrell?"

Terrell looked at his friend and then his watch.

"Okay, Kayla. It's after seven now. That means I'm gonna miss two hours on my paycheck. You gonna pay me back?"

"Shut up, Terrell, and let's go." She grabbed her purse and cut her terminal off. Her co-workers wished her good luck and Terrell wasted no time in getting her to the hospital.

"Which floor?" he asked as they got on the elevator.

"Fourth, labor and delivery." She groaned. He reached out and rubbed her shoulders. She looked at him and noticed the worry on his face. They got off the elevator and Kayla wobbled to the nurse's station.

"Hi, I'm having a baby," Kayla told the pretty nurse.

"Well, we're here to help you do that." She smiled at Kayla. "I'm Nicole and your name?"

"Kayla Hopkins. Karen Bray is my doctor." She felt another pain and grabbed the counter.

"Okay, Ms. Hopkins, follow me. You're already pre-registered so you don't have anything to fill out. Just sign. We can get that done after you're settled in the labor room. You need a wheelchair?"

"I think I can make it," Kayla told her.

"Okay. Mister Hopkins, you can wait in here while I examine your wife."

"I'm not Mister Hopkins. That's her father. I'm Mister Sims," he corrected her.

"I'm sorry, Mister Sims. Excuse me for making that assumption. You can follow Ms. Hopkins to the labor room. I know you're excited. Is this your first child?" she asked.

"Yes, my first baby," Kayla answered as they left Terrell and went into one of the birthing rooms.

Nicole helped her settle in and Kayla quickly felt comfortable with her. Kayla changed into a hospital gown and Nicole wrapped the monitor around her belly. Sounds of her baby's heartbeat filled the room. Kayla couldn't help but smile. *It won't be long now*, she thought. Nicole continued to examine her and told her to relax for a little while as she went to get Terrell.

"She's nice," Kayla said to Terrell when he came into the room.

"And she's fine. I like her."

"You okay, Mister Sims? Can I get you anything?"

"Um, your number. That is, if you'd like to maybe have dinner with me."

"I don't think now is the appropriate time or place for you to be flirting." Nicole laughed as she checked Kayla's vitals. "How are you gonna disrespect your child's mother like that?"

"God, Kayla, I swear. People call me your baby daddy so much that I'm beginning to believe it. No, Nicole, I am not the father of this baby. I am the lucky godfather."

"I thought you changed it to godpimp," Kayla told him. He looked at her like we wanted to hit her.

"Quit playing, girl. What kind of name is that? Godpimp?" He laughed lightly and Kayla opened her mouth in amazement.

"Well, you're a good godfather, bringing her to the hospital and waiting this long. Especially since she's not in active labor." Nicole wrote something down on Kayla's chart.

"What do you mean? I'm having contractions, aren't I?" Kayla wailed.

"Yes, but they aren't strong enough to make you

fully dilate. When I checked you, you were only three centimeters dilated. Now, you can stay for a couple hours and walk, maybe making you further along, but I don't think you'll have that baby tonight."

"Aw man, so you mean we've been here for nothing?" Terrell whined.

"Not for nothing," Nicole said and wrote her number down, giving it to him. "Let's just say I have a thing for godfathers."

"Told you I was a pimp." He winked at Kayla when the nurse left the room.

"Whatever. I can't believe I'm not having this baby tonight." She covered her face with the back of her hand.

"Kayla, Kayla. I got here as fast as I could. I brought your suitcase and Toby is bringing the camera. Thank you, Terrell. You okay? You need any ice chips?" Roni came rushing in.

"You could've took your time. She's not having the baby tonight. She's not in active labor," Terrell informed her.

"False alarm?" Roni asked.

"False alarm. Call Toby and tell him he may as well turn around." Kayla sighed.

"That's okay, Kayla. He'll come out when he's ready." Roni rubbed her friend's stomach and laughed. "Still comfy in there, li'l man?"

"Who wouldn't be? He's got it good. He got three squares and a warm bed," Terrell said.

"You make it sound like I'm a jail," Kayla told him as she sat up.

"You are. He can't get out, can he?" Terrell laughed. Kayla didn't find it funny.

* * *

Kayla decided not to return to work until after the baby was born. She spent the next day walking as Nicole had advised her to do. She walked around the neighborhood, she walked the mall, and she walked around the grocery store and Wal-Mart.

"Mama, what am I doing wrong?"

"Nothing, baby. You just gotta wait. He'll come when he gets ready," her mother told her.

"But Karen promised that he'd be here by tomorrow. And now you and Daddy are getting ready to go out of town. I wanted you all to be here." Kayla's parents were going to her aunt's house for Thanksgiving.

"You'll be fine, Kayla. I promise you we will be there to spoil our grandbaby enough. Look, I have got to get out of here. Your father has a list of things for me to do before we hit the road. I love you, Kay. And keep walking. Or you can always call Craig and have sex; that causes labor."

"Mama!" Kayla yelled into the phone.

"What? It's not like you haven't slept with him before. Now you need to. I'm just playing. Love you and call us if it happens before I call and check on you."

Kayla was even more depressed when she hung up the phone. All of her friends called or came by to make sure she was okay, but she knew they had plans for the holiday weekend. Yvonne was gone with her family, Tia was taking Theo to her grandmother's, and Roni was invited to the Sims' for dinner.

"Come on, Kayla, you should come," Roni told her Thanksgiving eve on the phone.

"No, I am too tired to move. I'm gonna stay in bed all day and be the warden for my son."

"You're crazy. I'll be over there after dinner," Roni told her.

"That's okay. I'll be fine. Enjoy meeting your future in-laws," Kayla mumbled. She climbed into bed and somehow found a spot comfortable enough to sleep in. The phone rang as she began to doze off.

"Hey, Beautiful. What are you doing?" Craig asked her.

"Trying to sleep," she murmured.

"Well, I'll let you go then. Call me if anything happens."

"Like what?" Kayla knew she was being mean, but she couldn't help it.

"Go to sleep, Kayla. I hate when you get like this. Call me if you need me." She heard the dial tone and put the phone on the receiver. She woke to the sound of the Macys Thanksgiving Parade and dialed Terrell's number.

"Hello," he groaned into the phone.

"Happy Thanksgiving, Terrell. Are you watching the parade?" she asked him innocently.

"No. What time is it?"

"Nine seventeen."

"Bye, Kayla. Call me after twelve. I can't believe you called me this early." Again, Kayla's ear was filled with the sound of the dial tone. She got up, took a shower and got dressed. As she was sitting at her kitchen table eating a bowl of cereal, her mom called to wish her a Happy Thanksgiving and make sure she was okay. That call was followed by

Roni, Tia, and Yvonne. By the time Kayla told everyone she was fine, she was tired all over again. The burst of energy she had when she woke up was gone and she was again having the pains in her back. She grabbed a blanket and relaxed on the lounge chair in the living room, watching television. She tossed and turned from the discomfort until she fell asleep. She thought she was dreaming when the doorbell rang. She sat up and looked at her watch. It was after seven and her back was killing her. She stood up and doubled over in pain.

The bell rang again and she called out, "Give me a minute. I'm trying!"

Taking careful steps, she slowly made her way to the front door. She didn't even look to see who it was. She just opened it.

"Happy Thanksgiving! I knew it was your due date so I decided to stop by and check on you! Kayla, what's the matter?"

She lifted her head and saw Geno standing there, carrying plastic bags, "My back is killing me, G."

"Come on. I'm taking you to the hospital!" He put his arm around her and helped her to his SUV.

"My bag, Geno. I need my bag," Kayla told him and he ran back in to get it.

While he was in the house, Kayla felt water run down her legs. She could not believe this was happening. She was standing in the middle of the sidewalk, legs straddled, when he came running out of the house. She looked at him, dazed and told him, "My water broke!"

"Don't move. I'll get some towels." He ran back

to the door, realizing he'd locked it and raced to get her keys out of her purse. He flew in and got some towels then ran back to Kayla. He covered the passenger seat and helped her in. Kayla flinched as he pulled out of the driveway.

"It's gonna be okay, Kayla. Hold on, baby." He sped to the hospital and rushed her to Labor and Delivery. Kayla was in agony the whole time.

"Hi, Kayla," Nicole greeted her. "You back for good?"

"I hope so." Kayla let out a long moan and Nicole grabbed a wheelchair. They got her into a room and when Nicole checked her this time, she frowned at Kayla.

"What? What's wrong?" Kayla asked her.

"Why did you wait so long to get here?" she asked Kayla and reached for the phone on the wall.

"I don't know. I didn't want it to be a false alarm again so I waited, and when I got up to answer the door, I couldn't walk."

"Page Doctor Bray and get her here. Her patient is fully effaced," Nicole said into the phone.

"What does that mean?" Geno asked.

"That means in about fifteen minutes she'll have a baby."

"What about my epidural and my breathing techniques?" Kayla asked.

"Too late, Kayla. Your baby's almost here. Are you gonna stay with her?" she asked Geno. He looked at Kayla and she reached for his hand.

"You don't have to do this, Geno." He looked at the fear in her eyes and knew he had to do this. There was no way he was leaving her side. She began to wail and writhe in pain.

"I'll be here. What do I need to do?"

"I gotta go to the bathroom. I need to get up!"

"That's your baby you feel, not your bowels." Nicole looked at Geno. "Grab her leg when I tell you to. Okay now, Kayla, on the next contraction I need for you to bear down and push. Ready? One, two, three, push." Nicole counted and Kayla screamed. It felt as if her bowels were being ripped from her body.

"God, I can't do this!" she yelled and sweat began to mix with tears on her face.

"Yes you can, Kayla. Look at me. You can do this," Geno told her. She shook her head fiercely at him, but he stopped her and moved her head up and down. "Yes you can."

"Okay, here comes another one. You ready?" Nicole said. "Push, Kayla, push! That's it!"

"I gotta stop! It's splitting me wide open!" Kayla screamed and panted.

"It's the head, Kay. I see the head. Come on! It's almost over. You're doing it, baby!"

"Looks like I made it just in time. Good thing I was with another patient upstairs. Hi, Geno." Karen burst through the door with a smile.

"Hey, Karen. Look. The head is right there," he said excitedly.

"I see. Now let's get him out. Come on now, Kayla. I need you to push for me. And go!"

Kayla bore down, chin on her chest, and pushed as hard as she could.

"That's it, the head is out! It's almost over, Kayla," Karen told her and she felt Geno's chin on her head. She closed her eyes as she heard his voice encouraging her to keep pushing, and then it was over. She heard the cry of her baby and she knew she had done it.

"Uh oh!" Karen said. "We made a boo boo!"

"What? Is he okay?" Kayla began to panic.

"She's beautiful," Karen said and put the wriggling, wet baby on Kayla's chest.

"She?"

"Yes, you have a beautiful baby girl. Geno, would you like to do the honors?" She held the scissors clamped on the umbilical cord.

"I don't think . . ."

"Do it, G. I want you to," Kayla told him. He reached and snipped the cord connecting Kayla and her daughter.

"Let's clean you up, Little Miss. Geno, you want to help while Karen finishes up with Kayla?" Nicole said as she took the baby. She put an ID bracelet on her little foot and on Geno's arm.

Just when Kayla thought the worst was over, Karen told her she had to deliver the birth sack.

"It's not another one in there, is it?"

"No, but it's gonna be some pressure." She felt Karen pulling on what felt like her insides and began to moan again. "All done."

"Seven pounds, three ounces. Nineteen inches," Nicole called out. "Vitals are great."

"I told you it'd be today," Karen said.

"You also told me it was a boy," Kayla said wearily. "I don't even have a name for her."

Geno walked over with the baby and handed her to Kayla. "What a day. What a day."

"It sure is. Congratulations, Kayla. You did good. Geno, you did good too!" Karen said as she was leaving. "I'll check on you later. Happy Thanksgiving."

Kayla was exhausted. They moved her to a regular room and she fell asleep immediately. When she woke up, Geno was still there, holding the baby.

"Hi, Mommy. You feel okay?" he asked.

"Yes, a little tired. What time is it?" she asked.

"A little after ten. I called Roni and she's on her way. She's mad because she missed the whole thing. You hungry?"

"Not really."

"Well, someone is. Nicole said you're going to breastfeed. I'm supposed to get her when you wake up. Here, hold her while I get Nicole." He passed the tiny little girl to Kayla and she could not help but smile.

"Hi, Sweetie. I'm your mommy. You ready to eat?" She kissed the top of her forehead and looked at her. She tried to see who the baby looked like. She was light in complexion, but Kayla knew that would change by the caramel color of her ears. Her eyes were closed, but Nicole said that they were brown. And she was bald, with the exception of a patch of hair on the very top of her head.

"Ready to do this, Kayla?" Nicole asked as she came in the room.

"I guess so. She's gotta eat." Kayla laughed. Nicole showed her how to hold the baby properly as she fed her, and Kayla felt like a pro as her daughter greedily sucked on her breast.

"Let me see him, let me see him!" Roni cried as she entered the room. "He's gorgeous. I can't believe I missed it, Kayla. How are you feeling? Did it hurt? How did Geno wind up here?" She didn't give Kayla a chance to answer. Geno came in with a

big bouquet of balloons announcing *It's a Girl.*
"You must have the wrong room," said Roni.

"You're crazy. How is she, Kayla?"

"It's a girl? How in the world? It's a girl!" Roni
looked from Kayla to the baby to Geno.

"Say hello to your niece, Aunt Roni." Kayla
passed the baby to Roni.

"Hi, Sweetie. You are so beautiful. You are
gonna be a diva, just like your mommy."

"Don't curse her, Roni," Geno said as he tied
the balloons to Kayla's bed.

"I can't believe I had a girl. She doesn't even
have anything to wear home from the hospital."
Kayla looked at Roni holding her daughter.

"That's the least of your worries. Aunt Roni will
have her hooked up. Now what you do need to
worry about is a name."

"Yeah, you need to pick one, Kayla, or she will
be Baby Girl Hopkins," Geno said. "What was the
boy's name gonna be?"

"Joshua Maxwell," Kayla told them.

"That was nice, but it definitely won't work for a
girl," he said.

"You got that right. What about Destiny?" Roni
asked.

"How about no. That's corny and everyone is
using that because of Destiny's Child."

"She's right," Geno said. "You had to think of
some girls' names before you knew it was a boy.
What were they?"

"Knock knock! Everyone decent?" Terrell stuck
his head in the door, followed by Toby. He looked
at the balloons and shook his head. "How'd you
manage that?"

"Ultrasound reading was wrong, I guess," Kayla told him and he gave her a hug.

"She's beautiful," Toby said as he looked over Roni's shoulders at the baby. "I guess you don't need the camera, huh?"

"Sure we do. This is a video worthy moment. Start filming. I'll be the host, of course. "Roni handed the baby to Kayla as Toby took out his video camera. "Today is Thanksgiving Day, and we have so much to be thankful for. We are here with Kayla Hopkins, who has just given birth to a beautiful baby girl. Kayla, what are you thinking about naming your precious daughter?"

"Her name is Jenesis Sade Hopkins. But her nickname is Day," Kayla said proudly.

"Day," Toby said. "I like it."

"It's not as tight as London," Terrell said recalling one of the girl's names he had suggested to Kayla early in her pregnancy, "But Jenesis Sade is pretty. And Day is player for a nickname."

"Beautiful Day." Geno took the baby from Kayla. He was amazed at her tiny body and thought the name suited her. Kayla had always talked about naming her daughter Jenesis with a J, after her mother.

"Now how did you wind up taking my place in the delivery room, Geno?" Roni asked.

Kayla and Geno recounted the events of the night for everyone until Nicole came in and announced that Kayla and the baby needed to rest. She took Day back to the nursery and everyone said their good-byes.

"Thank you again, Geno," Kayla whispered as he kissed her cheek before he left.

"I told you I would always be there for you, Kay. She's beautiful and so are you. I'll come back and visit both of you tomorrow."

"Okay. We'd both like that." Kayla closed her eyes.

"Kay and Day. What a pair." He chuckled as he walked into the hallway.

21

The hospital registrar came by the next morning to get the info for Day's birth certificate. Roni told Kayla she had called Craig and left a message on his cell phone that she had given birth and was in the hospital, but he still had not called or come by.

"Father's name?" the crabby white woman asked.

"Craig Coleman," Kayla answered.

"Is he here?"

"Not right now."

"We need him to sign the certificate if he is to be registered as the father. If not, a name won't be listed."

"He'll sign," she told her. She wanted Day to know her father's name, even if he opted not to be an active part of her life. She called his cell and again got no answer. When she hung the phone up, it rang instantly. Kayla thought it was him returning her call, but it was her parents calling to congratulate and let her know they were on their way.

"Hi, Kayla. You feeling okay?" Yvonne knocked as she came in the door. "Let me see my goddaughter. She's gorgeous! Hi, Day. Auntie Von bought this for you to take your pictures in and wear home."

"Thanks, Von. I told Roni last night that she had nothing to wear." Kayla looked at the soft pink and white outfit with the matching hat that Yvonne had given her.

"We got that all taken care of. Don't worry about a thing. You just rest up. When are they releasing you?"

"Tomorrow morning." Kayla sighed.

"What's wrong, Kayla?"

"I left messages for Craig but he hasn't called or come up here. I need him to sign her birth certificate."

"He'll show up. You told me he's changed, right? He's been coming around and he promised to be there for his baby. Just relax."

"Okay, Von." Kayla sighed. They dressed Day and got her ready for the photographers. The nursery had just brought her when Craig arrived along with Darrell.

"I hear I have a princess in here." He winked at Kayla. She was not amused.

"About time you decided to make an appearance." She scowled.

"Is this my new niece?" Darrell asked, "Hi, Kayla. It's nice to see you again."

"Can I at least hold her, Kayla?" Craig reached for the small bundle Kayla was clinging to as if her life depended on it.

"We've been calling and leaving messages for your trifling behind since last night and now you want to waltz in here and hold her like the proud papa?"

"I didn't get any messages, Kayla. I lost my cell the other night at the restaurant. We had mad dinner parties for Thanksgiving and I don't know what happened to it. I swear. The only way I knew was when Darrell called me a little while ago. We came straight here." He pleaded with her. She looked at him doubtingly and he looked at Darrell for support.

"He did lose his phone. So if that's what you were calling, he wouldn't have got the messages," Darrell added.

"Lying for your brother?" Kayla asked.

"No. The only way he knew was because Yvonne left a message on my voicemail a little while ago." Kayla looked over at her friend who shrugged at her.

"She looks just like you, Kayla. Hi, Princess. What are we gonna name you?" He rubbed noses with his tiny daughter.

"She already has a name," Kayla told him.

"How you gonna name her without my input?" He looked at Kayla.

"Don't go there," she warned him and he knew it wouldn't be worth the fight.

"Well, what is your name?" he asked the baby.

"Day," Kayla and Yvonne answered simultaneously.

"Day? What kind of name is that?" Craig frowned.

"It's her nickname. Her full name is Jenesis Sade Hopkins," Kayla informed him.

"Genesis, like the Bible?" Darrell asked as he took the baby from his brother.

"More like Geno," Craig said accusingly.

"First of all, it's Jenesis with a J, as in Jennifer, which is my mother's first name. And Sadie was my grandmother's name. That's how I came up with it. Secondly, Geno's real name is Antonio Giovanni. His nickname is Geno. So you can kill that thought before it even enters your mind."

"Jenesis Sade. Day. I think that is very elegant, Kayla. You picked a beautiful name." Darrell looked at her, seeing why Craig liked her.

"Okay. Since you've explained how you got it, I like it too." Craig rubbed her arm.

"I need for you to sign her birth certificate," Kayla told him.

"I know. What do I need to do?" He took a deep breath. He knew that news of Day's birth was gonna come out sooner or later, and now it was time to pay the piper. He had a plan, though. Looking at his brother holding his daughter, his heart filled with love, he knew this was the right thing to do.

"Sorry, I didn't know you had visitors," Geno said as he peeked in the door.

"It's okay. Come on in, Geno." Kayla motioned for him to enter. And he did with a big vase of pink roses and the biggest teddy bear Kayla had ever seen.

"Aww, Geno! That is so cute!" Yvonne stood to help him with his gifts. "Where did you find a bear that big?"

"If I tell you, I'd have to kill you." He smiled at her and passed her the flowers. She put them on the nightstand next to Kayla's bed.

"What's up?" he said to Craig and Darrell.

"Geno, this is Darrell. And uh, I think you met Craig," Yvonne said.

"Wussup?" Craig mumbled.

"Nice to meet you." Darrell smiled.

"Hi there, Miss Day. You're all dressed up." Geno walked over and looked at the baby.

"She had her first photo shoot." Yvonne laughed.

"The first of many. You just watch," Geno told them. "How you feeling, Kay?"

"Good. Our first night was okay," she answered.

"You ready to go back to Mommy?" Darrell asked Day as she began to squirm.

"Let me take her for a sec." Geno held out his arms and Darrell passed the baby to him. He paced the floor and rocked her, rubbing his face against hers affectionately. He turned and looked at Kayla whose eyes met his and they smiled at each other. Craig knew the look well. It was the look he gave Avis the first time he held his son. A look that said, "Look what our love for each other created."

Kayla looked over at Craig who was sitting, looking at Day's birth certificate. "You sign it?"

"No." He looked up at her.

"What are you waiting for, her eighteenth birthday?" Kayla chuckled.

Craig glared at Geno then looked her in the eyes and replied. "I want a blood test before I sign anything."

You could hear a pin drop in the room as all eyes landed on Craig. Even Day seemed stunned by what her alleged father had just said.

"What are you saying, Craig?" Kayla felt her blood go ice cold as she sat up in the bed.

"I think we need to give them some privacy," Yvonne said as she pulled Darrell's sleeve.

"Yeah, no doubt," Darrell told her as he stood up.

"You okay, bro?" he asked Craig as they headed out the door.

"I'm fine." Craig nodded.

"We're going to the gift shop for a while. Kay, you need anything?" Yvonne touched Kayla's hand. She knew that Kayla was offended by what Craig had said and she had good reason to be.

"No, you go ahead. Can you send the nurse in to take Day to the nursery, though? As soon as possible," Kayla told her, still staring at Craig. She did not want to expose her child to what she was about to say, whether she thought she could comprehend it or not.

"I'll get her right now." Yvonne hurried out of the room and gave the nurse Kayla's request.

"I'm here to pick up a package?" the cheerful nurse said as she entered the tension filled room.

"Yes, can you take her for a while?" Kayla asked.

"Sure thing." She smiled as Geno passed Day to her and she placed her in the bassinet. "We'll change her out of these fancy clothes and bring her back for her next feeding."

"Thank you," Kayla said. She watched the nurse wheel the baby out and then closed the door behind her. "Now, I'll repeat my question. What are you trying to say?"

"I'm saying I want there to be no question whether this child is really mine."

"*This child* has a name. It's Day. And I have no reason to tell you that you're her father if I had any doubt that you weren't," Kayla told him.

"Naw, Kayla. Here this brother comes waltzing in like he's fucking Father of the Year; you're looking at him like he's Romeo and you're Juliet. I'm not gonna be played out like some sucker taking care of a kid that might, just might not be mine."

"Have you lost your damn mind? I think you forgot something. I am not your girlfriend, lover, significant other or wife. Hell, I'm not even your mistress. I don't care if I look at Sam Sausagehead like he's the greatest thing that ever walked into my life. That's my business!" she yelled.

"Hold up, Kayla. You don't even have to justify that with a response," Geno said. "Look, man, if you want a blood test, that's your business. But believe me, if I was lucky enough to be Day's father, you'd better believe I am more than willing to step up to the plate and take care of my responsibilities. Quiet as it's kept, I was begging Kayla to tell me I was the father. I wanted to be. So don't come up in here trying to hate because Kayla and I are friends. And hell yeah, I'm acting like Father of the Year, because I was there when she was born, unlike you!" Geno sat down in the chair.

"Whether I was there when she was born or not . . ." Craig yelled.

"Hey, hey, hey! Y'all need to chill. I can hear you all the way down the hall." A voice stopped Craig before he could finish. "Whatever the problem is, y'all need to squash it. This ain't the time or the place."

"Who are you?" Craig gritted on the big guy who walked through the door.

"What's up, Terry? You're right, man. I didn't realize it had gotten out of hand." Geno stood and greeted his friend's brother.

"What's up? I'm Terrell, a friend of Kayla's." Terrell introduced himself.

"Another friend, Kayla?" Craig looked Terrell up and down and stood to leave. "Yeah, I'm definitely gonna need that test before I put my name on anything. You call me so we can have that taken care of. I'll holla."

"What was he talking about?" Terrell asked Kayla. Her head began to pound and she closed her eyes and sat back. She tried to make the room stop spinning but she couldn't.

"Kayla? Kayla?" She heard Geno and Terrell calling her name as she passed out.

22

Kayla could hear a faint beeping in the distance. She frowned as she tried to figure out what it was. Her eyelids fluttered as she opened her eyes. She looked around the room and remembered that she was in the hospital. *Day! Where is my baby?* were her first thoughts. She tried to recall what had happened. Her room was dark and as she looked out the window, she saw that it was pitch black outside. The beeping sound got louder and she turned to see that it was a heart monitor. There were several IV bags hanging by the head of the bed and running into her arm, and there was an oxygen tube in her nose. Her throat was dry and she pushed the nurse button.

"Hi, sleepy head," Nicole whispered to Kayla. "It's nice to see you finally awake."

"Can I get something to drink?" Kayla closed and opened her eyes, trying to focus.

"I'll be right back with some juice for you."

Nicole continued to whisper. She came in and gave Kayla a small can of apple juice and a straw. Kayla opened it and began to drink; she emptied it immediately.

"I feel funny. Like everything is foggy," she told Nicole.

"Probably the medicine they have you on. It's pretty strong. You gave us a scare, girl." Nicole talked low, confusing Kayla even more.

"Where's Day?" Kayla asked her.

"She's in the nursery. I'll get her for you in a little while. The staff has gotten quite attached to her over the past couple of days." She took Kayla's vitals.

"She was just born yesterday, Nicole. They can't be that attached." Kayla smiled.

"Kayla, you've been asleep for two days." Nicole looked at her.

"Quit playing. And why is it so dark in here? You are funny, Nicole. I see why Terrell likes you. Pass me the phone; I need to call my parents." Kayla looked on the nightstand and saw that there was no phone, "Where is my phone? And where is the TV? I know I have the bomb insurance. Isn't all of that covered?"

"Kayla, Karen had the phone, television and radio taken out of here. You can't have any visitors either, except for your mother." Nicole pulled a chair and sat beside Kayla's bed.

"Why?" Kayla was beginning to get frustrated because she didn't know what was going on.

"Kayla, your blood pressure shot up to one ninety eight over one twenty seven. You were a heartbeat away from a stroke. Your body shut down in order to prevent that from happening. That's why you passed out. You basically went into shock."

Kayla couldn't believe what Nicole was saying. She felt the tears fall from her eyes and she wiped them away. Nicole went and got her some Kleenex.

"But what about my baby? Who's been taking care of Day? I'm breastfeeding." Kayla sniffed.

"Because of the meds that they have you on, you can't breastfeed, Kayla. Not right now, anyway. But Day has been well taken care of."

"But, but, she's not gonna know me. Strangers have been taking care of her. We won't have a bond."

"Yes you will, girl. You're her mother; she knows that. And she hasn't been taken care of by strangers. Your mother comes and sits with you and her, and Geno does her feedings, too."

"Geno?"

"He's the only other one with a wristband for the nursery security. Your mother had to go through hell and high water to get permission to sit here with you knocked out in the same room." Nicole laughed. Kayla remembered the armband being placed on Geno's arm after he cut Day's umbilical cord. "Let me go call Karen and tell her you are doing better, and then I'll bring Day."

"Thank you, Nicole." Kayla looked at the beautiful nurse and was grateful for her.

"Sweetie, you're up." Jennifer rushed to her daughter's side and hugged her.

"Hi, Mommy."

"I am so glad you're okay. Your father is worried sick. He is going to be relieved." She rubbed her hand across Kayla's cheek.

"I'm fine, Mama. Did you see the baby?"

"She's beautiful. Just like her mother."

"Did they tell you her full name?"

"Her name is just as beautiful as she is. Thank you so much, Kayla. I am so flattered, and Gramma would be proud, too." Jennifer cried when Roni told her the baby's full name. She was hoping to have a grandson, but when she heard Kayla had a girl she couldn't have been happier.

"I guess I overdid it, huh, Ma?"

"Kayla, why in the world did you have all of those people visiting and all of that nonsense going on in the first place? You had just given birth, not signed a record deal. From the way I hear it, if Terrell hadn't arrived when he did, Geno and Craig were about to start fighting. You are lucky they didn't call security." Jennifer knew she was wrong to be laying her daughter out, but she was angry. Kayla could have died.

"Mom, Craig had the nerve to ask for a blood test," Kayla responded.

"Is it his baby?"

"Ma! Yes, it's his. I am not some loose floozy who sleeps with everyone. I know it's his baby."

"Then let him take the test. You didn't even have to go there with him. You know what the results would say, do you not?"

"Yes."

"Then take it. And when you take him to court for child support, you'll have all the proof you need!" Jennifer told her. "Who do he think he is, gonna question my baby's integrity?"

"You are crazy, Ma." Kayla laughed. Nicole

wheeled the bassinet into the room and Kayla happily took her baby. "She's gotten bigger!"

"No, you are the crazy one." Jennifer shook her head and silently said a prayer of thanksgiving for the recovery of her daughter and the birth of her grandbaby.

23

Kayla had just gotten out of the shower and was packing to go home. She was beyond ready to leave. She had been in the hospital five days, including the night that Day was born. She wanted to take her baby home and get on with her life. They had already brought Day from the nursery. Kayla made a mental note to send the nursery staff a thank you note and a basket of cookies from herself and the baby. They had been so attentive.

"Looks like you're ready to go," Karen said. Kayla was sitting on the side of the bed, waiting for her parents to pick her up.

"I've been ready," Kayla told her. "Day needs to go and see her new room."

"Well, I am gonna discharge you, but we need to get a few things straight before I sign these papers."

"Okay, what?"

"There are two young men outside who say they need to see you. Now, I have listened to both of them begging me to see you for the last two days. I have agreed to give them five minutes each. I am going to connect you back up to this blood pressure monitor and if it shows a high reading at any time while they are here, it's back in the bed and you will stay there. I cannot risk having you leave here and having a stroke. Understand, Kayla? You have a little one to care for."

"I understand. Who's outside to see me?" Kayla asked. She figured it was Geno and Terrell. They had probably been worried to death, and Kayla already knew that Geno came to see Day regularly.

"I'll send the first gentleman in," Karen said as she affixed the blood pressure cuff on Kayla's arm. "Remember what I told you."

"I will." Kayla took a deep breath and reminded herself to stay calm. She leaned over and checked on Day to make sure she was still asleep.

The door opened slowly and Kayla smiled at Geno as he entered.

"Hi, G. I knew you were here."

"You feeling okay, Kay?" He kissed her cheek and walked over to see Day. "Hey, Princess."

"I would probably be doing better if I was at home," Kayla admitted.

"Kayla, I'm so sorry for what happened the other afternoon. I was out of line and I was wrong. I know you think it wasn't my place to get into it with Craig, but when he made it seem like we were scheming on his punk ass, I got mad."

"Don't worry about it, G. It wasn't your fault. But I'm glad you're here. I want to thank you for looking after Day while I was sick. They told me that you gave her 'round the clock feedings and everything." Kayla wondered how he was able to get away from that crazy Janice to do it, but she didn't ask.

"That's my Princess. I didn't do anything you wouldn't do for me, Kayla. Hell, if it wasn't for you, I never would have finished school. I keep telling you that I will *always* be there for you. I'm not playing. No matter the circumstances." He sat next to her and put his arm around her. Kayla did not know what to think. She still loved Geno, there was no doubting that, but she did not know what he was trying to say and didn't want to make a fool of herself by asking.

"Time's up." Karen interrupted her thoughts before she had a chance to respond. She checked the monitor and looked at Kayla and Geno. "Very good, Kayla. No high readings. Now, Geno, I really need for you to make sure Kayla gets some rest while she is at home. Don't be calling her all times of the night and no surprise visits."

"I know. Karen, I know this sounds crazy, but are you sure there is no possible way that I could be the father? I am not saying that Kayla's not sure, but is there any possibility?" He looked at Karen, pleading.

"If the last time you were together was when you said it was, Geno, then there's no way. Now if you want to take a blood test then I'd be more than happy to have it done."

"No, it's just like I love her as if she's mine. She's only a few days old, but I know I couldn't love my own child any more. We have a bond," he said. It took everything in her power for Kayla not to breakdown and cry. She wished more than anything that Day could have been hers and Geno's child. It would have made a hell of a lot more sense than Day being the result of a one-night stand with Craig.

"Childbirth is a very bonding experience, Geno. And you already had a bond with Kayla. That's a lot of emotions, when you think about it. And Day will also have a bond with you, if you choose to continue. But know that bond comes with a lot of responsibility. You are talking about being a part of a child's life. That's nothing to take lightly."

"I know," he said.

"Kayla, you have another visitor waiting. And your parents are waiting to take you home as well." Karen opened the door.

"Goodbye, Kayla. I'll call before I stop by later." He looked at Karen for approval. "To see Day, of course."

"How about tomorrow? Give Kayla and Day a chance to get settled their first night."

"Okay. But I'm gonna call." He kissed Kayla, Day *and* Karen as he left.

"Ready for your next gentleman caller?" Karen asked.

"Send Terrell with his retarded self in." Kayla prepared herself for the smart comment she knew he would have when he came in. Karen shook her head and walked into the hallway.

Kayla could not help but frown when instead of Terrell, Craig walked in. She was about to curse him out when she caught a glimpse of the blood pressure cuff on her arm and began to breathe deeply.

"Hi, Beautiful." Craig spoke smoothly. He walked over and gave Kayla a hug, then touched Day's back. "And Little Beautiful."

"You are the last person I expected to be here," she told him dryly.

"Okay, I can't risk you falling the hell out again, so I'm asking you just to chill while I say my peace." He looked at her intensely. Kayla didn't want to hear anything he had to say, but she decided to let him talk so he could hurry and leave.

"Go ahead." She took another deep breath.

"Okay. I am sorry for saying what I did. It's just that I was looking at you and Geno and it was like it was *your* baby—*yours and his*. I know you wouldn't lie to me, Kay. And Karen confirmed what you said about the date of conception. I already made my peace with Geno, now I'm making amends with you *and* Day." He reached inside his jacket pocket and passed Kayla a folded piece of paper. She took it from his hand and slowly opened it. It was the registration for Day's birth certificate and he had printed and signed his name under the space for father's information.

"Thank you," Kayla whispered. She looked up at him and saw him standing next to Day.

"Can I?"

"She's your daughter. Of course you can." Kayla reached in and passed the baby to him. He gently rocked her in his arms.

"I want to be a part of her life, Kayla. I know you and I will be nothing more than friends, but I still want to be there for her and you. Please, give me a chance." He looked at her with that intense stare and Kayla could not help but smile.

"I don't have a problem with that, Craig. But I will not have you walking in and out of her life like some distant relative that she gets to see on birthdays and holidays. If you're gonna be a father, I have no problem with that. But I don't have time for your games, either," Kayla warned him.

"Alright, I understand. Well, I guess I need to let you finish up and get out of here. Do you need anything? Or does she?"

"No, we're fine for now. Thank you for stepping up, Craig." She took Day and placed her back into the bassinet.

"Well, call me if you need me." He gave her a hug.

"But are you gonna answer when I call? You know how you conveniently lose your phone sometimes." Kayla smirked.

"You're a trip." He opened the door and she could see her parents talking with Karen.

"Mister and Mrs. Hopkins, she's ready," he told them as he turned and waved to Kayla. "I'll call you later."

"Goodbye, Craig." Kayla waved. "Hi, Daddy. You ready to take all of us women home?"

"You'd better believe it. Where's my newest baby luv?" Her dad kissed her as her mother followed him into Kayla's room.

"I thought we took all of this kind of stuff home?" her mother said as she picked up a pink and white vase full of flowers that had been delivered earlier. She read the card then turned to Kayla and asked, "Who's Uncle Darrell?"

"Craig's brother," Kayla answered as she bundled Day up into the bunting Roni had sent.

"Well that was nice of him," her dad said as he picked up Kayla's suitcase.

"He's a nice guy," Kayla told them.

"Mom, can you please grab Day's pictures out of the drawer?"

"You'd better not forget them pictures," her father warned. "I gotta have plenty to take when I go back to work. My grandbaby," he said proudly as the nurse and Karen came in and Kayla sat in the wheelchair, holding her precious daughter.

"Thank you for everything, Karen," she said. "I couldn't have done this without you."

"Yes you could have. It just wouldn't have been as easy." Karen grinned. "Now, I have given your parents specific instructions, so I know you're in good hands. I'll see you next week in my office."

"Well, Day. We're finally going home." Kayla smiled and kissed Day's forehead.

24

Kayla's transition into motherhood came naturally. Her mother stayed with her for two weeks to make sure she and Day got settled. By the time she left, they had exchanged all of Day's blue clothes for pink ones and the nursery was still blue, but it now had pink accents.

"Mama, I can't thank you enough for being here for me and Day. You know you didn't have to do all of this," Kayla told her as she watched her pack her suitcase. Day was asleep in the porta-crib that Kayla had in her room.

"Please, Kayla. Wait until Day has a baby and then you'll know why I did it," her mother stopped packing long enough to say.

"Whew, that is over thirty years from now, Mama." Kayla raised her eyebrows.

"Yeah, that's what I thought when I had you. But somehow it didn't work out that way, did it?"

"I guess not." Kayla put her head down.

"Sometimes things work out better. Kayla, no

matter what the circumstances that got Day here, she is still our grandbaby and you are still our daughter. And we love you both very much."

"I know, Mama. I still feel that I somehow disappointed you and Daddy, though. I know you wanted me to be married first."

"Kayla, your father and I are very proud of you. You could be doing a lot worse, you know. We raised you and Anjelica to be productive, successful young women, and you are."

At the sound of her sister's name, Kayla felt her pressure rise. She had not spoken to her since the baby shower and she wanted to keep it that way. "At least *I* am," she said before she could stop herself.

"Kayla. Your sister is successful too, in her own right. Your guidelines for success are different from hers because you are two different people. But I am going to say this one last and final time. You are sisters and that fact will never change."

"Okay, Mama," Kayla said. She didn't want to argue with her mother so she just let it go. She knew that her mother would never believe what Anjelica had done if she told her the truth. The doorbell rang and Kayla went to open the door. Her father had arrived to pick up her mother.

"Hey, Daddy." She greeted her father with a kiss.

"Hey, honey. You doing okay?"

"Yes, I'm fine, Daddy."

"Where's my sweetie?" He walked into the nursery.

"Are you referring to me or the baby, John?" Kayla's mother asked her husband. He walked over and took her into his arms.

"Of course I was referring to you, Sweetie." As he kissed her, he peered into the crib looking for Day.

"She's not even in there, you big, fat liar." Kayla's mother pushed him away.

"Where is she?" he asked.

"In my room. She's asleep." Kayla led him into her bedroom. He went to pick her up but Kayla's mother protested.

"Leave her alone, John. We finally got her on a schedule. You can't wake her up. It'll throw her off."

"But I'm her grandpa. I get special, unscheduled visitation rights." He winked at Kayla and gently picked the baby up. He kissed her cheek and laid her back down, never waking her.

"Well, I guess we'd better head on home, Jen. Kayla, you take care of my baby luv and call us if you need anything." He put his arm around Kayla and they walked into the hallway.

"My bag is in the nursery, John. Grab it for me."

"Yes, ma'am," he answered.

"Thank you again, Mama." Kayla fought back the tears. She loved her parents so much and was grateful for them.

"I will call you when we get home. And don't you have a bunch of people running in and out of here fawning over that baby," she warned Kayla. Her daughter was all grown up with a baby of her own, but that would never stop Jennifer from being her mother.

"Okay, Mama." Kayla smiled.

"Let's go, Sweetheart. Love you, Kay. We'll talk to you later on tonight," her father called as they departed. As soon as Kayla locked the door, the bell rang again. Kayla laughed at her father standing outside her doorway.

"What'd you forget?"

"This is for you, Kay. Don't open it now, but put it to good use for you and Day." He put an envelope in her palm and rubbed the tops of her hands as he left for the second time. After she saw them pull out of the driveway, Kayla sat on the sofa and opened the card. It was simple, with a pink flower on the cover and a handwritten message on the inside.

> *To my daughter, Kayla, with love,*
>   *As you embark on this new journey, may the lessons of love, life and laughter that we have shared over the years be the compass that directs your life, as you are now a leader for your little one.*
>   *I love you and I am so proud of you,*
>
>   *Dad*

This time, the tears did not surprise Kayla as she removed ten hundred-dollar bills out of the card.

25

"What are you doing?" Geno asked Kayla.

"Watching cartoons." Kayla balanced the cordless phone on her shoulder as she bounced Day on her lap. She was sitting in the middle of her bed and was deciding what they should do on this fine December Saturday.

"Well, get dressed. I'm on my way to pick you and Day up," he said.

"What do you mean you're on your way? What are you doing home anyway, and where's your girl-friend?" she said in one breath.

"Just get ready. I'll be there in fifteen minutes." He chose not to answer any of her questions.

"I can't get myself and an infant ready in fifteen minutes. Are you crazy?"

"Jeez, Kay. Look, can you be ready in an hour?"

"Where are we going and what is the rush?" Kayla looked over at the clock and saw that it was only ten-thirty in the morning.

"Just be ready." He hung up before she had a chance to ask anymore questions.

"Well, Day. I guess we're going out for the afternoon." She looked into her eyes and kissed her chubby cheeks. At almost a month old, people said she looked just like Kayla, but Kayla didn't see it. "What shall we wear?"

Kayla put Day into her bouncer and went rummaging through her closet. She was almost back down to her pre-pregnancy weight, but because of her new, well-rounded hips and thick butt, her jeans still didn't fit right.

"I need to go shopping, Day," Kayla called out. The phone rang and she picked it up.

"Hey, girl. Theo and I are going to the mall. You want to go?" Tia asked.

"I can't. I'm going somewhere with Geno," Kayla mumbled.

"Geno? Where is his girlfriend?"

"I asked him the exact same thing." Kayla pulled out a pair of black stretch jeans and a red sweater. *Well, it is Christmas. May as well look festive.*

"Where are you going?"

"He wouldn't say. Just told me to be ready," she said as she went into Day's room and began to scavenge her closet for the perfect ensemble for her as well. She found what she was looking for and laid it on the bed next to her own outfit.

"Well, go and have fun. He must have had it out with his girl again. Every time she pisses him off he calls you. I don't see why he's with her crazy ass anyway."

"I don't know, girl." Kayla ran a tub of water and grabbed a towel for her and Day, and then got all of their toiletries, making sure she would have everything in arm's reach. She flicked the small radio she had on the shelf to the jazz station and it began to play softly.

"So, have you talked about getting back together?"

"Uh, hello. I just had another man's baby and he is living with another woman." Kayla could not believe Tia asked her that. She got undressed and then undressed Day.

"What? It's no secret that you and Geno still love each other. Hell, that's the reason Craig nearly flipped out at the hospital. I'll be the first to admit that neither of you are in the best circumstances, but you can't help who you love."

"That's not what Roni says," Kayla laughed.

"Humph, she's so in love these days that even her mama is shocked. I never thought I'd see the day. But ain't it funny how the two biggest players in the entire town hooked up?"

"I think it's cute. I am glad she finally found someone. You have Theo, she has Toby." Kayla took a moment to look at her naked body in the mirror. *I gotta work out harder,* she thought as she pinched her sides. "Yvonne and I are the only members left in the Lonely Hearts Club. Maybe we need to recruit new members?"

"Girl, please. Ain't nobody got a ring on their finger. Heck, I don't even think any of us are really ready for marriage."

"I am. And you are, too. Don't even try it. If Theo were to ask you to go and get married today, you'd be calling me to borrow my white wool suit," Kayla joked.

"Girl, please. Although you should let me have it anyway, because you can't get into it anymore." Tia laughed.

"You know what? On that note, I am hanging up."

"Bye, girl. Tell Geno I said hello."

Kayla picked Day up and went into the bathroom. She stuck her foot into the tub and made sure the temperature was okay. She carefully got in and lay Day on her chest as she cascaded warm water over her tiny body. Although she flinched at first, Kayla knew Day loved the tub. They were both treasuring the moment, when Kayla swore she heard someone calling her name. She sat up and before she could reach for the towel, the bathroom door opened.

"Kay!"

"What are you doing?" Kayla covered herself and Day as best she could, using her hands and Day's tiny body.

"My bad! I thought you had left the radio on in here." Geno smiled as he looked at her and the baby in the tub. "I was about to be mad because I thought you had left with someone else, and you knew I was on my way. Hey, Day, come here."

"Get out, Geno!" Kayla screamed.

"Why are you screaming? Give me the baby."

"No, get out." She was beyond embarrassed.

"Kayla. It's not as if I've never seen you naked before. Hell, I saw all that long before you gave birth. I saw all up *in* there while you were giving birth. Now pass me the baby. She's shivering." He laughed and grabbed the small pink towel off the rack near the tub.

"Get out of here. How did you get in here, anyway?" She reluctantly passed Day to him and he wrapped her warmly in the towel. He stood looking at Kayla as he rocked the baby.

"The door was unlocked. Need help getting out?" He grinned. Damn, he missed her.

"No, can you just get out?" She tried in vain to cover herself.

"Come on, Day. Let's give Mommy some privacy." He giggled as he turned and left the steamy bathroom. "Are these her clothes?"

"Naw, they belong to the other baby in there. What you think?" Kayla answered as she wrapped a fluffy towel around herself and stepped out of the tub. She let the water out and cut the radio off. Geno was sprinkling powder on Day's bottom when she entered the room.

"I thought I told you to be ready in an hour," he said without even looking up. Kayla grabbed her clothes off the bed and returned to the bathroom, closing and locking the door behind her.

"You're early," she said.

"It's twelve fifteen," he informed her.

I must've talked to Tia longer than I thought.

"Well, you know I have to get me *and* Day ready. I can't do that in an hour. You *did* call at the last minute. I still have to pack her diaper bag."

"Well, I already got her dressed. You just hurry up."

"I am. Did you brush her hair? And did you put lotion on her face?"

"Get dressed, Kayla. We're going to pack the bag," she heard him call out.

Kayla made sure he was out of the room and completed getting dressed. She was finishing up her makeup when she heard him talking to someone. She looked at the 'In Use' indicator on her phone and it wasn't lit. *Must be his cell phone,* she thought.

"I don't want to discuss it right now. Forget it. Look, Janice, I have to go," he said as Day began to whimper. "None of your business. I will call you later tonight. No, because I got stuff to do. Bye. You ready, Kayla? Day, your Mama is s-l-o-w, you know that?"

"I heard you, Geno. I'm dressed, if that's what you mean. I still have to pack the diaper bag," Kayla told him. She went into Day's room and grabbed the big diaper bag. Looking at the smaller, more compact one she asked, "Where are we going, anyway?"

"Just pack the bag and come on. You got a stroller?"

"We need a stroller? It's in the hall closet." She heard him fumbling and then the closet door closed.

"This is more like a baby limo. Day, you're gonna be riding in style, huh, boo? I bet you picked this big thing out, huh, Kayla?" He unfolded the monstrosity and then realized he didn't know how to fold it back up. Kayla came in carrying a huge, pink diaper bag. "We are just gonna be gone until tonight, Kayla, not the entire weekend."

"Shut up. I don't know what I'm gonna need and I want to be prepared." She went into the kitchen and grabbed bottles of prepared formula and extra cans, just in case. She picked up Day's extra pacifier off the table and then remembered to get the ice pack out of the freezer and put it in the bag. She looked at her watch and saw that it was now after one o'clock.

"How do you fold this thing back down?" Geno asked, still struggling with the stroller.

Kayla flicked a button with her foot and it collapsed instantly. "Ooh, that was so hard."

"Bring your smart mouth on before Day and I leave you here," he said as he grabbed the handle of the stroller with one hand and the diaper bag with the other one.

Kayla, Day and Geno spent the entire afternoon shopping. They walked the mall, buying Christmas gifts and enjoying the hustle and bustle of the season. Kayla and Geno had always loved Christmas shopping together. Actually, they loved all shopping together—Christmas, birthday, grocery, whatever the occasion. The mall was where they had their best times. It felt like old times, only now Geno was pushing Day in the stroller in front of them. A few people stopped and told them they had a beautiful baby and how precious their family was. Geno didn't correct anyone; he just smiled and thanked them.

"I am starving. What do you feel like eating?"

"I don't know. How about Chinese?"

"Red Dragon?"

"You really are trying to make this a tradition aren't you?" Kayla laughed as they arrived at their favorite post-shopping restaurant.

"No doubt," he said. He picked the baby up out of the stroller and put her on his shoulder as they waited to be seated. The doors opened and both Geno and Kayla were shocked when Avis, Craig and a small boy stepped out, arms full of bags. Craig was so busy talking on his cell phone that he didn't notice them.

"Oh, Craig, look at that pretty baby," Avis

squealed as she paused in front of Geno. "How old is she?"

When Craig looked up and realized whom she was talking to, the look on his face became sheer panic. He quickly closed his phone as Kayla stared at him, not saying a word.

"Three weeks," Geno answered, shaking his head at Craig.

"Oh, she is so cute. What's her name?" the woman directed at Kayla.

"Ask her father," Kayla smirked. Craig's eyes widened in shock and he could not believe what Kayla was doing. She turned and looked at Geno, wrapping her arm in his and rubbing Day's head.

"Jenesis, but we call her Day," Geno replied.

"Day, that is nice, ain't it, Craig?" She smiled at her dazed husband. He stood, not moving, too shocked to do anything.

"Are you gonna have me a baby sister, Mommy?"

"One day, Nigel. He been asking for a little sister for years," she informed them.

The waiter called Geno's last name and he placed Day back into the stroller.

"That's us," he said.

"Bye, Day," Avis gushed as they maneuvered past her. Kayla's eyes never left Craig's. It took all of her mental restraint to keep from saying what she was feeling. He was still with her. All this time he was telling Kayla that they were no longer together and they were. She was beyond furious.

"Man, that was weird," Geno said as they sat down.

"I can't believe his lying ass." Kayla shook her head. She looked at her sleeping daughter and took a deep breath. "I am gonna kick his ass."

"For what, Kay? I don't understand why you're so mad. You knew he was married." Geno shrugged. "I mean, I can understand you being uncomfortable, but mad?"

"He told me he was leaving her. He said they were no longer together," she responded. She couldn't believe Geno's nonchalance at the situation.

"So what if they're still together? As long as he takes care of Day, it shouldn't matter," he said.

"It does matter. He lied to me." She sat back and frowned. She was no longer hungry.

"Are you feeling this nigga, Kayla? Is that why you mad?" He looked over at her and lay the menu down.

"No."

His cell phone began buzzing and he looked at the caller ID. Ignoring the call, he put it back in his pocket. Kayla could tell he was getting frustrated. "Then you shouldn't care who he's wit' then. You don't need that nigga and neither does Day."

"Why not, G? Because we got you?"

"Yep."

"Really, did you forget you have a girlfriend? What? You think every time you get mad at her you can run to me? I don't think so. Neither my house nor my heart has a revolving door. I'm ready to leave," she told him.

"Fine. Let's go." They left the restaurant without eating.

The ride home was quiet, neither one saying anything. He carried the stroller and bags into the house, kissed Day goodnight and left, locking the door behind him.

It was after eleven when Kayla heard a knock at the door.

"Can I come in?"

"Hell, no! I know you have got to be out of your mind!" Kayla yelled back.

"It wasn't what it looked like, Kayla. We were just taking Nigel out Christmas shopping, that's all. I still have to be a part of my son's life," he told her.

"I didn't say you didn't, Craig. I can't believe you lied to me!"

"Lied about what? I am not with her anymore."

"I can't tell the way she was hugging up on you. And you trying to have another baby? I don't think she'd be feeling that way if she knew the baby she was cooing all over was *yours*, would she?"

"She didn't say we were trying to have another baby. She said Nigel wanted a little sister. Shit, he does! You're jumping to conclusions, dammit!"

Kayla thought about what he was saying and cracked the door open. She tried to remember what Avis said, verbatim, but couldn't.

"Let me in, Kayla. Please." He looked at her with that intense stare and she obliged. He followed her into the living room. "Where's Day?"

"Don't start with the small talk. It's after eleven. Where you think she is?" She sat on the sofa and he sat next to her. He began rubbing her back. She tried to shrug his hands off, but he kept on running his fingers across her shoulders. She had to admit it felt good.

"I'm sorry. But seriously, Kayla, I had to come over here and talk to you. I knew you wouldn't answer the phone if I called. I wanted to squash this shit before you blew it out of proportion."

"You know I was pissed when I saw you with her ass." She turned to look him in the face.

"You know I was pissed when I saw you wit' his ass." He raised his eyebrow at her. "And he was carrying my daughter. That's why I couldn't even say nothing."

"I thought you were scared I was gonna call you out."

"Shit, you almost did!" He laughed. "But I ain't mad at you, Kayla. I need for you to understand that I ain't tryin' to disrespect you. I care about you and Day. I just wish you would cut a brotha some slack. I told you, I'ma do right by you. Have I not been doing that?"

"You have," Kayla admitted. He would drop off diapers, wipes, and formula twice a week and he bought more shoes and outfits than Day could even wear. He *had* been doing right by them.

"So, truce?"

"Truce. But if I find out otherwise, you'd better believe it's on," she told him.

"I like when you talk like that. You know I love a woman wit' spunk. I know she 'sleep, but can I at least see my daughter?"

"She's in her crib."

Craig went into the nursery for a few moments.

"I gotta go, but I'll holla at you later, okay, Beautiful?" he said when he came out.

"A'ight." Kayla smiled at him. As mad as Craig made her, he still had a way of making her change her attitude toward him. He was definitely a smooth talker.

26

Day's first Christmas was an eventful one. Kayla bought more dolls, clothes and stuffed animals than she had planned, but Day was worth it. Her parents drove up to spend Christmas morning with her and then everyone was having dinner at Ms. Ernestine's with Roni and her family.

"Merry Christmas!" Roni, Toby and Terrell hugged and kissed as they came in, carrying armloads of gifts. Kayla did the introductions and put the packages under the tree.

"How is my goddaughter enjoying her first Christmas?" Terrell asked, looking at Day swinging peacefully in her swing by the Christmas tree.

"I think she's enjoying it. She's been 'sleep most of the day," Kayla told him. They laughed and exchanged gifts as Christmas carols played on Kayla's stereo. Kayla was headed for the kitchen when the doorbell rang again.

"Merry Christmas, Kayla."

Kayla's mouth fell open when she saw Geno outside. They hadn't talked since their falling out at Red Dragon two weeks prior.

"Merry Christmas," she told him.

"I hope you don't mind. I wanted to see Day and give her a gift." He smiled sheepishly.

"No, I don't mind at all. Come on in, Geno." Although they had fought, Kayla really missed him.

"Merry Christmas, everyone," he greeted as he followed Kayla into the living room.

"Geno. Merry Christmas." Her mother stood and embraced him and her father shook his hand. They were happy to see him. Kayla knew that deep down they wanted her and Geno to resolve their issues and get back together.

"This is for Day," he said, giving Kayla a large box.

"Thanks, G. But where's mine?" she asked him jokingly.

"When you become a mother, you lose all gift privileges." He grinned.

"I'm learning that the hard way," she told him. She opened the box, which contained several DVDs. *Cinderella, Snow White, Sleeping Beauty, The Little Mermaid, and Beauty and the Beast.*" Kayla announced the titles as she opened the gift.

"She is a princess after all," he told her. Day began whining in the swing and Kayla lifted her out.

"She needs to be changed," Kayla said, nuzzling her beautiful daughter.

"I'll, do it," her mother offered.

"No, you stay. I'll take care of her." Kayla took her into the nursery and began to change her.

"Long day for her?" Geno walked up behind her.

"Long day for me." Kayla rubbed her whining baby's head. Once again, the doorbell rang and Kayla shook her head. "Now who in the world could that be? Everybody's been here to visit already."

"Her father hasn't," Geno whispered.

"He's not coming. He said he had to work."

"Maybe he got off early," Geno suggested. Kayla felt the hairs stand up on the back of her neck when she realized the voice that was coming from the front of the house.

"God is punishing me. I know he is." She folded her arms and began to shake her head. Geno stood frozen, not wanting to move.

"Kayla, come out here. And bring Day!" her father called.

"She fell back to sleep," she told him.

"Just bring her for a few minutes, Kayla. She has a guest."

"I'll stay here," Geno said quietly.

"No! I don't want to take her out there," Kayla hissed.

"Kayla, did you hear what we said?" her mother said as she came into the room and reached for the baby.

"Mama, no. She just went to sleep. Leave her alone!" Kayla startled herself at the tone of her voice.

"Now, you listen here. I will not have you yelling at me like I am a child. It's Christmas and this is a time for family. Now, pick Day up and bring her out right now." Kayla knew her mother was not joking. She had never blatantly disobeyed her before and she wasn't about to start. She carefully picked Day up and held her in her arms, making sure not to wake her. She could hear laughter as she made her way down the hallway.

"Kayla! Merry Christmas." Anjelica held a fake smile on her face. Kayla just looked at her. "Geno! I didn't expect to see you here. Merry Christmas."

"Anjelica," he said and quickly excused himself, politely.

"Is this my new niece? Can I hold her?"

"She's asleep," Kayla said as she cradled Day's head and held her close.

"Well, I can see she looks just like her daddy. I can imagine your baby pictures looking just like her, huh, Geno? Oh, what was I thinking? You're not her father, are you?"

"Anjelica, that is enough," her father said.

"I'm sorry. It's just that seeing Kayla and Geno together with the baby, they look so natural. I haven't the slightest idea why they ever split up. They make such a nice couple," she said maliciously. Geno couldn't stay a minute longer. He quickly got up and got his coat.

"You're leaving so soon, Geno?"

"Yes, I think that's best," he said, making sure not to look at the hateful woman.

"I'm quite sure you have a lot to celebrate today. I hear congratulations are in order. Have you set a date?"

"What are you talking about, Anjelica?" Roni asked. She had been watching Anjelica since she arrived and she knew she was up to no good.

"He's engaged to my friend's sister. Janice, Janice Miles." She smiled knowingly. The entire room got quiet and waited for Geno's response.

"What is she talking about, Geno?" Kayla rolled her eyes at Geno. "What the hell was that all about, G?"

"She was just tripping, Kay. That's all. You know how Anjelica is." He shrugged.

"You're engaged to Janice, Geno? And you didn't even tell me?"

"I'm not engaged, Kayla."

"Is she wearing a ring?"

"Yeah."

"Then you're engaged, Geno." Kayla was so hurt that she wanted everyone to clear out of her house so she could be by herself.

"Kayla, let me explain. It's not what you think," Geno began.

"There's nothing to explain." Kayla smiled. "Congratulations. Well, I know you must be going and I don't want to keep you from your fiancée. Thank you so much for your gifts and I hope you have a Merry Christmas."

"I guess I should leave now, huh?" Geno frowned.

"I think that would be best."

"Kay, I'll call you later."

"Don't bother," she said dryly. She couldn't even look at him.

"Merry Christmas, everyone," he said as he departed.

"Mama, do you want to open your gifts now?" Anjelica turned and asked her mother.

"I don't think so. I would like to see you in Kayla's room though." She motioned for Anjelica. Kayla's sister rose and tossed her hair as she exited down the hallway.

She could hear her mother's voice getting louder from the bedroom and she looked over at her father, who was sitting on the sofa. "Did you invite her here?"

"That's your sister, Kayla. She don't need an invitation to your house." Her Dad looked at her like she was foolish. "It's Christmas Day and the family is to be together. What is wrong with you?"

"I don't care what day of the year it is, Daddy. Anjelica is still a conniving, mean, hateful dog and I don't want her in my house."

"Kayla! Now I know you and her don't get along, but she is still your sister." Her Daddy frowned.

Kayla could not believe her father. Once again Anjelica had come into her house and disrespected her and yet her parents were still defending her. Kayla wouldn't have cared if they were Siamese twins. She wanted Anjelica out of her house. She walked into the kitchen and leaned against the refrigerator.

"You a'ight, Dawg?" Terrell asked her after a few moments. Kayla forgot he was still there.

"Anjelica does this shit all the time and they still act like she's God's gift." She was too mad to cry, even though she wanted to.

"Stop tripping, Kay. I'm talking about Geno. I know you're pissed."

"Uh, that's where you're wrong. I'm happy for Geno. I am glad he has finally found someone to spend the rest of his life with," Kayla lied. She could not believe he was engaged to someone else. Her heart felt as if it had been ripped out of her chest; it took everything she had to not curl into a ball and cry. But she was determined to be stronger than that.

The phone rang before she could go on. She snatched it up without checking the caller ID.

"Hello," she snapped.

"Dang, Merry Christmas to you too, Beautiful." Craig laughed into her ear.

"Yeah, whatever," she replied.

"I guess Santa damn sure wasn't good to you. How is my gorgeous Day? She enjoying her first Christmas?"

"Yeah, she is."

"Well, can I come through and bring Day her gifts? And you too?"

"You bought me a gift?"

"Of course. You are the mother of my child. And a good mom too, I might add."

"Well, I have company right now, but I'll call you when they leave."

"Bet. I will check you later."

"Bye." Kayla found herself smiling as she hung up the phone. Craig bought her a gift. She had no doubt that he was getting Day gifts. But he had gone so far as to get her a gift, too. She was digging that.

"Who was that?" Terrell asked.

"Craig." She shrugged.

"Why are you smiling?" He looked at her funny.

"He got me a gift."

"So did I, but you ain't smile like that. Don't do nothing dumb," he warned.

"What are you talking about, Terrell?"

"I mean, I know you're pissed at Geno and here this nigga is buying you a gift."

"I am the mother of his child. Besides, it is Christmas."

"Whatever. Just be mindful of the games niggas play."

"Okay, Terrell. Ain't nobody playing no games.

Damn, it's just a Christmas gift." She laughed because he was always suspicious. They went back into the living room where her mother and sister had rejoined her dad.

"Kayla, I want to apologize," Anjelica began.

"Save it. Mama, Daddy, we need to get ready to head over to Aunt Ernestine's. I have to get back here so Day can spend time with her father." Kayla ignored her sister completely, hoping she'd get the picture.

"Well, your father and I have decided to head to Aunt Margie's for dinner. You go ahead to Ernestine's and tell her we send our best," her mother said.

"Well, I'll talk to you all later." Kayla kissed her parents as they left behind her sister, who made no comment. She closed the door behind them and breathed a sigh of relief.

"Your life makes the soap operas look boring." Terrell shook his head. "I wouldn't have missed this for the world."

27

Kayla made it home by nine o'clock Christmas night. She called Craig as soon as she got in.

"Dang, you just now getting home?" he whined.

"Yeah."

"Is Day still up?" She could hear a lot of people in the background.

"I still haven't given her the last feeding. If you come now, you can do it. Where are you anyway?"

"Uh, I'm not that far. I got one stop to make and then I'll be there. Just keep her up until I get there."

"You'd better hurry. When she gets hungry she gets demanding."

"Like her Daddy. I'll be right there." He laughed.

"Yo, Craig, you got something good for me?" She could hear a woman laughing in the background.

"Who is that?" Kayla demanded. He had been swearing to her that he was no longer with Avis and she never questioned him about other women. Maybe she should.

"Nobody. Give me fifteen minutes, Kay, and I'll be there." He hung up.

Kayla changed Day into her pajamas and set her in the swing, hoping she would be content until Craig got there. She had just begun to get feisty when the doorbell rang.

"You're right on time," Kayla said as she opened the door. Craig's arms were full of wrapped boxes and gift bags. "What did you do, rob the mall?"

"It's my baby's first Christmas. What do you expect?" He followed Kayla into the living room and placed the gifts under the tree. He walked over to the swing and picked Day up. "Hi, Day. Merry Christmas."

"I have no room for all of this stuff. I can't believe this." Kayla looked at the mass of gifts under the tree.

"Open them for her while I feed her and put her to bed, Kay," Craig said, reaching for the bottle sitting on the table. He sat down and began to feed Day, looking like a natural. Kayla knelt down beside the tree and began opening gifts. Craig bought Day any and everything for an infant age six months and up. He had musical activity sets and games, toys that attached to her stroller and car seat, he even bought her a piano that she could kick and play with her feet. Kayla laughed every time she opened a gift. She was delighted when she opened a small box that contained Day's first pair of earrings.

"Diamonds, of course," Craig informed her.

"Just like her father," Kayla commented, noticing the studs he wore in his ears. He stood and took the sleeping baby into her room and placed her in the crib.

"I'll be right back," he said and opened the door.

"Where are you going?" She jumped up to go behind him.

"Chill. I gotta get your gifts out of the trunk," he told her. She sat back down and waited for him to return. He came back with another armload of packages.

"I know all this isn't for me." She raised her eyebrows at him.

"Merry Christmas, Kayla. These are from Day." He passed her three large boxes. She was too shocked to even thank him. She just began to open them one by one. The first one contained a beautiful, ivory cashmere sweater and matching leather pants.

"Oh, my God. Craig."

"Keep opening." He laughed. She opened the second box and found an ivory Coach bag and wallet. Kayla could not believe it. She had never bought herself a Coach bag because her mother had told her that there was no point in spending more money on a purse than you had in your wallet.

"One more from Day," he said, sliding a longer box toward her. She opened it to find a pair of ivory leather boots. She sat back on the sofa, stunned by what he had just given her. No man, not even Geno, had ever given her such elaborate gifts. Stuff like that only happened to Roni. "What's wrong? I got the right sizes, right? You don't like it?"

"I love it. I'm just surprised. I never expected this," she said.

"Well, you still have your gift from me to open." He pushed a long box into her hand. She carefully opened it and lifted a thick, gold chain out, holding a heart-shaped charm with a diamond. "Open the heart."

Inside there was a small picture of Kayla holding Day in the hospital. She had given him a copy of it after he started being a good father. She felt the tears swell in her eyes and tried to brush them before they fell.

"Look at the back," he whispered in her ear as he stroked her hair. She knew she could not take anymore, but she looked anyway. There were three small words engraved on the back of the charm: *Kay & Day.* She fell into Craig's arms and cried. All of the emotions she had gone through that day came pouring out at that very moment. Craig just held her and let her cry.

"Thank you, Craig," she finally said after she had gotten herself together.

"Kayla, you are my daughter's mother and more importantly, you are my friend. I give you mad props because you deserve and earn your respect. You don't hassle me, you let me know in a proper way if I ain't handling my business and you are a damn good person. Hell, I been feeling you from the moment I met you and you know this. But I have my issues; you know that. I just want you to know that I care about you and appreciate you, even though I ain't that nigga Geno," he added.

"You don't have to be Geno. I appreciate you too, Craig. You have really surprised me. I thought you were gonna be one of these M. I. A. dads. You know, missing in action, but you proved me wrong." Kayla wiped the remainder of her tears and smiled at him. Craig's cell began to vibrate and he took it out and looked at it.

"Look, Kay. I gotta dip. But check this out, I would like to take you out tomorrow night if it's cool. If I get my moms to watch Day, you wanna go grab a bite at Dolce's?"

Kayla did not have to think twice. Dolce's was the premiere spot for dinner. She knew reservations had to be made at least two weeks in advance, so she figured Craig had either been planning this for a while or had some connections because he was a cook.

"That would be nice. I would love to go." She stood and walked him to the door. He bent down and caressed her neck as he hugged her. She tilted her head so that her lips met his. She closed her eyes and felt her mouth open as he began to suck on her bottom lip. She didn't want to stop and knew he didn't either, but the vibration from the phone stopped him.

"Mmmmm, see you tomorrow night, Beautiful. I'll pick you up at seven," he whispered and kissed Kayla once more on her forehead. *Too bad he don't act right, or else he just might be the one for me,* Kayla thought as she went to try on her new outfit and boots.

28

"I need to talk to you," Geno said when Kayla answered the phone. She had been avoiding him for weeks now and he still hadn't let up.

"For what, Geno? I ain't your fiancée, you don't need to talk to me about shit." Kayla grabbed her purse and the diaper bag. She and Craig had an appointment with a childcare provider and she knew she couldn't be late.

"Kayla, I swear. I thought we were much cooler than this. You don't return my calls, and on the off chance that you do answer the phone, you still won't talk to me. I'm getting real pissed." Kayla could hear that Geno was frustrated, but she did not care. He wasn't her man; let Janice deal with him.

"Look, Geno. I am on my way out the door, I have an appointment and I can't be late." She picked up the carrier, where she had already placed Day, and opened the door.

"Look, Kayla. I gotta go outta town for a few

weeks, but I need to see you when I get back. Face to face. This is an entire month's notice, so you have plenty of time to clear your schedule. You owe me that much, Kayla. And I wanna see Day, too."

Kayla sighed. Geno was right. She did owe him the opportunity to apologize to her face to face. "Fine, Geno. Just let me know when."

"The last Saturday in March."

"Fine. I gotta go." She hung the phone up and rushed out to meet Craig. Kayla was scheduled to return to work the first week of February. As much as she hated to leave her baby, she knew she had to go back to work in order to survive. She had diminished her savings down to almost nothing and although Craig was a good provider for Day, she still needed her own income to live comfortably. Tia had told them about a woman named Ms. Cookie who had an awesome childcare center, but she was always full. Craig had told Kayla to let him worry about getting Day in. She had no idea what he did, but he had called Kayla that morning and told her to meet him at Ms. Cookie's for their tour and interview. The neatness and cleanliness of the center impressed Kayla. There were four different rooms; three of them set up with cribs and tables. The other was a multi-purpose room, holding a large screen television and shelves of toys and books. The unique thing about Ms. Cookie's center was she exclusively kept infants up to age two.

"Well, we will see you all next week then." Ms. Cookie smiled as she walked them out.

"You mean she's in? I thought you had a waiting list." Kayla was stunned.

"She has a very persistent father." Ms. Cookie nodded. "I can respect that."

"Thanks, Ms. Cookie. We'll see you next week." Craig carried the carrier to the car and strapped Day in.

"What did you do?" Kayla asked him, incredulously.

"I got my daughter in school. I handled my business."

"How?"

"Don't worry about all that. You said you wanted her in, now I got her in. She's in and I paid her first month's tuition up front, so you don't have to sweat that either. Now I got some other business to handle. I'll be by there later, and tonight I'll do the three a.m. feeding." He winked and kissed Kayla as he jumped into his new Jeep. He told her he had gotten a major raise because they sold the restaurant to a new man, and rather than see him quit, he offered Craig double what he was making. Kayla waved as he drove off. The sight of a red car caught her eye and she turned, but it was gone. She had been seeing a red Benz following her for a couple of days now. The tag read LIBRAGAL. She knew Avis drove a red Benz. She scolded herself for being paranoid and got into her own car.

She knew she had a surprise planned for Craig. Karen had already given her the okay to have sex, but she wanted tonight to be special. She raced home to prepare. She covered her bed with the navy blue satin sheet set that Tia had given her for Christmas and placed candles all over the bedroom and bathroom. She thought about cooking but decided against it when she remembered she had no culinary skills. So she ordered some Chinese delivery. Once the food had arrived, she called Craig to see what time he would be coming and reminded him to pick up some wine and strawberries. She already had whipped cream in the fridge. She put a slow jams CD in the stereo, double checked Day and waited for her soon-to-be re-lover's arrival.

"Damn, I shoulda got Day in school earlier." He laughed as Kayla opened the door. She was wearing a blue, silk kimono and matching slippers. Her hair had grown out to its original length and she had it pulled on top of her head. She had sprayed herself with Escada, knowing it was his favorite scent for her to wear.

"Maybe. Come on, dinner's ready." She turned to go into the kitchen.

"Oh no. I hope you ain't cook." He groaned.

"You'll have to come and see." She rolled her eyes and he followed behind her. The table was laid out beautifully and she had the variety of oriental dishes in her glass serving plates and bowls.

"This is beautiful," he commented as he sat down.

"You get the wine and strawberries?"

"Yeah, right here. Give me a corkscrew so I can open the bottle."

She passed him the opener and reached into the cabinet to get two glasses. She could feel him walk behind her and reach around her waist. Her body got hot and she had to catch her breath.

"Here," she said as she turned around, holding the two glasses. He took them from her hand and placed them on the counter with one hand, pulling her to him with the other. She put her arms around his neck and stood on her toes. His arms felt so good around her as he lifted her up off the floor. She wrapped her legs around his thick waist and they kissed each other hard. Kayla found herself biting at his mouth, matching his heat. She had never wanted anyone so bad in all her life. She could feel him through his pants as he carried her to the bedroom. Once there, he laid her on the bed and looked around at the sensual surroundings Kayla had created. He didn't waste any time removing his clothes and climbing next to her. She had already removed her robe and he was staring at her sexy body. She was now even thicker than the first time he saw her nude body. Her breasts were fuller and her nipples were inviting his touch. He took his time running his fingers all over her body and nibbling her every crevice. She moaned in delight as he blew erotic kisses over her body. He kissed and licked from the top of her head to the arch of her foot, which he teased with the tip of his tongue, causing her to squirm. He knew what he was going to do next and so did she. His tongue found his way into her now melted openness and the wetness invited him home. He enjoyed the invitation and let it be known. Kayla found herself lost in the ecstasy he was taking her to. She tried to be mindful that their child was now sleeping in the next room, but could not stop herself from calling his name and letting him know she was there. Just as she caught her breath, he mounted her and began riding her gently. She bucked at first, because it was painful, but soon began to enjoy the ride, her hips rising to meet his. It was Craig who began to moan this time as the heat and wetness from her body began to contract around his thick muscle each time he entered. He began to thrust faster and faster, the sound of their bodies connecting and the scent of their lovemaking making it even better. As they had the first and only time they had ever made love, they reached their climax together and with each other's names on their lips.

"I love you, Kayla," Craig whispered. Kayla didn't know what to say. She knew she cared for Craig, he was after all the father of her child, but deep down, she knew she still loved Geno. But he was with another woman. What was the use of holding on to those feelings? *Can I love two men at one time?*

"I love you too, Craig," she said as her mind told her heart to shut up. He kissed her once again and rose from the bed, walking into the bathroom. He returned with a warm cloth for her to clean herself up. "Thanks, but I think I need a shower after that one."

"We did get kinda funky. I think I'll join you. That is, if you don't mind."

"I don't mind at all." Kayla grinned as he pulled her up. "Start the water. I need to check on Day."

She peeked into the dim nursery and made sure Day was still sleeping. *I can't believe she slept through all of that,* she thought. She walked into the room just in time to hear Craig talking on his cell phone.

"Damn, man. I told you I couldn't meet up tonight. I got something to do. We just have to handle it in the morning. Man, naw. Because. Look, meet me in ten minutes and your ass better be there when I get there. Whatever."

"Who is that?" Kayla asked, causing Craig to damn near jump out of his skin.

"Don't be sneaking up on a brother like that,

girl." He turned and smiled at her. "That was Darrell. I gotta go meet him at the crib right fast."

"But I thought we were gonna take a shower."

"Look, give me thirty minutes, Baby. I promise
you I will bathe you from your head to your feet,"
he said as he pulled on his jeans and Tims. He
looked so sexy. Kayla sat on the side of the bed and
rolled her eyes. "Thirty minutes. I promise, Kay."

He kissed her and nearly ran out the door, leaving her sitting on the side of the bed. He returned
two hours later and climbed into bed, wrapping
his arms around Kayla as she slept.

29

"Hello." The call was coming from Lynch Financial Group and Kayla knew it must either be a telemarketer or a wrong number.

"Can I speak to Kayla?"

"Yes, you may. Who's calling?" Kayla indirectly corrected the unknown female caller. She was waiting on Roni to arrive so they could go to lunch with the rest of their girlfriends.

"Avis. Avis Coleman." Kayla's heart began to thump in her chest. She knew this day was coming, but she still was not prepared. She took a deep breath and closed her eyes.

"This is she."

"I need to ask you a few questions." She could hear the ghetto attitude and New York accent in the woman's voice and knew that it was not gonna be pretty. Craig had assured her that he and Avis were finished, but she still had her doubts.

"Go ahead. I am listening."

"Are you and Craig fucking?" she asked. Kayla

cringed at the crudeness of her question. She decided to attempt the intelligent way out.

"Craig and I are dating, if that's what you want to know. As far as us having a sexual relationship, well, I feel that that's none of your business, especially considering the fact that you two are no longer together."

"None of my business! Bitch, have you lost your mind? That's my husband. We may be taking a break right now, but we are still and always will be married. I just wanted to know for my own sake and my protection if you are fucking him, because I still am."

"Well, thank you for being concerned enough about me to let me know that. I will take it all under advisement." Kayla figured the dumb girl probably had no idea what the word "advisement" meant, and knew that her calmness was pissing her off even more.

"Let me give you a little more facts to take under ad . . . ad . . . *advisement,* since you wanna be so gotdamn funny. Craig is my husband!"

"You already told me that twice," Kayla said calmly.

"Listen to me, trick! I am his wife and I am the mother of his son. You will never be me. I have his seed. You may be his *piece* for right now, but I have his son. He will be taking care of me forever. You are nothing to him! I am everything!" she screamed. Kayla tried to remain calm and not let the worst of her come out, but this ghetto bitch had said the wrong thing.

"Guess what? He might have me be his *'piece,'* as you call it, for a little longer than you think, my dear. You see, I would never want to be your funky, uneducated ass for nothing in this world. Not only do I have my own, but I got his seed too, boo. I am the mother of his daughter." Kayla hung the phone *up thinking, let her think about that.* When Roni came through the door Kayla was still *fuming.*

"You ready? What is wrong with you?" Roni looked at her friend who was so mad she was almost feverish.

"That stank ho Avis called me." The phone rang and Kayla read the caller ID. "This is her again. She's calling from her job. Hello."

"I know you are a liar, bitch. You know Craig is out in the streets blowing up and you trying to take him for what he worth. I know your so-called daughter ain't his. But you know what? You keep trying me and I am gonna really fuck you *and* your baby up."

"Listen, I don't take to threats too kindly, so let me warn you. Don't let your mouth write a check your ass can't cash. Don't call my house again." She hung the phone up and grabbed her purse. The phone began to ring again. "Let's go before I have to get ugly."

"You should let me talk to that bitch," Roni said as she grabbed the diaper bag and the car seat. "Aunt Roni knows how to handle hers, right, Day?"

"Mommy knows how to handle her own, too!" Kayla slammed the door as they left.

After a wonderful lunch with her friends, Kayla returned to find that she had thirty-eight new calls on her caller ID and twelve new messages. She looked at the small screen of the phone and there were different numbers, but they all came from Lynch Financial Group.

"I don't believe this. She called almost forty times and she left twelve messages."

"No she didn't. Play them on speakerphone so I can hear them," Roni told her. Kayla played each message. They were all full of profanity and threats to her and Day. She told Kayla she knew where she lived and was gonna kill her. She even offered to meet Kayla somewhere so they could fight like "real women".

"You really are crazy. Ain't no nigga worth fighting over," Kayla replied to Avis' voice. But there was something else about the messages that bothered Roni.

"Kay, what does she mean about Craig making big money in the streets now?"

"I don't know. She said something about that to me earlier. I thought she was talking about the raise he got at the restaurant."

"I don't think so. I betcha that nigga is hustling. You see, a woman like her ain't gonna be sweating him like that if he just a cook. And you said she drives a Benz. Unless she's a big time broker at Lynch, she wouldn't be driving a Benz. He's hustling."

The phone rang again as Kayla was thinking about what her friend had just told her.

"It's her again," she told Roni.

"Let her leave another message," Roni told her.

"I am, but in the meantime, I'm gonna get her ass." Kayla called the phone company and got her number changed immediately. She found the toll-free number for Lynch Financial Group and called them. "Yes, I need to speak with Corporate Security, please. Thank you."

"What are you doing?" Roni frowned.

"Outsmarting the dumb bitch. She is so stupid. Watch this. Hi, my name is Kayla Hopkins and I need to report harassment by one of your employees. Her name is Avis Coleman. Yes, well Mrs. Coleman has called my residence several times today from your company and even left threatening messages on my voicemail. As a matter of fact, hold one moment and I will play them for you." Kayla clicked to the other line and dialed the voicemail number, playing the messages for the manager. "As you can see, these messages are time and date stamped, and if you compare that to Mrs. Coleman's schedule, you will see that they were made on company time. Now, I am sure you are paying Mrs. Coleman to do something other than bother persons such as myself. I have contacted the authorities as well as my attorney, and you will be hearing from them soon. I am calling you to ask Mrs. Coleman as a courtesy to refrain from contacting me. Yes, that's fine. Let me give you my new telephone number for them to call me. I had to go through the inconvenience of changing it due to this unfortunate circumstance. Yes." Kayla gave him the number and he assured her that the company's attorney would call her as soon as possible.

"Work it, girl. Be smarter than her!" Roni snapped her fingers at Kayla and she tried not to laugh.

"Thank you. And one more thing, can you let Mrs. Coleman know that it is a federal offense to use profanity over telephone lines in a threatening manner? The telephone company could prosecute her and have her home lines permanently disconnected. You have a wonderful day as well." Kayla tossed her head back with laughter as she hung the phone up.

"A woman after my own heart. I trained you well." Roni hugged her girlfriend. "One down, one to go."

"What do you mean?" Kayla asked.

"We're gonna find out if that brother is dealing. Come on. We'll drop Day off at Tia's." Roni jumped into the car. They dropped Day and explained to Tia that they had some emergency business to take care of. Tia just shook her head and took the baby and the diaper bag.

"Where are we going now?" Kayla asked.

"To Toby's. He'll know someone that could tell us if Craig is hustling."

30

Roni sped through the streets and pulled up behind Toby's Lexus truck. They hopped out and walked to the front door, ringing the doorbell. They waited a few minutes but there was still no answer. "I know he's here because he has to be at the club by eight. What time is it?"

"Six forty," Kayla answered. "I thought you had a key anyway."

"Not yet. 'Yet' being the operative word. He must be 'sleep." Roni laid on the doorbell, ringing it five or six times in a row. They finally heard footsteps coming toward them. "About time."

"Wha . . . Hey, what are y'all doing here?" Toby opened the door slightly, wearing some sweats and no shirt. Kayla tried not to stare at his muscular, chocolate body, but it was hard.

"Hey, sweetie. We came by because we need to talk to you. It's an emergency." She reached to open the door but Toby stopped her.

"I . . . I was uh, about to jump in the shower. Why don't y'all meet me at the club?" he quickly suggested.

"I told you it's an emergency. And why aren't you answering your home phone? I tried to call on my way over here."

"I was asleep. Look, I need to go get dressed. I'll check y'all at the club." He stood behind the slightly cracked door. A movement in the background caused Kayla to frown, but she didn't know what it was. She was gonna find out, though. She looked again and realized it was a foot, without a shoe, dangling off the sofa.

"That's cool. Come on, Ron. You know I gotta pick Day up in a little while. We'll check you later, Toby." She pulled at her girlfriend's jacket and gave her the look. Roni didn't know what was up and was about to go off on Toby, but she followed Kayla's lead.

"A'ight, Kay. I'll see you later, Ron. I love you." He watched them get into Roni's car and shut the door.

"What the hell was that? And why are you rushing me? You know Day is with Tia. She could stay there a month and she and Theo wouldn't care."

"Somebody's in there, Ron. Pull behind that car over there and we're gonna walk back and see who it is. Come on!"

Roni did as she was told and they crept back up to Toby's house. Sure enough, as they peered through the front bay window, they could see Toby hugging that fat nasty Darla on the sofa. Kayla could not believe Toby. He was just as bad as the rest of the trifling, lying men. She turned to see her friend's reaction and saw that Roni was not by her side. She quickly looked around and spotted her in the driveway next door, picking up a skateboard. Before she could react, Roni had tossed the board through the bay window, scaring Toby and Darla. They both screamed and ducked, not knowing what was happening. But Roni didn't stop there. She found a brick and headed for Toby's truck.

"Roni!" Kayla screamed. But the tears that were streaming down her face blinded Roni. She could see more hurt than anger in Roni's eyes and Kayla knew that made her more dangerous. Roni had vowed never to be hurt by any man.

"Veronica! Stop right now. I mean it. Don't make me stop you!" Toby ran after Roni but didn't make it to her in time. The brick seemed to be floating in slow motion as it crashed through his rear window. Kayla grabbed Roni's arm and dragged her to the car, rushing to get away from the now livid Toby. Kayla jumped behind the wheel and tried to think of where to go. They drove around in silence. Roni's eyes glazed over with sadness. Kayla knew the only place to hide. She pulled behind the back of Jett Black. They knocked on the back door and Ms. Ernestine opened it, letting them in.

"Y'all must have really gotten into trouble. Coming through the back door." She smiled at them, then policed Roni's forlorn face. "What happened, baby? What's wrong?"

Kayla followed mother and daughter into Ms. Ernestine's decked out office and explained what had just transpired between Roni and Toby. Kayla thought Ms. Ernestine would be mad enough to kill Toby, but she just laughed.

"My baby is finally in love. I never thought I'd see the day."

"I am not in love with him," Roni told her mother defiantly.

"Yes, you are. If you weren't, then you would've cussed him out rather than vandalize his property. It's nothing wrong with being in love, Roni. That's not a bad thing."

"I got played. I can't believe I got played." Roni began to cry again.

A knock at the door surprised them all.

"Ms. Ernestine, it's a man named Toby out here to see you and he is fine," the shampoo girl, Tameka, came and announced. Roni looked at her mother with a panicked look on her face. Ms. Ernestine touched her daughter's arm and let her know it would be okay.

"He doesn't know you're here. I am not gonna let anything happen to you, you understand?"

"Yes." Roni nodded at her mother. She sat behind the large desk and looked at Toby in the surveillance camera her mother had, displaying the center of the shop. Ernestine Jett kept watch over her shop even when she wasn't seen.

"How you doing, Toby?" Her mother walked up and gave the handsome young man a hug. "What brings you all the way over here? And on a Friday night, too? Aren't you supposed to be spinning records at Dominic's?"

"Yes, ma'am. I came to see if you've seen or heard from Roni," he asked her wearily.

"No, I'm sorry. I can't say that I have. Something wrong?" she asked.

Toby looked around at the crowd of women and then mumbled, "Is there somewhere else we can talk? Somewhere private?"

"We can go in my office. Just give me a minute to clear some stuff up," she said. "Be right back. And Meka, you can look but you'd better not touch."

"What are you doing, Mama?" Roni hissed as her mother re-entered the office.

"Go in the bathroom and wait, both of you. Don't make a sound," she told them. Kayla and Roni went into the small bathroom adjoining the office and held their breath.

"I hope your mama knows what she's doing," Kayla whispered.

"Lord, help her to calm him down so he won't call the cops," Roni prayed aloud.

They listened as Ms. Ernestine and Toby came back into the office.

"Now, what's going on, Toby? And why is my daughter missing all of a sudden?"

"She showed up at my house unexpectedly this evening and I was trying to help a friend of mine out. A female."

"A friend?"

"Yes, ma'am. This friend of mine has some heavy issues going on right now and I was helping her deal with them. I told Roni I was kind of busy and thought she had left, but the next thing I know she busts my window with a skateboard and bricks my truck." He dropped his head toward the floor.

"Are you sure it was just a friend? Roni has never been the jealous type. Did something else go on that you aren't telling me?"

"No, I mean I will admit that the female and I do have some history, but I swear to you, Ms. Ernestine, I would never do anything to hurt or disrespect Roni. I love her with all my heart, and believe it or not, I have never been faithful to anyone until I met her. I know that she is my soul mate and I am not gonna risk losing her for nothing and nobody. I want to marry her. That is, if I have your blessing. But I have to apologize to her for earlier and get her to forgive me."

"Let me get this straight. You were comforting a friend at your house and Roni got mad and broke your house window *and* your car window and you want to apologize and propose to *her*?"

"Yes, ma'am." He looked at her like he was confused.

"Toby, are you sure nothing else happened?"

"I swear. The girl was upset because she found out she was pregnant and the father wants nothing to do with her. I was just being a shoulder for her to cry on."

"And it's not your baby?"

"Absolutely not. I haven't been with anyone since I met Roni and we got together in July. I just need her to forgive me for not explaining and trying to be hush-hush about the whole situation."

"I think she'll understand. I will do what I can to find her for you. I believe that you love her, Toby, and as crazy as both of y'all are, I think you're made for each other. She tears up *your* stuff and *you* want to apologize. I have heard it all."

"Thanks, Ms. Ernestine. I appreciate it." Toby hugged her and left out.

"Girl, if you don't get your behind out here and call that man. Lord, I finally got a wedding to plan!" She hugged Roni and Kayla. Both were still in shock from what Toby had just said.

"And Terrell calls me Drama Queen." Kayla shook her head at her friend.

31

"Where have you been and where is my child?" Craig demanded as Kayla pulled up to her house.

"She's at Tia's. What is your problem?" Kayla flared at him.

"God damn Avis has been blowing up my pager and cell phone. She says you got her fired. What the hell is your problem? I told you to stay away from her."

"First of all, I didn't go looking for her, she came looking for me. She called *my* house harassing me and threatening me and Day."

"Day? How the hell did she find out about Day?"

"I told her."

"You did what? I know you didn't. Don't tell me that, Kayla. You told her? So basically what you did was give her a valid reason to take my ass to court for child support and alimony. I told you not to talk to her dumb ass."

"Look, you two need to take that into the house.

You don't want your neighbors to call the cops," Roni encouraged.

Kayla had forgotten that they were standing in her driveway like common folk. She quickly unlocked the door and went inside with Craig on her heels.

"I didn't give her anything. I am not gonna walk around here like my child is some deep, dark secret to be denied. And her stupid behind would still have a job if she would've left me alone like I asked," she yelled at him. His pager went off and he pulled it out and looked at it.

"I got a errand to run. I will deal with this shit later," he mumbled.

"Before you go, let me ask you a question. What restaurant are you working at again?"

"What?"

"What is the name of the restaurant?" She looked him in his eye to see if he could lie to her face.

"I don't have time for this. I'll call you later." He stormed out of her house. She looked at Roni and told her to come on.

"Where are we going?" Roni asked as they raced to the car.

"Follow him. I don't care what you have to do. Run red lights, stop signs, just stay behind him."

Roni followed the SUV like a pro. She kept a safe distance and trailed Craig until he pulled in front of a row house on one of the side streets all the way across town.

"What up, Craig? You got that for me?" A tall, dark figure wearing a black jacket approached Craig as he got out.

"You paged me, Fred. If I ain't have it I wouldn't

have come. Now, you got my money? And hurry up. I got other business to attend to," Craig grumbled as he reached under the back seat and got a small bag out. Kayla watched in disbelief as the transaction took place.

"Here, man. Now where's my money?" Craig walked toward the shadowy figure.

"Right here, Player!" He reached into his jacket, but instead of pulling out money, he pulled out a nine millimeter and shots rang out. Kayla opened her mouth and thought the screams were coming from her mouth, but it was Roni's voice. The slim man looked around and ran off, stopping only to pick the package up from Craig's bleeding body.

32

Kayla rocked back and forth, cradling Craig's head in her arms. She began to pray and let him know he was going to be all right. She tried to look for a sign that he understood, but he never opened his eyes. She could hear the sirens in the distance coming closer, and the flashing lights were soon dancing across Craig's face, but she still rocked and prayed.

"Ma'am, we need to get to him. Are you okay?" the paramedic asked her. Kayla didn't answer. She continued to rock.

"Kayla, let them help him. Please." She heard Roni's voice in the background. She felt someone gently lift him from her arms and she watched them check for life. It was like she was in a movie.

"Are you okay, ma'am?" again someone asked. "Were you struck anywhere?"

Kayla didn't realize what they were talking about until she looked down and saw that she was covered in blood. She shook her head at the police officer.

"It's not my blood. It's his. Is he going to be okay?" She watched as they began performing CPR.

"They're gonna do everything they can to save him. We need to ask you and your friend a few questions."

"Can we do it later? She needs to make sure he's taken care of first, as well as herself." Roni put her arms around Kayla. The attendants placed Craig on a gurney and lifted him into the back of the ambulance.

"I need to ride with him." Kayla pulled away from her girlfriend and ran toward the vehicle.

"It's okay. She can ride," the officer assured Roni.

"I'll follow you in my car," Roni yelled.

It seemed as if the ride to the hospital took an eternity. Kayla listened as they made comments in regards to Craig's condition. She tried to understand what everything meant, relying on her memory from watching episodes of ER. Most of it was still foreign, but one phrase was clear.

"He's crashing!"

They scrambled, poking Craig with needles and trying to stop the pouring blood from his chest. Kayla closed her eyes and prayed harder and harder. She could not believe that the father of her child was dying before her eyes. It was too much to take.

They rushed Craig into the operating room and told Kayla to wait. She didn't know what to do. The nurse came over and asked if she was Craig's wife. She thought for a moment and shook her head.

"I'll call his brother," she said quietly.

"Okay." The nurse smiled.

Kayla picked up the courtesy phone and dialed Darrell's house. She could hear the panic in his voice when she told him Craig had been shot and he needed to get there right away. He told her it would be okay and he was on his way. Kayla sat on the hard chair beside the phone and tried to think.

"How is he?" Roni asked her quietly.

"They haven't said yet. I don't know."

"He'll be okay, Kayla." Roni tried to comfort her friend and began to pray herself. This was why she didn't date thugs. She had been there when they told her mother that her father had been shot over a dime bag of weed. She was only seven years old. She decided right then that her mother deserved better and so did she.

A little while passed and Darrell came into the waiting room along with two people who he introduced as his parents.

"Where is he? What did they say?" Craig's mother asked.

"They haven't come out and said anything yet," Kayla told her. "He was shot three times, and one of those was in his chest."

"My God. Where did this happen? And who did it?" She cried, looking to Kayla for answers.

"We were on Brighton Street. We followed him. He didn't know we were there," Kayla tried to explain. "It was a guy . . ."

"Brighton Street. Why was he over there?" she interrupted.

"He was dropping something off to the guy and the guy pulled a gun."

"Jesus, I knew he had started selling again." Craig's father sat down and sighed.

"You don't know that, Eddie. He might have just been in the wrong place at the wrong time." She shook her head at her husband. She didn't want to think that Craig had gone back to dealing in the streets. He had stopped that a long time ago.

"Mister and Mrs. Coleman? I'm Doctor Win." The young Korean doctor came into the room, his scrubs covered in blood.

"Yes. How's my boy?" Craig's father jumped up and asked.

"He's stable. The bullet barely missed his heart. We've stopped the bleeding, but these next twenty-four hours are critical," he informed everyone.

"Can we see him?" Diane asked.

"You can, for a few moments. We are transporting him to intensive care. But you do need to know that he is in a coma."

"No! How long will that last?" Eddie looked solemn.

"We can't tell you. He may regain consciousness tomorrow; he may never wake up. As I stated earlier, the next twenty-four hours are critical. I'll tell the nurse to come and get you when he's moved." Dr. Win went back through the doors, leaving everyone to digest what he had just told them.

"He's gonna be fine," Kayla said. "I prayed and asked the Lord to heal him. Now we just gotta have faith."

"That's right."

"Oh, God! Oh, God! Where is he? Craig, Craig!" Kayla heard someone yelling from the corridor.

"Ma'am, ma'am. You are going to have to wait in there with the rest of the family. The doctor will in-form you of his condition," the nurse said loudly over the wailing voice. The door opened and Avis nearly fell through the door, crying as if Craig were already dead.

"Oh, God! Diane, did they say how he was? Oh, Craig, please be okay," she gushed and fell into Diane's arms.

"Avis! Get yourself together," Eddie grabbed her by the arm and told her. Avis turned to him and wept even louder.

"Ma'am, you are going to have to calm yourself. There are other families in nearby waiting rooms and you are causing a disturbance," the nurse warned.

"What the hell is she doing here? Did she shoot him?" Avis rolled her eyes at Kayla. "I thought this was a family waiting room. She ain't family! I am his wife! She is his whore!"

"Avis! That's enough. Now is not the time nor the place," Eddie warned. Kayla stood up and looked at Roni.

"I think it's time for me to go."

"You damn right. You shoulda been gone a long time ago, heifer! You know this bitch called and got me fired today, Diane? Now that I'm in her face, she wanna run off. Naw, be a real woman. Face me, you skank."

"Get out, Avis! My son is clinging to his life and you want to come in here and embarrass him and his family by acting a loudmouth fool. I don't need that, and neither does my son. I am telling you to leave right now or I will have you escorted out." Diane stood and looked Avis in the eye.

"So now you gon' defend her? I think you forgot who your daughter-in-law was. Better yet, the mother of your grandson," Avis said in a threatening manner. For some reason, Diane seemed slightly intimidated. Whatever was about to go down, Kayla wanted no part of it.

"We're leaving. I'll call later to check on Craig," She said to Eddie as she and Roni headed toward the door.

"I'll walk you all down," Darrell said.

"So now you wanna leave? Before you even get to see him? Typical." Avis spat the words at Kayla and it took all of her remaining restraint not to swing on the fat cow.

Kayla quickly walked out into the hallway and into the parking lot. Suddenly, she felt someone rushing toward her and she turned just in time to see Avis charging at her. She felt the punch Avis threw as it landed on her cheek. The pain jolted her but she recovered in time to dodge the next punch she threw. All of the anger that had been pent up came gushing out and she proceeded to whip her ass like she had been wanting to all day. Although the woman was bigger than Kayla by about eighty pounds, she was slower, too. After receiving a few blows of her own, Kayla sucker punched her and knocked her to the ground, then dove on top of her fat body, aiming strictly for her face. She showed no mercy.

"Kayla! Kayla!" She heard Roni screaming. The funny thing was that neither she nor Darrell tried to stop her initially. They let her get her hit on for a few minutes until someone yelled that security was on the way. At that point, Darrell lifted Kayla off Avis and carried her to Roni's car. They sped off before he could say a word.

33

"Kayla, Terrell's here to see you." Roni knocked and stuck her head in the door of Kayla's bedroom.

"It's cool. He can come on back." Kayla sat up in the bed and clicked her television off.

"Hey. You okay?" Terrell looked at her sympathetically. She couldn't do anything but nod. It had been six days since Craig had been shot. He was still in a coma. Kayla hadn't had the strength mentally or physically to go and see him. She just lay in her bed, occasionally watching television. Her parents had come and taken Day back with them for a few days, and Roni had been staying at her house and looking after her. Although she had tried, Kayla still could not get herself together.

"How's he doing? I mean, have you heard anything?"

"He's still in ICU. He's stable but he still hasn't woken up," she told him. "How are you doing? You look terrible."

"Man, I just been having issues of my own. You know what I mean?" He sat on the side of Kayla's bed.

"Terrell Sims with issues? I don't believe it. This I gotta hear. What's going on?" she asked him curiously.

"I was told I'm about to be a father."

"What? Nicole's pregnant! Congratulations. What's the problem?"

"She's not the only one." He looked down at the comforter and shook his head sadly.

"What do you mean? I don't understand." Kayla was confused.

"I have two children on the way by two different women, one of whom is *not* my girlfriend."

"And who is the other?" Kayla knew Terrell was serious about Nicole. He'd assured her of that when she asked him Christmas Day. He even admitted to being in love with her.

"Darla."

"STD Darla? I know you're playing." Kayla remembered seeing her hugged up with Toby the night Craig was shot, and what Toby had explained to Ms. Ernestine about the situation.

"I wish I was. And she ain't trying to get rid of it, either. I don't know what I'm gonna do. I love Nicole. I want her to have my baby. Hell, I love her and want to *marry* her." He looked at Kayla.

"No you don't. Don't even sit there and lie. If you loved her you wouldn't have been fucking Darla." Kayla was pissed at what Terrell was saying.

"It's not like that, Kayla. I do love Nicole."

"So you accidentally fell into Darla's twat? Is that what happened?"

"No. I mean, with her it was an ego thing. You

see, before Christmas Nicole didn't have time for a brother like I needed. That 'me-time' that I gotta have. With Darla, I could go out to the club and then swing by her crib and she would have a sandwich and some chips ready on the table for me. She'd be waiting for a nigga to hit the door and she would slob me down from the jump. I had my own special Kool-Aid in her fridge, sweetened to my liking. She knew how to treat a brother like a man. Nicole never did stuff like that."

"What does Darla do again?"

"She does hair I think. Oh, and she work somewhere else, too. I forget where."

"So you went to her because Nicole was working full-time at the hospital, going to school part-time, and didn't allow you to disrespect her by staying out all night and coming to her crib to eat and sleep whenever you felt like it. Is that what you're saying?"

"No, not like that. I just—I don't—man, my life is so messed up right now."

"You damn right. You blew a perfectly good relationship with an educated, hard-working, respectable woman so you could have 'me-time' with a part-time hairdresser that your brother used to screw. Not only is that pathetic, Terrell, it's nasty. And now she's about to have your baby. And you think my life is drama-filled?" Kayla was disappointed in her friend. He was supposed to be smarter than that. "And if you know you ain't care about that girl, why didn't you wrap it up?"

"I did. At least I thought I did. I don't know, Kayla."

"So you don't even know if it's your baby."

"She says it is."

She looked at Terrell and remembered how he had been there for her over the past few months with all she had been going through. She could not believe she was treating him the same way she didn't want to be treated when she found herself pregnant. She had no right to judge him.

"I don't know what to tell you. I do know that if Nicole forgives you, she's a good one and you better spend the rest of your life making it up to her."

"If she forgives me, you'd better believe I'm gonna marry her."

"You'll be okay, Terrell. I'm here for you. You're my dawg!" She took his hand.

"Thanks, Kayla." He smiled at her.

The phone rang and Roni answered it before Kayla could read the caller ID. She was still trying to help Terrell make heads or tails of his predicament when Roni came into the room.

"Kayla, it's Darrell. Craig has regained consciousness."

Kayla was quiet the entire ride to the hospital. After the last time she was there, she didn't know what to expect. Darrell did call her, so she hoped that was a key indicator that Avis would not be there. She held her breath as she entered Craig's room. His parents and Darrell were all standing over him as she walked in. He was still hooked up to tubes and machines, but his eyes were open.

"He . . . hey, b . . . be . . . beautiful," he stuttered. Kayla smiled at him.

"Hey yourself. You scared the hell out of me."

"I know. I scared the hell out of myself," he said and closed his eyes. Kayla wanted to confront him about the entire incident, but she knew this was not the time. The nurse came in and told them that he needed his rest.

"Kiss my beautiful Day for me," he managed to say.

"I will." Kayla squeezed his hand. They left him and met with Dr. Win in the hallway.

"Well, he's out of the woods. He has a lot of healing to do, but that will happen in time. There was no permanent damage done," the doctor assured them. "He will remain in here another ten days, but we'll move him to another room. He's a lucky young man."

"Thank you, Doctor Win. Thank you for all you've done," Diane said.

"We really do," Darrell added.

"You all take care and I'll check on him later." The doctor left them standing in the hall.

"How you holding up, Kayla?" Eddie asked her.

"I'm fine. I guess I can go back to work next week," she told them.

"I am sorry for all that has happened, including my ignorant daughter-in-law." He rubbed her shoulders.

"It's not your fault nor your place to apologize. I know how to handle trolls like her."

"I second *that*. Lord knows you handled her in the parking lot last week." Darrell laughed. "You tore her fat ass up!"

They all told Kayla about the damage she had done to Avis. She ripped her weave job out and broke her nose. Diane said she *still* had a black eye.

"I'm sorry. But you do know that she tried to jump me. I don't fight unless I am pushed."

"Don't worry about it. Darrell told us what happened. She just got what she been deserving for a while now. I just hope you watch your back. That Avis is a snake and this won't be the end."

"I will. I'll be back tomorrow to check on Craig." Kayla hugged all of them.

"Thank you, Kayla." Diane nodded. "I know this entire situation has not been a very good one, but you have handled it like a lady and that says a lot about you and your character. One more thing."

"Yes, ma'am?"

"When do we get to meet our granddaughter?" she asked Kayla. Kayla didn't know what to say. "We know."

"I, who . . ." Kayla began.

"It doesn't matter. When do we get to see her? We hear she's beautiful."

"Whenever you want," Kayla told them. She felt the weight she had been carrying around for days lifted off her shoulders. *Maybe things are gonna be okay after all,* she thought.

34

Kayla was getting dressed for her first day back at work when the phone rang. She checked the caller ID and it was an unavailable number. She knew that when Ms. Diane or Darrell called from the hospital that was how the number came up, so she answered it.

"Hello," she said, but there was no answer. She held the receiver a few moments longer but still heard nothing. She hung up the phone. The same thing happened three additional times and Kayla was getting pissed. When the phone rang once more, she snatched it up and yelled.

"Why the hell are you playing on my phone?"

"Whoa! Kayla, it's me. What is going on? Are you okay?" Geno asked. Kayla was relieved. She was almost in a panic. She knew it was Avis, but she had no idea how she could have gotten her telephone number.

"I'm okay, G. Somebody keeps calling here play-ing on my phone."

"I thought this was your new number. I had to beg Roni to give it to me."

"It is. I was gonna call you and give it to you myself, but everything has been so hectic around here."

"I know. I heard what happened. How are you holding up?"

"I'm okay."

"Thank God you and Roni weren't hurt. Your mom still has Day?"

"Yeah. She's gonna be there another week and then I'm going to get her. You still out of town?"

"Yeah, I'll be back next week. I still want to talk to you. I need to explain a few things."

"Look, Geno. I keep telling you that you don't owe me an explanation." Kayla saw that she only had half an hour to get to work. "I gotta get outta here. I have to be at work by twelve-thirty. I'll call you later."

"Promise?"

"I promise." She hung up the phone and finished getting dressed.

"Well, look who finally decided to join the realms of the working class." Terrell grinned when she made it to her desk.

"Ha ha." She stuck her tongue at him.

"Naw, Dog. I don't even wanna go there with you. I should've known that was your car in the parking lot. Who else would have 'Kay&Day' on their tag? You got personalized plates. Bad idea."

"Why? You got 'em." Kayla looked at him smugly.

"I ain't got the kinda drama you got, either," he answered.

"No, but you got drama of your own though."
She winked at him.

"Don't go there."

"I didn't, you did." She smirked as he rolled his
eyes at her. She sat at her desk and looked at him
innocently and he could not help but laugh.

Kayla's first week back was a light one. Her su-
pervisor told her to take it easy and she did. She
would leave work every day and go visit Craig, although it was way past visiting hours. He seemed
to enjoy her visits and they would laugh and talk
like they were at her house instead of the hospital.

"Have they told you when you can leave yet?"
she asked him Friday evening.

"No, not yet. I think the doctor is juicing me for
my insurance money." He smiled.

"You'd better be glad you have insurance," Kayla
told him. She wondered who he got it through, *the
Dealers' Union?* She figured that now was as good a
time as any to ask him what she wanted to know.
She had waited long enough. "Craig, are you selling drugs?"

"What? How am I gonna be dealing from a hospital bed, huh? Yeah, after everybody leaves I go
and stand on the corner and sell anesthesia." He
tried to make her laugh.

"Before you got shot, were you dealing?" She
was not gonna break. She needed to know the
truth.

"I was dabbling. I wouldn't call the little bit of
business I was doing dealing."

"Why, Craig?"

"I mean, after Day was born and I left Avis,
things got real tight. I had not only one daycare

bill. I had two. Avis was always crying about money for her and Nigel. And then you were so cool that I really wanted to do right by you. I wanted to make you and Day happy." He looked at her and reached for her hand.

"Don't put this on me, Craig. I did not tell you to start selling drugs. I would never tell you to do that. You could've gotten a second job at McDonald's if it was that bad, and I would have been fine with that. Please don't try to make me feel like you did this for me. You can't make no money for me and Day from a coffin or from jail, which is where you're gonna end up if you don't stop."

"Kayla, believe me. I just wanted us to be a family. I love you and Day, Kayla. I am so sorry that I messed up this bad. Please forgive me."

Kayla looked at his beautiful eyes and they were pleading along with his mouth. She did not know what to do or say.

"You gotta promise to stop, Craig. I don't do hustlers. I don't care how much money they have. I don't do jails and I don't do funerals. Now, the choice is yours."

"I'll quit, Kayla. I promise."

The word "promise" reminded her that she had promised to meet Geno at the Deck. He had finally convinced her that she needed to see him so they could talk.

"I'll be back tomorrow." She bent over him and kissed him gently.

"What time?" he asked.

"Around ten."

"I'll see you then, Beautiful. I love you."

"I love you too, Craig," she said as she left. She

thought about him as she drove to the restaurant. If he was willing to give up that lifestyle then she was willing to give him another chance. As she pulled into the crowded parking lot, her cell phone rang. She didn't recognize the number.

"Hello."

"Kayla, where are you?"

"Geno, I'm at the Deck. Where are you?" She looked at the clock to make sure she wasn't late. The numbers read ten-forty. They were scheduled to meet at ten forty-five.

"I'm gonna have to meet you a little later. Uh, I left my phone and I gotta swing back and get it. Is that okay?" he asked her. She could hear someone laughing in the background.

"Look, Geno, I don't have time for your games, okay? You go and handle your business and I'll check you some other time."

"Kayla, wait. I gotta talk to you."

"Good-bye, Geno." She clicked her phone off and drove home. Pulling into her driveway, she realized that she had left her purse in Craig's hospital room. *I'll just leave it until in the morning,* she thought, but then decided to go and get it.

She quietly got off the elevator and sneaked past the nurses' station. Luckily, there was no one there. She proceeded down the hall and when she got to his door, she heard him talking to someone.

"I know, boo. I'm sorry that happened, really I am. I know she had no right and I'ma check her on it. Look, I'm just tryin' to do and say whatever so she won't take me for child support. You know we don't need that shit right now. Let me handle Kayla. I know what to do. As a matter of fact, baby,

I already got her thinking I'm quitting the game. Hell no, you know I got too much invested in the streets to do that shit. But if she think I ain't hustling, she ain't gon' be having her hand out for no money. I'm gonna do everything outside of killing her ass to keep her from taking me to court. Trust me. Yeah, I told you I got this. Avis, baby, I know. I do love you. You're my wife and nobody can take that from you. You the mother of my firstborn son. You're my queen. I just want us to be a family again. I just want to make you and Nigel happy. I love you, too." She heard him hang up the phone and turned, accidentally bumping into a nurse.

"Can I help you?" she asked, startled.

"I, I left my purse in his room and I need it. Can you get it for me?" Kayla asked, still stunned.

"Sure. Be right back," she smiled and said.

"Don't tell him I'm out here. I don't want to go in."

"No problem," she said. The nurse returned with the purse in hand and gave it to Kayla.

"Thank you," she said and rushed out the hospital. She sat behind the wheel of her car and could not move. She didn't know what to do. She picked her cell phone up and dialed Geno's number.

"Hello." A female answered.

"I'm sorry. I must have dialed the wrong number. I was trying to reach Geno."

"You dialed the right number. He accidentally left his phone on my bed a little while ago. I'll let him know you called," she said and hung up in Kayla's face. Again, Kayla was dumbfounded. She felt as if her life were falling into pieces. She quickly dialed another set of numbers into the phone.

"Hey."

"I need to talk to you," she told Terrell.

"What's wrong, yo?" he asked. "You a'ight?"

"Can you please meet me at my house, Terrell?"

"I'm in the middle of something right now. Can I call you back?"

"Yeah, that's cool," she said.

"You sure you a'ight?" he asked her again.

"Yeah, I'm cool. I'll talk to you later." She quickly hung up the phone and her bottom lip began to quiver. She started to cry. She had no one to talk to. She knew that her girlfriends were probably tired of her and all of her problems, and she definitely could not call her mother. Kayla called the only other person she knew could help her. She closed her eyes and prayed to God.

"Lord, please help me. I am at my wits' end and don't know what to do. I am tired of putting my trust into these men and they are dogging me every time. I have no one else to turn to. Please help me."

She wiped her face and drove herself home. She took a quick shower and got into the bed.

As she began to dream, she felt a spirit of peace come over her as God told her, "That's your problem. You are trusting man when you should be trusting Me."

"Thank you, God," she said and entered into a deep slumber. She thought she was dreaming when she heard the sound of glass breaking from outside her house. She sat up in the bed and rubbed her eyes. There was another loud crash and she rushed to the front of her dark house, peeking out the front window. At first she could not find the source of the commotion and then her attention was drawn to her car. She knew she was dreaming when she saw it. She ran to the front door and flung it open.

"No!" she yelled as she looked at the vandalized mess. Her windshield and all of her windows had been broken. Her lights were smashed and the hood was dented in, her tires flattened. She scurried into the house to call the police, but when she picked up the phone there was no dial tone. She reached for the light switch but when she flicked it, it was still dark. She could make out a shadow going into the nursery. She crept into the kitchen and unexpectedly felt someone behind her.

"Avis!" She turned and screamed.

"Guess again, bitch!" the figure said, lunging at her. She grabbed the attacker's arms as they reached for her and flung them away. She tried to run toward the bedroom but felt hands around her neck. They were strong and forceful. Kayla knew that this was not the same person she had fought with a week ago. She struggled to get out of the grip, but couldn't. She reached for the knife set that she kept on the counter, but her assailant flung her the other way. "Trust me." God's words rang in her head. Thinking quickly, Kayla kneed her perpetrator in the groin. The attacker bent over in pain and Kayla grabbed the butcher knife. Her enemy grabbed another weapon and they charged at each other. Kayla felt the piercing heat of the blade as it penetrated her chest. But she was not to be outdone. She forced the knife into the attacker's body as hard as she could. They screamed simultaneously and Kayla began kicking and stabbing at the same time. As her knee connected with the body, she realized that it was a woman. She fought with everything she had until the shadow fell before her. As she realized who had attempted to take her life, Kayla passed out on the floor.

35

"**D**awg, you gonna be alright. Hold on." Kayla could hear Terrell in the distance. He seemed so far away. Kayla could not breathe. She tried and tried, but she could not get any air into her body.

"Her lung has collapsed," she heard someone saying. "Get her to the hospital, now!"

Kayla decided not to struggle to breathe any more. *God, I am trusting You. I need You to breathe for me because I can't.* She closed her eyes and suddenly she could breathe. She thought about her beautiful daughter and her parents, she thought about her friends and co-workers. She thought about Craig and Avis and Geno. All the things in life she had accomplished and the goals she still had. She reflected on her drama-filled life and the lives of those around her. She was grateful. Grateful for the strength and tenacity to stand when others couldn't, and to try again when she failed. Come what may, Kayla loved her life and wasn't ready to

give it up. *Okay God, I think I'm ready to breathe now.*
She opened her eyes and focused on where she
was. She knew she was in the hospital, that was a
given. She looked over and saw her mother sleeping in the chair.

"Ma . . ." She tried to speak but there was a tube
down her throat. She hit the side of the bed rail to
wake her mother.

"Oh my God, Kayla. Wait a minute, I'll get the
nurse." Her mother rushed out of the room and
returned with the nurse. The nurse took her vitals
and then told her to blow so the tube could come
out. Kayla obeyed and blew as the nurse pulled the
long, plastic tubing out of her mouth. She went
into a coughing frenzy and they gave her some
water.

"Are you okay?" the nurse asked after Kayla was
calm.

"Yeah," she whispered. "What happened?"

"You were attacked, baby. But you're gonna be
okay," her mother said with tears in her eyes.

"Day?"

"Day is fine. She's with your father. I need to call
him."

"Tired." Kayla shook her head and closed her
eyes again. This time when she woke up, Terrell
was sitting where her mother last was.

"Yo, you finally up?" He smiled. She nodded at
him. Her memory was much clearer now. She remembered hearing his voice in her kitchen and
him picking her up off the floor. She could hear
him calling 911 and giving her address.

"Thank you. How did you find me?"

"I rode by your house after I finished handling

my business. I saw your car was all messed up and your door was open. Your neighbors were standing outside like they were scared to come in, so I did. I found you and old girl on the floor." He gave her the details from his viewpoint. "You got her pretty good, yo. I'm proud of you."

"Where is she?"

"Still in ICU. They're gonna transport her to county jail soon as she's well enough."

"I still don't understand why she did it." Kayla told him.

"Well, from what I understand, your boy told her he didn't love her and broke off the engagement. He admitted he was still in love and wanted to be with you and Day. She flipped."

Kayla tried to figure out what Terrell was telling her. "Janice? Janice did this?"

"Yep. But get this. Remember your prank calls?"

"Her?"

"Yep." He nodded.

"But how did she get my number or even my address?"

"Anjelica. She gave up everything to her. She set you up," he said. As much as Kayla disliked her sister, she was still hurt by Anjelica's vindictiveness. "I'm sorry, dawg."

"Not your fault," Kayla said with tears in her eyes. "Thank you. Have you seen Day?"

"Yeah, she's out there with her father. Let me get her." He winked at Kayla and left before she could stop him. She still had not told him about what she overheard on the phone and she didn't want to see Craig.

"Hey, Beautiful," the deep voice said, and Kayla

closed her eyes. As she opened them, she smiled. She saw Geno standing next to her bed, holding her beautiful daughter. "You ready to come home?"

"Geno. Terrell told me Craig was out there."

"Would you rather see him than me? 'Cause me and Day can leave." He smiled as he walked over to her bed. Kayla pushed the button and the bed raised to a sitting position.

"Quit playing. Bring my baby here. Hi, sweetheart." Kayla took Day into her arms and lay her across her chest, disregarding the pain she felt from her stitches. She kissed and nuzzled the infant against her cheeks.

"She missed you, Kay. How're you feeling?"

"Alright. I still can't believe what happened. I hate Anjelica. I don't care if she is my sister. The sad part is that as much as I hate her, I would never do to her what she has done to me." Kayla felt the tears as they ran down her cheek.

"It's okay, Kayla. Please don't cry, baby. This is as much my fault as it is hers. I should have been up front with Janice from the jump. I knew I was still in love with you and couldn't marry her."

Kayla was still stunned by the fact that Janice tried to kill her.

"Then why did you buy her a ring, Geno?" Kayla looked at him, waiting for an explanation.

"I didn't buy her a ring, Kayla. She started talking about getting married after Thanksgiving and then began wearing her grandmother's wedding ring. I never even asked her to marry me. But I never told her I wasn't gonna marry her, either. I just let her think I would because I didn't want the confrontation."

"You never proposed?" Kayla was secretly pleased.

She wanted to be the only one Geno ever asked to marry.

"I've only proposed to one woman, Kayla. The one I'm in love with." He touched her forehead and she closed her eyes. She could smell his cologne and wanted to be in his arms again, but she knew this wasn't the time.

"Am I interrupting?"

Kayla opened her eyes and looked over in the doorway. Craig was sitting in a wheelchair.

"What do you want?" she asked him. After all she had been through, she still remembered overhearing his telephone conversation with Avis. He was the last person she wanted to see. Geno stood protectively by her side.

"They told me you were conscious. I had to make sure you were okay." He proceeded to roll into her room.

"I'm fine. Geno, can you excuse us for a moment?"

"Sure thing, Kay. You want me to take Day?" he asked her, rubbing the baby's back. Craig did not look thrilled.

"No, she's fine. This'll only take a few moments." Her eyes never left Craig. She was ready to set his lying ass straight. She was never one to be made a fool of.

"I'll be right outside." He nodded.

"Kayla, I'm so glad you're okay, baby. I can't believe that nigga. His girl stabbed you and he got the nerve to be up in here, wit' my baby? He better be glad I'm in this wheelchair." Craig rolled over to her bed and grabbed her hand. Kayla snatched it away quickly.

"Don't touch me!"

"What the hell is wrong wit' you, Kayla? Shit was all good between us, and now you trying to act brand new. What's wit' this change of attitude?" He frowned at her. This was not the way he thought this was gonna work out and she knew it.

"Where's your wife?"

"What? You know me and her ain't . . ."

"Don't lie to me. I am so sick and tired of your lying that I don't know what the hell to do.. I heard you talking to her on the phone, Craig. I heard everything, EVERYTHING!" Kayla felt her voice getting louder as she talked. "You no good, dope dealing, cheating mothafucka. Well, you know what? You can go to hell and take your fat ass wife wit' you. I don't need you and neither does my daughter."

"Hold up, Kayla. I was trying to keep her calm. I would say anything so she would leave us alone. Don't you see that? It wasn't you I was lying to, it was her."

"I don't give a damn. Get the hell out! The next time I see you will be before a judge," Kayla told him. He had a look of defeat on his face. The door was pushed open and Geno stuck his head in.

"Everything okay, Kayla?"

"I'm leaving, man. Just know that this ain't the last of this bullshit, Kayla. All I wanted was for us to be a family and to do right. But you so stuck under this mothafucka that you can't see that. It's all good, though. You do what you gotta do and I'ma do the same. Believe that."

"You threatening me, Craig?" Kayla's nostrils flared in anger. Craig didn't answer her. He just touched Day's arm and wheeled himself out of the room. Kayla knew there was something to what he said, but she was determined to not let it bother her. Craig was so full of it, she didn't know when to take him seriously. She could only hope that this was one of those times he was just talking.

"So, now what?" Geno looked at her. Kayla really didn't have an answer for him. She knew she loved him, but could she really trust him? She looked down at her sleeping daughter and was grateful for her. She recalled what the spirit had told her the night she was stabbed. *Trust me.*

"Now we move forward," she told him.

"Together?" he asked her, hopefully. To make sure she knew what he meant, he got on one knee next to her bedside. "I love you, Kayla. I love Day. I want us to be together.

"You begging?"

"Kayla," he said threateningly.

"I'm just asking. Day and I want to know. Are you begging?"

"I'm begging," he answered and kissed her fully. She looked down at her squirming daughter and saw that she was smiling.

Epilogue

It was a week before the wedding and Kayla was too excited to breathe. She had checked and double-checked everything. Things were going perfect, too perfect. That was what worried her. She and her bridesmaids were meeting at the boutique for their final fitting. As she pulled into the parking lot, she had the feeling that she had forgotten something.

"My shoes," she said out loud. She quickly made a U-turn and headed out of the parking lot, stopping when she spotted Roni and Tia pulling into the lot. She pulled beside them, rolled down her window and told them, "I forgot my shoes."

"I'm not surprised," Roni said.

"I'll be right back. They're right by the door at home," she said.

"Hurry up. I gotta meet Theo later," Tia warned.

"I will." Kayla sped down the street and made it home in a record ten minutes. She quickly hopped out of the car and went inside. She could hear

Geno talking to someone on the phone and walked into the bedroom where he was. His back was to the door and he hadn't heard her come in.

"No, I'll tell her. It's okay. I know. We'll be there as soon as we can. Okay, goodbye."

"Who was that?" she asked as she walked behind him and put her arms around his waist. He jumped because she had startled him.

"Damn, Kay. You scared me." He looked at her and took her into his arms. She could tell something was not right by the look on his face.

"What's wrong?"

"Sit down, Kayla. I gotta tell you something." He motioned for her to sit on the side of the bed, his eyes never leaving hers.

"What's wrong, Geno? Did you forget to take the check to the limo company? I told you to drop it off last week or they wouldn't be able to hold the limo. You know . . ."

"Kayla, that was your Aunt Lorrene."

"What did she want? I know she ain't tryin' to bring a whole bunch of people to the wedding." Kayla smiled, but Geno didn't smile back. She knew this was more serious than the limo or the guest list. "What's wrong, Geno?"

"Kayla, she called for your parents. Anjelica . . ."

"I don't want to hear about it. I don't give a damn who calls; she is not to come to my wedding. I never want to see or talk to her again. That's final." Kayla went to get up but Geno stopped her.

"Kayla, that's not what she was calling about. Baby, Anjelica's dead." His head fell and he looked down as he said the words. They sounded so final.

"What?" Kayla was confused. She began to gasp in small breaths as she tried to think. Maybe she didn't understand what Geno was saying. "What did you say?"

"Baby, Anjelica's dead. They found her body a few hours ago in her apartment." Geno looked at Kayla. She had the strangest look that he had ever seen.

"No, she's not. This is just another one of her stunts she's pulling to get some attention. This is her way of spoiling my wedding next weekend," she assured him. She tried to breathe, but could only gasp.

"Baby, she committed suicide. We need to get to your parents' house as soon as possible."

"She's really dead?" Kayla asked. Geno only nodded. She began to shake her head and he pulled her to him. She buried her face into his chest and cried, "No!"

On the day they were supposed to wed, Kayla buried her sister. The church was filled to capacity for what was scheduled to be a momentous occasion, but was now one of tragedy. As she sat on the front pew beside her parents and her fiancé, Kayla looked at the ivory casket that stood where she was supposed to be standing to say "I do." Her mind was filled with memories of growing up with Anjelica. Kayla tried to remember only the good times, but they were few and far between. After the choir sang and the minister gave a moving eulogy, the casket was reopened for the family and friends to give their last good-byes. People hugged Kayla and her family after they had their last viewing. Anjelica looked beautiful in a gold, Oriental style dress, holding a red rose.

Finally, it was time for Kayla to say good-bye. Slowly, she walked to her sister's casket, escorted by Geno. She leaned in and gave her a kiss on her cold cheek, whispering "I love you" as the tears streamed down her cheeks. As she took her seat, Craig came down the aisle, holding another rose. He walked up to the casket and placed the flower next to Anjelica's sleep-like body. After he paid his respects to Kayla's parents, he walked up to Geno and whispered loud enough so that Kayla could hear what he had to say.

"You ain't the only one that had both of them, Player!"

Drama Queen Reader's Guide Questions

1. How does Kayla's relationship with her parents affect her decisions in life?
2. Is it possible to enter into a new relationship even though you still have feelings for an ex-lover? Is that fair to the new person you are involved with?
3. Once a relationship has ended, should you maintain a relationship with your ex-lover's family and/or friends?
4. Kayla had more of a sister bond with her girlfriends than her own blood sister. Is this typical?
5. What part does the male ego play when it comes to insignificant relationships with females, i.e. Terrell/Darla/ Toby?
6. Was Yvonne's reaction to Kayla's pregnancy warranted by their friendship?
7. Was Roni's defense of Kayla's situation to Yvonne valid?
8. Did Roni overreact when she saw Toby with

Darla at his house? Did Toby's suspicious behavior provoke her actions?

9. When Terrell told Kayla about Darla's pregnancy, was Kayla's reaction a surprise? Was she being a hypocrite, considering her own situation?

10. Can a man and a woman really be just friends? Ex: Kayla and Terrell.